CRITICAL ACCLAIM FOR
Down by the River

"A full-bodied, fully imagined novel."
—*New York Times*

"O'Brien succeeds magnificently. . . . *Down by the River* is observant, luxurious. As a novelist, O'Brien has never been more psychologically acute; as a lyrical stylist she is a match for anyone living, and a worthy heir to her great forebears in Irish literature."
—*San Francisco Chronicle*

"O'Brien has a devouring eye for detail."
—*Newsweek*

"O'Brien faithfully, unerringly depicts the fullness of human experience. *Down by the River* is a dark story, full of horrifying scenes and abject suffering. But the novel, like the central character, is ultimately defiant."
—*San Diego Union-Tribune*

"Viscerally terrifying. A moving addition to O'Brien's impressive body of work."
—*Los Angeles Times*

"A forlorn, unsparing novel of rural despair . . . a heady blend of insight, intellect, and poetry."
—*New York Times Book Review*

"A riveting and resonating story. . . . O'Brien creates a stark, unflinching story. . . . A simultaneous poetic sense also imbues the narrative with beauty and grace."
—*Publishers Weekly*

EDNA O'BRIEN is the author of eighteen books, including *House of Splendid Isolation, Lantern Slides, A Fanatic Heart, The High Road,* and *The Country Girls Trilogy* (all available in Plume editions). Born and raised in Ireland, she currently lives in London.

Edna O'Brien

DOWN BY THE RIVER

A PLUME BOOK

PLUME
Published by the Penguin Group
Penguin Putnam Inc., 375 Hudson Street, New York, New York 10014, U.S.A.
Penguin Books Ltd, 27 Wrights Lane, London W8 5TZ, England
Penguin Books Australia Ltd, Ringwood, Victoria, Australia
Penguin Books Canada Ltd, 10 Alcorn Avenue, Toronto, Ontario, Canada M4V 3B2
Penguin Books (N.Z.) Ltd, 182–190 Wairau Road, Auckland 10, New Zealand

Penguin Books Ltd, Registered Offices: Harmondsworth, Middlesex, England

Published by Plume, an imprint of Dutton NAL,
a member of Penguin Putnam Inc.
This is an authorized reprint of a hardcover edition published by Farrar, Straus and Giroux, Inc.
Published by arrangement with Farrar, Straus and Giroux, Inc. For information address
Farrar, Straus and Giroux, Inc., 19 Union Square West, New York, New York 10003.
First published in 1996 by Weidenfeld and Nicolson, London.

First Plume Printing, March, 1998
1 3 5 7 9 10 8 6 4 2

 REGISTERED TRADEMARK—MARCA REGISTRADA

LIBRARY OF CONGRESS CATALOGING-IN-PUBLICATION DATA
O'Brien, Edna.
Down by the river / Edna O'Brien.
p.   cm.
ISBN 0-452-27877-5
1. Fathers and daughters—Ireland—Fiction.   2. Pregnant women—
Ireland—Fiction.   3. Single women—Ireland—Fiction.   I. Title.
[PR6065.B7D69   1998]
823'.914—dc21   97–37248
CIP

Printed in the United States of America

PUBLISHER'S NOTE
This is a work of fiction. Names, characters, places, and incidents either are the product of the
author's imagination or are used fictitiously, and any resemblance to actual persons, living or
dead, events, or locales is entirely coincidental.

'Darkness is our souls do you not think?
Flutier. Our souls, shame-wounded by our sins.'

—James Joyce, Ulysses

'And thy belly be like a heap of wheat set about
with lilies.'

—Song of Solomon

✠

A FRESH CRIME

Ahead of them the road runs in a long entwined undulation of mud, patched tar and fjords of green, the grassy surfaces rutted and trampled, but the young shoots surgent in the sun; flowers and flowering weed in full regalia, a carnival sight, foxglove highest and lordliest of all, the big furry bees nosing in the cool speckled recesses of mauve and white bell. O sun. O brazen egg-yolk albatross; elsewhere dappled and filtered through different muslins of leaf, an after-smell where that poor donkey collapsed, died and decayed; the frame of a car, turquoise once; rimed in rust, dock and nettle draping the torn seats, a shrine where a drunk and driven man put an end to himself, then at intervals rubbish dumps, the bottles, canisters, reading matter and rank gizzards of the town riff-raff stowed in the dead of night.

'Blackguards,' her father said. He always said that when he passed these dumps and vowed to look into his forefather's deeds and get his ownership straightened out. They walk in silence, the man several leagues ahead, his soft brown hat a greenish shard in the bright sunlight, a bold rapparee, his stride animated with a kind of revelrous frenzy, traffic growing fainter and fainter, a clackety river beyond and in the odd gusts of wind the under-sides of the larches purling up to show ballroom skirts of spun-silver. The road silent, somnolent yet with a speech of its own, speaking back to them, father and child, through trappings of sun and fretted verdure, speaking of the old mutinies and a fresh crime mounting in the blood.

The man carried a measuring tape – one he had borrowed – the girl, a tin can to collect blackberries. It was too early, berries on the stalks showed rawly pink, little excrescences purposing to come forth in a pained fruition. His spirits were buoyant because he was going to sell some of his fallow bogland, put it in plastic containers marked 'antiquity' and ship it. The brainwave had hit him the previous evening when he read in the paper about foreigners hankering for bog.

'It beats Banagher and Banagher beats the bank,' he had said. In Europe and beyond, men went out on Sundays, shedding their city constraints in search of the bemired underworld. One such lucky party of pioneers had come upon a man thousands of years old and while knowing it to be a matter of gravity, nevertheless brought away a portion of him, his little shrivelled bags, which in the paper were given the Latin name of Testa.

'We might even dig up a little man ... A cave man,' he said.

'I hope we don't,' Mary said.

He leapt to his task, threw off his jacket, as soon as they got there, extending the metal ruler down the moist seams of black-brown soil and hurrahed when it landed in the mire of the water. He shouted the measurements and she shouted them back to make sure that she had heard correctly. Pounds, shillings and pence danced before his eyes, carpets for her mother, her poor moiling mother, a bicycle for her and then getting carried away with his estimations he spun the metal tape in a wide and apostolic arc, a wand, pronouncing his claim over the deserted but fabled landscape, over furze and fern, lakewater and bogwater, bogwort, myrtle, sphagnum, the warblers' and the bitterns' cry; his empire. He struck out with it then waved and dandled it to verify both his powers and the riches which had lain so long, prone and concealed, waiting for the thrust of the slane. He fished in one bog hole, then the next, hooking on green scum and a frail cress with tiny white fibres, which he placed at her feet.

'Fancy a snack,' he said and presently he was combing a third lodge of water for a big fish, no more of your scutty little minnows, a salmon, eight, nine pounds in weight, something to get his bait into. Warming now to this charade he lifted the rod, shook it free of water, knelt to fix to it those juicy worms which had been suffocating in his trouser pocket since morning.

'We'll make a fire and we'll roast him ... Who was that fellow ... I know ... Finn Mac Comhill who ate of the salmon of knowledge ... We'll be the same,' and easing the rod down he watches for the tell-tale ripples, the rings of water in the space above the fish's nostrils.

He was acting like he acted with visitors, a spiral of gaiety that was sometimes short-lived and often followed by some argument about horses or the exclusivity of the family motto. Might before right, that was his.

'Go on ... Get the fire going,' he said and drew himself backwards in a mimicry of someone tugging at a formidable weight.

'We'll cook it at home,' she said, persisting in the game.

'We'll cook it here,' he said, and with his free hand did a shoo in her direction to get her moving, to gather kindling and bank the fire with the strewn turf that lay around like consignments of mauled pampooties.

'Eureka ... Eureka,' he said and told the world that either he would break that fish or that fish would break him. On impulse then he decided to let the bucko stew a bit, and dropping the rod he wedged the metal case under a stone, then searched for cigarettes which he hadn't brought, said 'blast, blast', then came behind her where she was bent down lifting the burnt logs among the cinders from a recent fire.

'Daytrippers,' he said.

'Yes. Daytrippers.'

'I wonder why they came in here.'

'To see the scenery.'

'You can see scenery anywhere but you can't get as lonesome a place as this.'

He asked her to try and guess what those daytrippers might have eaten.

'Oh ... Anything ... Hard-boiled eggs ... Potatoes.'

'And after the spuds comes the strawberries,' he says and starts then to feel the stuff of her dress, pinching the bodice underneath it. In the instance of his doing it, she thought she had always known that it would happen, or that it had happened, this, a re-enactment of a petrified time. To impede him she stood up and made fidgety bustly movements, remarking that they had better be getting back, pretending not to notice the snapping of the elastic, his jesting with it, allowing it to snap back and forth, jesting of flesh and ruched thread, then not that at all, a hand on the gusset, his splayed hand lifting her up and off, like it was the swing boats, going out, out, a sherbety feeling, out into the cumuli of space.

'Is that nice?'

'I don't know.'

'Is that nicer?'

'I don't know.'

'What are little girls made of?'

'I don't know.'

'Sugar and spice and all things nice – say it, say it, Mary.'

'Sugar ... and spice ... and ... and ...' the voice growing pipey and the mountains and sky bumping into one another.

'Say it ... Say it.'

'We'll lose our fish,' she says.

'He has the worm ... He's OK, come,' he says, the voice softer now, hiving up her dress and walking her backwards, his arms cumbent so that she has to droop on them, her eye catching an old Ovaltine tin with a picture of a lady with a saffron mantilla, veering her away from the light, onto a cushiony incline with a ring of gorse above it, his figure falling through the air, an apotheosis descending down into a secrecy where there was only them, him and her. Darkness then, a weight of darkness except for one splotch of sunlight on his shoulder and all the differing motions, of water, of earth, of body, moving as one, on a windless day. Not a sound of a bird. An empty place, a place cut off from every place else, and her body too, the knowing part of her body getting separated from what was happening down there.

It does not hurt if you say it does not hurt. It does not hurt if you are not you. Criss-cross waxen sheath, uncrissing, uncrossing. Mush. Wet, different wets. His essence, hers, their two essences one. O quenched and empty world. An eternity of time, then a shout, a chink of light, the ground easing back up, gorse prickles on her scalp and nothing ever the same again and a feeling as of having half-died.

Her pink canvas shoe had fallen into the water and she lifted it funnel-wise to free it of ooze. He looked at her, a probing look, looked through her as if she were parchment and then half-laughed.

'What would your mother say ... Dirty little thing.'

He crosses to the lake, wading through the thick lattice of bulrushes and she thinks he is washing now in the brackenish water, swabbing himself with the saucer leaf of the water-lily and that on him will linger the sweet lotus of that flower.

Everything is drying, coagulating. It is a plasma. She will wash in the river, wash and rewash and pleat herself back together. She will throw the knickers far away down in the fairy fort. She does not know what has happened. And there is no one that she can ask. An image floated up then to startle her, something she had once seen and thought of as being quite harmless; it was a cake at a party which seemed to be uncut but when she brought her face up close to it, every piece had been severed, every severed piece, side by side, a wicked decoy.

Climbing the roped rickety gate that leads from the bog road to the outer road she wobbles, grips a tassel of flowering dock, and the coral seeds crushed to shreds she puts in her pocket. Only they will know. No one else will ever know.

Except that they will.

In the City far away men of bristling goatee beards, men of serious preoccupied countenances, move through the great halls, corporeal figures of knowledge and gravity, the white of their wigs changing colour as they pass under the rotunda of livid light, ribs of yellow hair, smarting, becoming phosphorescent, powerful men, men with a swagger, a character personified by the spill of the gown or the angle of a coiffed wig, their juniors a few paces behind them laden with briefs and ledgers, the whole paraphernalia of the law in motion, some already at the bench, others walking slowly to the appointed courts, men of principle who know nothing of the road or the road's soggy secret will one day be called to adjudicate upon it, for all is always known, nothing is secret, all is known and scriven upon the tablet of time.

✠

FRUITS

It was Saturday. She was let stay in bed. Her mother felt her head. Scalding. Scalding.

The sun made little incursions of light, bluing Our Lady's blue cloak and emphasising the white disc of her chest. Dust on the linoleum moved in whorls like it had life in it. She would mop the room when she got up. Swish the side of the mop, the feathery part, over the grey-blue linoleum with its motifs of trodden berries. She did not look at Our Lady. Our Lady knew. Maybe her mother knew. Maybe Tara knew. Maybe the teacher that she liked knew, maybe that was why he was so abrupt. She would never have a boyfriend. 'I'll never have a boyfriend, ever.' She didn't get crushes on young boys, like Tara did. But she had a crush on the new teacher who had come to the vocational school. His name was Augustine and he had a beard. She imagined if he lay in a hayfield, little pismires getting in there and tickling him and his asking his sweetheart to tease them out. He was engaged. She had gone to the school and had him called out to give him a message.

Her mother said that if he was looking for accommodation they had spare rooms. Her mother had not said it expressly, she had merely said that the money from a room could help defray expenses. Also another person to sit with them at night would mean there were fewer rows. He seemed baffled at being called from his office and alternated between smiling and blinking. He suffered from involuntary blinking. She had made a hash of the request, saw that he saw that there was scheming in it. He hadn't. It was simply that he was far too happy where he lived, enjoying a nightly luxury that no one, not even himself, could explain, a succubus who ministered to him while he slept. He had digs in a room above a shop, enjoyed the company of the men who drank after hours and discussed everything that transpired in the town and up the country, every stir. Most nights he was given a snack, a cold beef sandwich or a slice of cake, and then to his bedroom and at totally unpredictable times, his visitor, pulling the covers back, planting this constellation of kisses, hungry kisses on his lower quarters, his coming awake to commune with her, only to find her in flight, sometimes catching a glimpse of a bit of white nightgown.

He felt certain that it was Moira the shopgirl. It had to be. Yet nothing in her daylight manner gave her away. She would be up early, racing from the shop to the kitchen, frying rashers, getting cakes of bread in the oven, adjudicating on the weather and calling up to him, 'Your breakfast, professor.' It was with a great formality she stood over him and poured his tea. He spent hours watching her, he watched her carry crates of beer and plonk them on the counter, then shout to a potboy to come and sweep the place; he watched her peel the muslin from the big cooked hams and put them on the slicers; he watched her slice; he watched her take a fillet of fat with a breadcrumb and sugar coating, lick it and put it in her mouth. He watched her scratch herself. He watched her barge at the postman who was too lazy to get out of his van to deliver the letters. She would not be drawn out on any subject, except the weather. He thought of laying a trap for her such as leaving a suitcase in the middle of the floor which she would trip over, but then thought why spoil it. Her mouth it was that made him certain. In an otherwise homely face, her mouth was maddening, like blubber, red, the red of raspberry wine, practising on itself for its night-time forays.

'Actually, I'm fixed up,' he had said to Mary and she slunk away, believing that she had made a fool of herself.

'I made a fool of myself ... Didn't I?' she said to Our Lady and then promised to do a novena so that they would get someone for the room. The sound of the roaring was so fierce and escalating that it was like fire. Her father was taking it out on her mother on account of her being let stay in bed. She ducks under the covers. It follows her there. She cannot hear the exact words but that is of no matter, she waits only for the sound of things crashing and then the silence, the pounding silence which always follows when her mother has fallen to the floor or onto a chair. Yet there is neither a falling nor a silence, just the anger crackling and magnifying.

Some time later her mother came up to report. Her father had caught some boys raiding the orchard, one bucko up in the pear tree, shaking the branches, another gathering the spoils and a third looking through the hole in the wall, the lookout. Her father had marched them into the kitchen to read the riot act and threatened them with the guards. Her mother re-enacted it, her father writing down their names, their ages and their abodes, when he knew very well they all lived in the cottages, then describing how they were white as sheets and one of them having to go out during the interrogation, got short-taken.

'I thought it was you,' Mary said.

'I was in stitches,' her mother said.

'I thought he was shouting at you,' Mary said.

Her mother went on laughing. A strange hard brittle laughter. She did not like her mother then.

You can think more than one thing about the same person at exactly the same time. You can think oodles of things and they are all different and they are all true. Her mother was a plantation of evening foliage and evening flowers, lush and copious, dark red dahlias; her mother was that bit of stone wall with stained-glass windows that no one could see through; her mother was the Chinese lady in the picture with the dagger in her hair and pursed knowing lips; her mother was the woman who sat on the table when that doctor came and made free with her, was allowed to swing her legs, then feel her calves, then slip off her shoes and she being told in a strained voice to go off and play. You can think more than one thing about a person at the same time and they are all true, but one thing seems to be truer, the clandestine thing.

Her mother told her that she was to get up, that her father wanted her to do a message.

'What message?' she said, bridling.

'The fresh air will put the roses back in your cheeks.'

'What message?'

She almost told then, she was almost ready to blurt it out.

FLESH

Run. Run. Run. Then it can't happen. A road with umpteen cars and lorries, yet a road with bends, blind corners where anyone might be lurking. Her father had told her to go and ask your man with the stallion if he could bring the mare. The man's phone was banjaxed.

'You'll be better once you're up,' her mother said, the old appeasements about fresh air and roses in the cheeks.

Passing the cottages, a mother of one of the truant boys launches into a spiel, half song, half tirade, cursing those with orchards, landed people with not a drop of Christian blood in them; a big woman, bare-sleeved, her hands raw from tubs of washing, her arms spawned with freckles, the vaccination marks glaringly white. With a stick she beats a tartan rug that is hanging on a line, marvelling at the motes of dust that come streaming out.

Once out of the village and up the country road the breeze gets headier. It is like paws on her cheek, touching her. Everything makes her jump. Butterflies run on ahead and she tries to keep up with them, the sage green of their drawn wings dangle as if pollen was spattered on them. She only knows the man's first name – it is Eamonn. He has a red face and after his wife left him it was said that he killed her German dog with his bare hands and that it was left outside the barracks, its neck doubled back and its mouth bloodied. A loner ever since.

'No. No. No.' The sound comes out piping. Her voice answering to a young man in a grocery van who has slowed down to offer her a lift.

'I'd rather walk,' she says a little less frantic.

'Sound,' he says and drives off, giving a chirpy hoot. It is like that. Everything and everyone is liable to attack her. She is a leper. What to do about Holy Communion next day. She has decided that she will go to the altar and when the moment comes to take the host she will lower her head. She knows that after a few Sundays the priest will notice and will come to her house or her school. Each day unbeknownst to her mother she has gone to the river. She has brought salt in a paper bag and in a shallow part of the river she has sprinkled it, then squatted in it.

The slip road is a lattice of green with bushes and briars on either side. She passes pebble-dash piers with a bed and breakfast placard and further on there is a little pony, tethered to a hazel tree, standing sullenly in a heap of dung, flies buzzing and circling around him. In the field beyond, mares and their young are lying in pairs, sunning themselves. At that moment a foal starts to gallop and the mother follows, the two of them doing the radius of the field, a shifting and flowing mirage of white and off-white limbs, a decorousness in their tracks, yet queerly hysterical, then stopping all of a sudden to look about, as if to receive an accolade. The foal suckles the mare quietly, so quietly there is not even a gurgle, and the mare, seemingly indifferent to it, munches greedily on the grass and swallows without chewing.

Through the open door of a bungalow, she sees a playpen, pink, the pink of strawberry milkshake, the rungs festooned with toys and baubles which are also pink. A little boy with red cheeks and one very red squashed earlobe is playing with a fire engine, lifting the frail white ladder up and down, getting vexed with it, then going into a fit the moment he sets eyes on her. His mother comes into view, a young woman in a dirndl skirt who lifts him out and says, 'There, there,' while kissing him all over. The woman and her husband have just moved to the neighbourhood to take over the management of a supermarket. Mary has noticed them at mass, the only married couple to sit together.

'My father sent me over to ask if he can bring the mare later on.'

'Frank,' the woman calls. She has come to the wrong house. He is in grey pyjamas with the cord missing so that he has to hold them up. His bare chest has the hard fawn indentations of walnut-shell and his hair is tousled.

'You've come to the wrong house,' he says, and points to one further up with a tractor in front of it. The mother eases the child back into the pen where he now punches each and every bauble, so that it is like a toy-fair sprung to life, a jamboree in which pink shutters open and close, a cash register dispatches its drawer, a pink ball swings on a pendulum, a vanity mirror does somersaults and throughout, a strange aged guttural voice repeats, 'Babyee ... Babyee ... Babyee ...' Husband and wife stand side by side laughing and there is between them such a harmony, an insatiable love, as if they are kissing, even though they are not. The small space between their bodies is a compression of desire and heat, and when they look at the child they are looking with the same eyes, the same doting eyes, and when they look at Mary they want her to be gone, their snug world is that complete.

'Does he have a cross dog?' she asks.

'You wouldn't know what he has ... He's so odd,' the husband says and runs off shouting, 'My toast, my toast.' Mary can smell it as she walks away.

The man with the stallion is bandaging a mare's tail, doing it briskly as a surgeon might, while the little piebald pony is being led around her, nuzzling her, glorying in it. A woman with dark glasses is standing by a bright blue horsebox and the man with her, her groom, is shielding a lit match with his cap while she draws on a long black cigarette.

'She's on, she's on ... She's casting,' Eamonn shouts as water begins to gush from the mare, like a tap freed of its washer, yet the lips from which it pours are the scarlet red of freshly drawn blood, which open and close in a kind of winking frenziedness. He calls to the young boy to get Mike Tyson from the boil house and be quick about it or it'll be all over.

There is something slow and ceremonious about the passage of the stallion across the rectangle of weeds and grass to where the mare is standing, in it the immutable ritual of courtship.

'He'll be all pie to her at first ... The Latin lover,' Eamonn says, and the stallion, as he comes alongside her, runs his neck silkily alongside hers, lingering, then sniffs at her flank without regard to the rushing water, while at the same time the little teaser is led away, her head down as if she has just disgraced herself. The white of the stallion so close to the burnished chestnut of the mare resembles the painted halves of twin centaurs. Then he mounts her, his frame like a cupola, covering hers. It is uncannily still, no sound at all, the mare not moving, not even blinking, merely gazing out, as if at something immemorial, even the men very still, no sound except for the prancing, a dainty prancing at that, of the hind legs of the stallion as he passes into her, his possession of her a long glide, as though being sucked hungrily and moistly by every particle of her, her eyes softly gazing and the sense now of something happening, that primal transaction of entrails and juices, the moment contained, another life beginning in the dark secret spheres of her, away from sun and sunlight, and even away from the source which gave it and which is now withdrawing from her, strangely indifferent and dulled, an entity on four feet being led away. In her, something biding, immobile, a rock-like stillness.

'Did you enjoy that,' Eamonn says to Mary. She looks down at her shoes. She does not want him to see that she is crying.

'My father wants to know if he can bring the mare.'

'Tell him tomorrow ... And tomorrow ... Mike's had his wedding today ... Not that he'd mind ... They say you can kill yourself with drink or drugs but not with sex,' he says and shouts across to Dorothy to ask her if she agrees.

'I wouldn't know, Eamonn,' she calls back.

'The mare gets most of the fun,' he says and nudges Mary to see how she is taking the joke. He sees the tears and laughs loudly.

'Christ ... You must live in a doll's house,' he says. She wants to explain that it is not from fear, that it is something beyond fear, something else, but she cannot, because she knows that no matter what words she uses he will not understand. That she knows. That is how it is. His boots, upturned and stumpy, are like the boots of the man on a Toby jug except that they are covered with muck.

'My father said to ask how much.'

'He knows how much from the last time,' he says and winks as she goes, tells her to hang around and learn the facts of life.

In a gust of wind the hail came, sudden and slantwise, it blew across the treetops and left a sort of silver spume on them and the sides of the saplings billowed and caved with it, then cushioned out and caved again and in the field as she passed by, the stallion stood stock still, head high, the hail like a pearled toga flung across his back, shanks and hooves in a fresco of pink-tinted blossom.

✠

THOU SHALT NOT KILL

Gubu. Gubu. Gubu. Roisin, their visitor from the city, gloats on the word, repeating it with different intonations and making faces to emphasise her disgust.

'Grotesque, unbelievable, bizarre, unjust.'

The women look, listen, crossing and uncrossing their legs, shifting their haunches, the elderly ladies on chairs, the thinner ones squeezed onto a sofa, intrigued and not a little awed by the brusqueness of her manner, her militancy, the necessity for them to recognise the urgency of why she has come, the catastrophe which is happening all around.

The room itself is roasting, her invective adding to the heat, so much so that the ornaments seem to quiver and the two cranberry vases of which Noni is so proud, and each of which houses a chaste white tulip, look on the point of toppling over. Noni imagines water leaking onto the lace antimacassars and thence to the new salmon-pink carpet which she is paying on the instalment for. Sally, who is herself expecting a child and in no way prepared to hear about the slaughter of the unborn, wishes she had not come and wonders if she could go out. Rammed down their throats are the details of the tiny thing, when it starts to make a fist, suck its thumb, get hiccups, swim, do somersaults and even sneeze. It is making her queasy. Johnny was right. She should not have come. A baby was a mystery and it should be left so. Roisin is holding up two pictures, two contrasting pictures, a contented baby, curled up in a womb, and a torn baby, its body mangled, pools of black blood in the crevices and in the empty crater of its head. Arms go up, forearms go up which Roisin pulls aside, forcing them to look, to witness the butchery done in England and elsewhere by a clique of killers. She dilates on the methods – curetting, suction, salt poisoning, Caesarean.

Fearing that she might have been too strident she now holds up a photograph taken from a painting of Our Lady, Our Lady's eyes sunken from incessant weeping, her fingernails dirty from rooting in trash bins to find the foetuses and save them from dogs and human scavengers. She kneels before each one now, a tremor in her voice, asking them to look into their hearts and ask themselves if they could endure the thought of any child ever being slaughtered again. She recites the words that such a child might, in its last mangled moments, scream out.

> *'I won't see the sky or the birds in the trees*
> *I won't sing a lullaby or feel a cool breeze*
> *I love you dear mummy, of course I do*
> *And I thought dear mummy you loved me too.'*

The women in their cardigans and garish frocks, their different lollopings of perfume and hairspray, sit stiffly, terrified of her, and look down at the sad eyes and the dirty fingernails of Our Lady. She tells them that the artist who painted the picture completed it in a matter of hours, though normally her work took months, because Our Lady's hand guided her.

Mrs Morgan, the retired midwife, holds the image to her lips, repeatedly kisses it and thinks, 'If only, if only we had a crusader like Roisin long ago.' In her long toiling years, childless years, she recalls the babies she delivered, the anguished mothers asking why they had to be women, her shouting at them to push, push, that first miracle cry, that infant's pierce, which did not, however, make up for the silenced creatures she had found in drawers and wardrobes and in bolster cases, like sleeping dolls; a little baby boy in a lavatory bowl, twins with binding twine around their necks, outside in a haggart, a brazen strap of a sister saying itinerants must have left them.

Murderers in legal closets, pagans in Strasbourg, a network conspiring in the greatest holocaust of all, the abortion holocaust. She is walking, striding, in her coffee-brown trouser suit, her bracelets jangling, estimating by the expression in their eyes their commitment or their shiftiness, almost certain of the ones who will enrol and the ones who will slink away.

'Your children shall be the olive fruits around your table,' she says to Maeve, the prettiest of the group and the most refractory. They outstare each other, two determined young women, their hair identically coloured with henna lights; enmity. Maeve suddenly laughs, to rile her.

'Why do you laugh?'

'I bet you'd love to know,' Maeve says, thinking that Joe will kiss her when he comes off shift, kiss her all the way to the car and have her knickers off as soon as they get into the back seat. 'You're too good to me, Maeve,' is what he will say if he wants a certain thing.

'Got to see my young man,' she says, and goes out, spluttering with laughter.

It is not at all how Noni imagined it. She imagined tributes for her spick and span house, the blazing fire, the big logs, the spread in the kitchen, savouries under the hood of the stove to keep warm, knives and forks, daintily wrapped in a paper napkin as they might be for a wedding or a twenty-first. Wines and port wines and the cut glasses on the tray, the lustre of rainbows on them.

'It's home ... It's what we call home,' she had imagined herself saying in answer to these manifold tributes, secretly chuckling at having given her husband strict orders not to come back until after eleven o'clock, not to darken her door until every motor car was gone. On and off during the day she gave a satisfied hoot as she recalled his cringing mien, asking her what he was to do until eleven o'clock and her telling him that no doubt he would find something to do, somewhere to plank his backside.

Those three sessions with the counsellor have given her her mandate. She wears the trousers now and has mastery over that pig of a man to whom she has been married for twenty-five years. Deciding to do catering for the factory and for private parties has brought her independence, that and a stint on Saturday morning doing the altar in the chapel. She holds the chequebook, pays the television rent, pays the licence fee and hides that remote so that he can no longer flick the channels. Their battles have ceased. She cooks her own tea in the evening, rashers and fried bread, or a Spanish omelette, cleans the pan so that when he comes in from his job with his brown paper parcel of chops or sausages he has to find the pan, melt the fat and start all over again. She has allocated to him utensils, cups, saucers, three pieces of cutlery with yellowish stains like rancid egg yolk. A sort of truce after many bitter years of rowing, the earlier years when he struck her, the later ones when he raised his fist and longed to strike her, culminating in an atmosphere of glares. Silence now and if some necessity for speech arises, such as a slate falling off, or his aunt from Canada phoning, the information transmitted through another, usually a passing child. Gone the time when she cowered, dreaded his key in the door at night, drunk, banging things, threatening to kill her, all that is past now and there is a truce, a hating truce.

'Ronan won't be joining us,' Sheilagh had said. Sheilagh would be first, in her apron and her cork-soled sandals, cringing, saying she should have changed into something good.

'Ronan has been sent a-packing,' she had said, knowing only too well that Sheilagh's is one of the hobs he hatched on, portraying the aggrieved husband with a witch for a wife.

'Answer that door,' she had called to her abruptly, she herself having had to tear to the kitchen because the sausage rolls were on the point of burning. It was the midwife, Mrs Morgan, who had to be helped down the hall, waddling and puffing, saying she did not know which was worse, her lungs or her arthritis. Needed humouring. They had to ease her down into the best armchair, her bandaged legs ballooning out in front of her, her walking stick flying out, pronouncing her nephew to be the best in the country, and without him she could not stir. And so it was, ting-a-ling-a-ling, every other minute, coats having to be put somewhere, introductions, some of them overdressed, that Maeve one with the sleeveless blouse to show her armpits and Kitty making such a production of the carrageen soufflé she had brought, boasting of how she had soaked the seaweed, then blanched it in lemon, holding it out for each and all to admire.

Everyone was on tenterhooks, waiting for Roisin, their guest of honour, and for Father Gerard, who had convened the meeting. They had talked of this and that, the young mechanic crashing his car, survived by his wife and six children, with another on the way, conjecture as to whether the long hours he worked had made him fall asleep at the wheel, dismay that his wife was insisting on having the baby at home. In hushed tones, there was mention of another young girl, a country girl who was expecting and had told her parents that she would not have the child adopted, a story all the more offensive because they themselves had adopted her at a late age and had sacrificed their lives for her. Wrangling followed about the rights and wrongs of adoption, in the end people deferring to the midwife who said the church could always find a good home for any child.

'Father's here ... Father's here.'

It circulated like a chirrup and some did little things to their hair or touched up their lipsticks as he came in. To see him in his slippers with his big wide smile, and stains on his slacks, made Noni want to run and put her arms around him because he seemed so helpless and even his jumper was helpless and needed mending.

'*Mea culpa, mea culpa,*' he said all around, then sat and in a low sympathetic tone almost like a sermon, described how a young lad, over-fond of his drink had come to the sacristy door to ask him in the name of God to give him the pledge. He could easily tell how the poor boy had been led astray by others, coaxed to go a few miles away to quiet shebeens for quiet after-hours drinking and made to drink till morning. Naturally he wanted to help him. He told him the few remedies he knows, prayer, or a lozenge, or a drop of Lucozade, and afterwards the boy knelt and swore that he would not drink again.

'But you'll have a drop of wine, Father,' Noni said.

'Shouldn't I give good example?' he said.

'Oh this is social drinking,' she said, dispatching Sheilagh to collect the tray while also saying 'Hands up for the vino.'

Those who declined put their hands to their chests, confessing that they might get too fond of it, citing the case of women who carried gin bottles in their handbags and chewed peppermints or cloves to disguise their breath. When they clinked glasses, Lorna surpassed herself, began raving about her Spanish holiday, Spanish food, tapas, dinner at ten o'clock, gypsies with tiered skirts and fresh poppies on their garters.

'For God's sake, Lorna,' Noni called across.

'Lovely fragrance,' Father Gerard said, bringing the glass to his nose and asking if he would be right in thinking that it was an Orvieto.

'Close ... Close,' Noni said because with her developing knowledge of wine regions which she gleaned from a colour supplement she knew that it was a neighbouring district. He put the glass to his mouth allowing his tired, milky eyes to roll upwards, swallowed and recalled a night, some years back now, in a *pensione* in Italy when the couple next door to him started a fierce argument, or so he thought, his trying to avoid hearing it, only to discover after half an hour that they were locked in their room, and he had the presence of mind to come outside to their door and shout in to them, shout, '*Chiave, chiave.*' He smiled as he explained to them that *chiave* was Italian for a key. He then suggested to the captive couple to put their key under the door so that he could try it from the other side and presto it worked. In the little celebration which followed they drank Orvieto and the man, who was a wine dealer, gave him a thorough education in different vineyards, promised to send him a case, which, as he said forlornly, never arrived.

'You've travelled so much,' Kitty said.

'Not a great deal,' he said, although then conceding that he had been to most countries in Europe and also California.

'And do you speak many languages, Father?' she asked, tiddly already.

'A spattering,' he said, and tried to recall the few words of Russian that he knew, words which he learned from an Orthodox priest in Georgia, sitting up one night in a jasmine garden, exchanging views and praying for the faith to be restored to Russia. They had prayed until breakfast time, a bouquet of prayers he called it.

'Father, you will never guess what these are,' Kitty said, holding up a plate on which were the broken bits of uncooked spaghetti no bigger than matchsticks. He peered down, sniffed them, looked puzzled and asked if they might be for use in some game such as 'Fox and Goose'. There was laughter then.

'I'll tell Father,' Noni says, galled that the glory might be snatched from her, she who, after all, had got up at dawn to clean the house, who was at the supermarket before they opened to get the best cheeses and who was bitterly disappointed to learn that they had run out of sausage sticks and had a brainwave to use the broken-up spaghetti sticks to hold the bits of bacon and the cocktail sausages. He said that it had to be one of the most ingenious things he had ever heard of.

It was at that moment Roisin arrived, letting herself in through the back door, her tread so light that everyone jumped, and most were startled to see such a beautiful girl with such lovely hair and such very special eyes, grey eyes that shone, as if silver polish had been poured into them.

She was prettier than her photos. Her photos were in the paper because of her having been to Rome and having had an audience with the Pope. They craved to know of it. Girlishly she could only repeat that it was the most beautiful thing in her whole life and that His Holiness had given her a sense of being right and on the right path and had implored her to spread the word of his *Evangelicum Vitae.*

'Was this in English?' the gawpy Sheilagh asked.

'No, I learned Italian.' Again they marvelled, praised her application and went on to be even more astonished when she told them that she had gone first to Krakow where he had been an archbishop, wanted to make the pilgrimage and retrace the journey of his whole life, from his priesthood in Poland to the episcopal See of Rome.

Yes, at first they had found her charming, warming her hands by the fire, reminding herself of each person's name and accepting the plate of food, but asking that the potato salad be taken back. It was when she began preaching that they became afraid; they saw something else, the eyes with the hardness of enamel, outrage in her voice, insistence that they look at the gory photographs, that they read the literature, that they know exactly how the brutal operation is done.

'What if a girl is raped?' Linda had asked her.

'An abortion won't unrape her, all an abortion will do is compound the crime,' Roisin said, nettled.

'A point well made,' Father Gerard said to calm things.

'Or ...' Kitty asked, but can scarcely bring herself to say the words. It had to be conceded, she had said quietly, that scandals not only existed in dirty rags of newspapers, but happened to families, families all over, so that one read of girls drowning themselves, or giving birth in graveyards and leaving the infant to die.

'Oh, the incest tosh,' Roisin said.

'How dare you accuse me of tosh.'

'Wasn't that what you were getting at.'

'Yes.'

'It is sad, of course, but there can be no exceptions.'

'Ever.'

'Never.'

'Suppose a girl in that state walked in here now and said "I'm going to throw myself in the river," what would you do, what would we do?' Linda asked, rash rising in her neck.

'She wouldn't ... They have a hormone which stops them.'

'Who says?'

'It's medically proven.'

'You think you know it all, well I'm going to tell you ... You know nothing ... And I'm not going to be railroaded.'

'Will someone put their hands on her,' Noni said, furious.

'And?' Linda says.

'Throttle you.'

Father Gerard rallied then, said he did not think it was fitting for anyone to get overheated, said that the important thing and the momentum of the gathering was Roisin's arrival, her fervour among them, the gospel which she had come to spread. He asked them to remember the Holy Father's words to her – *Evangelicum Vitae*.

'May I tell a little story,' she said then, deferring to the priest and to Noni, who both nodded and begged her to sit down. Her voice was much softer, as if she was reading from a children's book.

'It was a Saturday, she and her comrades were at the same appointed spot, holding up the leaflets, asking passers-by if they could be of help, when a young girl in an oilskin coat began to shout and harangue them, telling them they had no business making passers-by feel so dirty or so criminal. It was not long however before the young girl broke down. Her story was quite simple. She was going to England the next day to have it done and somehow, somehow they managed to console her, they managed to persuade her, they managed to find shelter for her and she did not go after all. A year later she returned to the same spot with a little boy in her arms and that little boy did not have to compose a poem and say *"Oh Mummy I thought you loved me too."* '

'Beautiful ... A beautiful parable,' Father Gerard said, sprinkling his hands as if there was Holy Water on them, blessing them and drawing the meeting to a close. He assured her that she need not fear, that good work was instigated.

'Father ...' Noni asked, with exaggerated deference, 'do you mind if I put on a song?' The words were in Gaelic and few of them understood it. Father Gerard smiled upon hearing the first few lines and whispered aloud that it was his favourite song as he began to translate the lines which told of lovers hoping to meet under a thorn tree but fated not to.

'It's so sad ... It's too sad,' Kitty said.

'I sang that song once to a countess,' Father Gerard said, tender now, in a mood of reminiscence, recalling a holiday with his sister, a walk in the Black Forest and how they met this count and countess who invited them back to their *Schloss* for the night and how after dinner his sister urged him to sing and he sang that song which brought tears to the countess's eyes.

'A noblewoman ... Very tall ... I can still see her in my mind ... A lovely fox fur wrapped around her ...' he says and regrets as well the passing of the beautiful old love songs.

'I have to go, Father ... I have a long drive ... Will you pray for me,' Roisin says, gentle now, apologetic.

'And will you pray for me,' he says, begging her to know that priests need prayers too, that priests can fall by the wayside.

'You were an inspiration to us all,' Noni says, ushering the group to rise and applaud, and in the doorway Roisin makes a fist and asks them to keep remembering the picture of the happy infant, the one that swam and sneezed and did somersaults and made a little fist at life.

A PAGAN PLACE

Tara's bedroom is her igloo, crammed with stuff, a fox fur, beads, purses, coloured posters of her favourite groups pinned to walls and ceiling so that she can commune with them. The 'Keep out' sign in two languages is meant for her dope of a brother. Sometimes she kisses the bare chest of the young men on the poster and then again, in a bad temper, tears them from the wall, stamps on them and calls them Wet Wet Wet.

'Lock the door,' Tara says. 'Lock the door, my little brother may try to get in. He has the hots for you. Drew a picture of you. And keep your back to it.' She is waving a razor which she has just bought.

'What are you doing with that?' Mary asks her.

'I've got to, I've simply got to,' she says, pulling it from its wrapper and holding it across her belly, wondering where the bikini line begins.

'You'll hurt yourself.'

'It's got to be done. Men . . . They don't want all that stuff in their mouths.'

'Tara, you're mad.'

'You've been in love, you know.'

'It was an infatuation.'

'Us waiting outside the school for him and he coming out and just saying, Hi, girls.'

'Are you in love, Tara?'

'Two.' She lifts both fingers and does a mock cry of despair, says no one in the world realises how painful it is, the dilemma it poses to be in love with two men at the same time.

'Which two?'

'You know, Danny and...'

'And...'

'It came on, the night of the disco, this rush for the DJ, suddenly I saw him in another light. God, he was so cool up there, the cling of his jeans, so masculine.'

'Isn't Danny masculine?'

'Sure he is on the hurly pitch, in his togs. Did I tell you someone wrote on the blackboard "Tara loves Danny". I nearly died. I came into the classroom, sat down, saw it and everything went flying, the desk on top of me. "Are you all right," he said, "Oh fine," I said ... He felt sorry for me. He said you and me can go with him to the next match on the team bus ... The trouble is, what worries me is he's all hurling ... He dreams hurling. He eats raw eggs and things to be fit for hurling. DJ is different, smooth, chats me up.'

She has wedged the razor out of its packing and is testing the sharpness on the down of her lips.

'Could you do it for me,' she asks.

'I couldn't, I can't.'

'But you'll stay with me while I do it.'

'I'd rather not.'

'Every film star does it and every rock star and every model. I expect their managers do it. The only bloody thing is there's no proper instructions, all it says is that it's moisturised with aloes, it's like a cocktail.'

'Don't face me while you're doing it, face the other way.'

'God, you're a wimp,' Tara says, turns and starts to chatter about DJ whose real name is Dieter, gloating over his tan, something Danny could do with, but deciding that both are hunks.

'Did you kiss either of them yet?'

'Maybe,' she says and shrugs, adding that a girl cannot tell for certain whether they are good at it just by kissing. 'Did I tell you what I said to my mother?'

'She has a set on me ... She glared at me when I came in.'

'She thinks you're a bad influence ... Anyhow, she flew at me when I said to her, "Mummy, suppose you marry someone and he's no good at it, what then?" She went every colour. I don't think

Daddy and her ... I never hear a sound ... They're like corpses in there. I did a doodah.'

'What?'

'Made a complete fool of myself with DJ ... I said to him, "Do you want to come out with me," and he thought about it and he said, "You've a nice body, Tara, but you see it wouldn't be fair to my girlfriend in Germany."'

'You asked him to come out with you.'

'Ask and you shall receive. Look under the mattress, there's something there I want you to read for me. It's all about S-E-X. I got it in town. God, how I want to be in town. They just walk around in anything, pyjamas or slips or anything. Two people kissed the whole way up the main street. It was excellent kissing, it just went on and on. I was so jealous, raunchy. Mary, my best years are passing and your best years are passing, remember that. I saw these two really old people in the disco Saturday night; they were thirty or forty and they had the gall to get up and dance. Ouch. And snog. I don't want to be thirty or forty, ever ... Ouch it's hurting, for God's sake read it to me.'

Mary reads stiffly, as if from a school book.

The hymen which partly blocks the vagina is the gift-wrapping proving that the product is untouched.

Turn him on with a sassy walk or your fave raunchy film.

Start by gently massaging his inner thighs and get him to massage your inner thighs.

Then, the tonsil hockey.

Slather ice-cream on him and lick it off ... Slow tempo.

Get what you want in bed and more.

One hour's worth of sex burns off one hundred and fifty calories.

Get him to pull out in time.

Keep asking yourself am I climaxing.

The average female orgasm lasts five seconds – beat the record, make it ten. Remember it is one of the surest ways of getting rid of that nagging headache.

'Jesus, hide it, hide it.' They could hear her mother's footsteps, her mother's voice saying it was time Mary MacNamara went home, lessons had to be done, a supper had to be prepared.

'Bye ... Bye.' Tara's voice calling to her along the road becomes fainter and fainter. Then it is lost. A lorry with a load of bullocks is parked by their gate. They were bawling at being packed in together, or else because of dimly knowing where they were destined for, the abattoir. From the fields the cows returned their cries, one cow in particular, demented because her calf had been taken away that morning. In front of the nettlebed, two dogs, their own and a stray dog, walking around each other, sizing each other up. The damp grass came up to her ankles.

The whistle was like a lasso, lassoing her into the fort of trees where he stood. He wore a trench coat and a scarf down over part of his face; then the whistling grew softer, sweeter, a signal which said, 'Don't be afraid, you know what I'm after.'

It was pitch dark in there. Not sight, not words, only touch. Touch telling her what to do. Almosting it. Touch decreeing the momentum, of fast or slow. Her mouth not large enough. The thrust, like it might choke her; the girth that of her mother's deodorant knob but of a different taste. Rapidity. Then volitionless. Sea foam, sea horses, a lavering in her mouth and soon after, a different whistle, a curfew, to be off, to go home.

She knelt and cleaned her mouth and her tongue on the grass and the dew. Getting up she began to reel and had to find her way home by the feel of the trees which she passed. The fits had already started. They came and went but intensified the moment she saw her mother, her mother asking, What, what?

Her mother did not know what to do. When her father came in from counting cattle she met him with, 'She's having fits.'

'Fits. What kind of fits?'

'She's choking, she saw something but she doesn't know what.'

They felt her pulse. She was lying in front of the fire on the corduroy cushions while they waited for the doctor to come. She was asked if she wanted something, if she wanted biscuits. She would not speak. Nothing would drag a word out of her, not threats, not coaxing, not their kneeling down and whispering. Her tongue was gone. It lay there like the tongue of an old shoe. It was stiff and defiled. Her tongue had become an enemy. Her mouth an enemy too. They handed her a sheet of paper and a pencil. She wrote down that there was a lorry parked with animals in it. She did not see anyone in it, only the beasts in the back.

When the doctor came she was put in the dining room. Everything was cold in there, the silver was cold and the scoop in the coal scuttle kept tapping, up down, up down. Her father and the doctor's driver had set off with sticks and flashlamps. Outside they were now hollering and hitting out at bushes and the trunks of trees.

The lady doctor told her not to be afraid, said they would just have a little chinwag. At first she was very patient but then clacked her teeth and went, 'Tch, tch, tch.' She did not like girls who were stubborn. She decided then it could be a case of deafness and that she would have to syringe the ears. She had a little tin bowl, kidney-shaped, in her doctor's bag and called out in a peremptory voice, 'Boiling water, please.' It was like having a bolt going from one ear to another through her skull. Afterwards, she could hear everything clearly, too clearly; she could hear the air sidling through the room, then sifting like flour dropped from a sieve.

'She doesn't know yet, Bridget,' the lady doctor said then, lingering on her mother's name in a show of solicitude.

'Nothing.'

'Sometimes the mind just clamps up,' and her voice trails away, admitting to feeling bested.

The cushions have been put back on the bedchair and Mary is made to sit now, a princess's throne, little blandishments, cut cubes of toast and a mug of cocoa.

Their voices hushed and raised by turn, their disgust, their simmer, their vicious threats all come to the same thing, the same non-thing. They are pretenders to one another. No one looks anyone in the eye lest they betray themselves. In the sockets of the eyes different densities of dread. They know without knowing.

She recalls the smell of that black silk scarf, with the diamond patterns on it. It smells of mothballs. One day she will look for it, or maybe she won't.

✠

SPHINX

'There was a big fire, all colours but mainly orange. I don't know who'd lit it. Maybe me. The axe was brand new, like the ones in a fairy tale, the blade silvery. It did the work of its own accord. It had only to be told which bit to hack off and it did it. It was a man that was being cut. The pieces were on the floor. They were laid out like vestments. His eyes wouldn't shut, not even when a pendulum was swung back and forth. They were like the sheep's head's eyes in a saucepan, big and glassy. They stared. It was a new tongs and it was easy to lever the bits into the fire. He got roasted, his legs first, then his shoulders, then his other parts. The head was the last. The head took a long, long time. It didn't want to burn. It got a griddle in the end.'

It was as if the woman herself had spoken the words although it was Mary's lips which moved and said them. They were in the woman's caravan, a chenille curtain above the door to keep out the draught. Her mother was in the field outside walking up and down, up and down. This woman was their last resort. At first they had talked a bit, the woman asking her why she liked flowers so much and even knowing that she liked snowdrops the most of all. Then the woman lit a candle and put music on, strange, ethery, and before long went into a sort of a trance and said 'Tell me your nightmare, Mary, tell me your nightmare.' And she did.

When the woman, Olwyn, had first come to the neighbourhood people shunned her and awful things were said about how she harmed people. Her caravan was moved from one site to another and eventually her son came from abroad and made some sort of arrangement with the guards to let her park in the Cáoiserach, the pauper's grave, because no one else would venture there. She kept bees and sold the honey in the local shop, that and sweaters which she knitted and which fitted either man or woman.

'It's a bad dream,' Mary said, looking away. She could feel the woman yawning and trying to bring herself into another state, a more awake state. Then she was putting her feet back into her fleece-lined boots.

'Maybe it's a good dream.'

'It's not ... It's bad.'

'Better dream a bad thing than do a bad thing.'

The woman did not ask who it was, all she did was mix pink powder with jam into a paste and give it to Mary to swallow.

'You won't tell my mother, will you.'

'Why would I tell your mother that which is between us, our secret. You know between every two people in the world there is a secret waiting to be shared and if that happens they are linked. It does happen sometimes, but very seldom.'

'What will you tell her?'

'That you must go away and stay away.'

Her mother does not like being told this and her objections are strenuous and twofold, one is money and the other is that Mary is all they have.

'It would break her father's heart to see her go.'

'Then hearts are going to break,' Olwyn said, conceding that of course no one could forecast anything, only God, God knew how the wind blows, or the embryo fares in the womb of a woman.

Mary sat with her father by the fire, the colours were gorgeous, the flames massive, every description of flame, but at the rear stacked against the chimney wall were two tall ashen sods like tombstones.

'Why do you want to go away to school?'

'It's only for a while.'

'Why don't you stay at home with us ... Why don't you?'

✠

CONVENT

Everything about the convent reassured her. The spick and span atmosphere, the smell of wax polish and wraiths of incense smoke which drifted from the chapel windows each evening after benediction. Smells that wiped out other smells, that dead donkey, the clamminess down in a bog hole, the stuffiness of a room at night, adjoining bodies. There were girls all around in the vast dormitory but she was separate from them. No one touched her. She would become pure. Her other life was over, her second life had begun. Her other life finished the day she left home. Going through the front gate she did not look back. She knew that inside the house they would be crying, either in the same room or in separate rooms.

Passing the town and the town's sulky dogs, passing the bank with the creeper on it that was the colour of ripe strawberries, she had this presentiment that she would not be seeing it again, except that she was wrong. The strawberry creeper had made her think of strawberry jam and how much she loved it and how the fruits were thick and squishy, whereas those in the punnets were watery.

The world she arrived to was strict. Rules met her as she got out of the car and carried her case down a flight of steps and through a concrete passage and up similar steps and she thought, 'I will remember these steps forever.' They were of hard blue limestone with little indentations and little pimples, and she wondered what it was that was so momentous about them. A nun with a list of names checked her name, then ticked it off and told her to speak to second sister. The second sister consulted a different list and told her the saint's name of the dormitory she was assigned to. They were cold and frowning. New girls trudging up the polished stairway swooned and wept as if they were going to prison. The supper consisted of egg salad and single slices of cheese, shaven very thin. It was musty. She thought of the strawberries while she was eating it.

Her mother's first letter arrived almost at once. She was told to go to the parlour and collect it. She was also told that letter writing was restricted to one a week. The parlour smelt holy as if the wax polish was blessed. Her mother said – 'We miss you, I went down to the river to cry as I did not want your father to see me crying. Your father is not hard-boiled, I want you to remember that.'

She shone at lessons and when a nun praised her she blushed. Sister Aquinas praised her the most. The words uttered nasally were like an accolade from another sphere, a heavenly sphere; this nun, tall, aristocratic, singling her out and reading aloud bits of her composition as an example for others. On her copybook, glowing, ebullient remarks and a very deep purple ink that was also a sign of recklessness.

The nuns sealed inside their garments and their guimps were not women, they were snow creatures, and she thought of them as being excavated thousands of years hence, like the ice man in Austria. When she looked at the young postulants she thought she would like to be a nun. She and Sister Aquinas would meet constantly then, in chapels, or in the polished corridors and at night when all rose from their pallet beds to prostrate themselves before God. The postulants' skins were like roses, dog roses, subject to a change in colour, sometimes as if cochineal was dropped onto them from a dropper and other times pale as albumen as if they had suffered a shock. The older nuns had warts and some had traces of moustache. Sister Aquinas, although older, was not like that, her skin was sallow. She lived for when they met, especially when they met by accident, and sometimes she received a little smile and other times Sister Aquinas kept her lids down.

Only her mother's letters kept hauling her back. They were cries for help. The handwriting itself and the words both pierced. Her mother had had shingles and could scarcely hold a pen as two of her fingers had lost their power.

'I haven't drunk tea in seven weeks and no desire to eat. I think I died. Got up in my sleep at night and found myself in other rooms, all alone and afraid. Believe it or not your father makes the fire every morning and cleans out the ashes. He cried after you left. As for tablets, there is a chemist shop inside of me. I feel the cold a lot. I open the back door and shut it again. The cold is like an animal that wants to come inside. No one knows what it is to be getting older. If I were young as you and you were as old as me you would know what I am saying.'

Mary wrote back each Saturday but the words were stilted. She did not know what to say. No one was saying the thing which was most in their hearts. No one. Not her mother. Not her father. Not Sister Aquinas either, Sister Aquinas was sometimes curt, made fun of her in front of other girls because she asked to be excused from drill. They thought she was a spoilsport. But it was not that. She was trying to have no body, to elude it.

STRAWBERRIES

It was during the rosary it happened. A nose bleed, so violent and untoward that it gushed as water might from a town pump. She tried to stop the flow, first with her own hanky and then with the loan of a hanky, but she couldn't. As well as streaking down her face and chin it was also flowing backwards and she thought she would choke. Two girls next to her helped her out and a nun followed. They laid her flat on the recreation hall floor but that did not stop it. They put a dictionary under her head and still the blood came with a vigour. She believed it was a sign. The entire quota of her woman's blood was coming out now, and ever after there would be no more blood, she would have shed it all, she would be clean and porous as a wafer. The red tiles would be the redder for it; it would seep into the glaze and the dye.

Girls came and gawped, some fearing she was going to die, some kneeling to ask if there was anything they could do. Sister Aquinas was summoned to console her. It was like hearing a voice through a cloud of ether, quite calm, telling her not to be afraid, then feeling her pulse, then putting a large bunch of keys at the nape of her neck. There were long keys and short keys, cold at first, but soon they got warm and still the onflow and her head becoming very light as if certain incidents were being leached out of her.

She was brought strawberries as a treat. Sister Aquinas had sent a lay nun to fetch them. They were tinned strawberries, sweet, mushy, gulpable and they reached to the blob at the back of her throat which she had wanted lanced and then lifted out with forceps, to remove a memory taste. It had happened. A segment of strawberry had replaced it.

'Drop down on dew, ye powers from above and let the clouds rain on the just, let the earth be opened and bud forth a saviour.' Sister Aquinas had had the words written out for her on a piece of buff parchment, the capital letters painted in carmine red. She took it and looked at it and said the words again.

'Do you talk to the nursing sister about your woman's things?' Sister Aquinas said. All the others had gone up to bed and the dormitory lights were out, just the two of them with a little torch, like two people bivouacking.

'No.'

'Have you had your woman's things?'

'Sort of.'

'What does that mean?'

'Do nuns have woman's things?'

'Oh yes ... We're women ... Fifty or sixty of us up there ... All nuns and all women, with our women's things and our women's woes and our little spites and our little victories. If you asked me would I enter the convent again were I to know what it entailed, would I, would I, if I could have seen the future in a flash of light.'

'Would you?' Mary asks.

'I didn't say you could ask.'

'I thought you did.'

'I'm glad you've come to us ... It gives us something to look forward to,' Sister Aquinas said quietly, and her hands reached out and touched the face and the keys at the back of the neck, the hair above it warm and matted, but lightly, so lightly it was as if she were a chimera and the touch itself gossamer.

'This is the nicest day of my life, it's like a daydream,' Mary said, her shyness gone because of her head being emptied of all that blood.

✠

BRIDGET

Bridget goes to the river to think. She can think there and she can cry. The river lures her to itself. Many's the time she went in search of geese and goslings, only to find Mr Reynard had been, only to find bits of yellow gosling fur that he had spat out. Long ago.

She comes for another reason. There is something she wants to say. Maybe she can say it to the river. There is no one to talk to. There never was. A voice is telling her that she is not right. She will be leaving them soon, leaving her poor family to their own devices. She is afraid to go. There is no one. There is only herself and the cells, the growing, multiplying, murderous cells.

With approaching death there comes questions and recollection. The little pod called her life. Girlhood. School. Her wedding. Speeches. Her wedding night. Giving birth. And those visits, those lawless visits that she lived for. Knew his stuff he did, with his stethoscope and his ample hatching hand. She lived for those visits, monthly they were. He knew when to come, knew when a woman was ripe, must have gleaned it from his medical lore. Rarely any preliminaries, except that time when he took off his pigskin gloves that were the colour of castor oil. Sat her on the kitchen table and felt her legs, her swinging legs; then that licking sensation and the sounds, wild and strangled in the empty, biding kitchen. A reason for living. A reason for dying. Then his being sent away, far away, struck off the register. No one knew why. All that, long since put to rest or so she thought, but not so, with the steely hooves galloping in. Death. The blackest of words. Two judgements, the immediate one and the everlasting one reserved for the last day. The last day.

Those that thought they knew one another, husbands and wives, sons and daughters, kith and kin, bathed in their shame.

If only the river could wash the soul the way it washed clothing or the body. Her shoes are in her hand, her stockings likewise, and she has found the raised ridge of stepping stones which she has not crossed in so long a time. Her balance is not what it was. She calls out to someone, her arms extended like a lady in a picture holding the scales of life.

The wolfhound whom she had always dreaded met her on the drive, circled her, snapped at her ankles, and showed its teeth when she pelted it with the stones which she had picked up. Betty looked through the window and for a minute it seemed that she was not going to come down.

'I won't come in ... I won't come in,' she says, when eventually the door is drawn back and a sausage cushion kicked to one side.

'Come in, you're all wet.'

'If anything happens to me, Betty, will you look after Mary, will you promise me that?'

'Why should anything happen to you?'

'You think I'm mad but in the past week two people sent me nightdresses ... one is a woman I haven't heard from in years and the other is a relative in Dublin.'

'And what's so wrong with that?'

'They are dressing me, I think, maybe, for the next world.'

'Come in, you're drenched ... I have a good fire on.'

'No, I won't.'

The things she has come to say are too confused and too loathsome. Or has she just come to talk around them, like a hen going around a bush before it lays.

Either way she does not go in. She is better alone with the river or with her fowl.

✠

CHRISTMAS

Afriend called Chrissie invited Mary to go home with her at Christmas. There would be Midnight Mass and most probably a drinks party on Christmas morning. Their house was by the sea. Chrissie's mother was English and she and her husband were separated.

Her mother took it well, said in a letter that of course they would miss her and that her father had taken it badly but that Easter was not far off. She had posted her gifts. In the box which she was allowed to open in the nuns' parlour there were felt slippers, fawn with blue rosettes, a dressing gown cut down from one her mother had had, seersucker, which meant it would not crease, and money in a wallet which her mother had made at night class. She explained that the wallet would at first be very stiff but that with wear it would be like a glove. The note attached was wrenching – 'God grant I'll see you some time again.'

Chrissie's house was not quite on the sea; it was the first of a row of houses that led down to a quay and from the very upstairs window there was a view of boats that had been dragged up for the winter, boats and fishing nets like seaweed strewn over the dark rocks. Seagulls everywhere. She was at the top of the house and Chrissie was one floor down in the room next to her mother. Chrissie's mother was tall and cold with a tortoiseshell hairband in her blond hair. When the telephone rang, moments after they arrived, Chrissie's mother ran to it and then carried it out into the hall. The table was already laid, Chrissie's mother saying that they would eat early because growing girls needed their beauty sleep. The room had a chill to it. Chrissie's mother insisted on keeping the fireguard on.

The dinner was spinach and a pork chop which had a kidney in it.

Christmas Day did not turn out as envisaged. They called on a family after mass and were given coffee and homemade shortbread in a big cold gaunt room with a spinning-wheel in one corner and a view of the sea. There were no ships in sight, the sea itself was storm-tossed. Their presents were at home under the tree yet to be opened. Chrissie's mother had got three slices of turkey which were cooking slowly in a gravy, and the sprouts already peeled and diced were in a bowl, squeezed together, like the fat green beads of a necklace.

'Oh, let me, let me,' Chrissie said, begging to open the champagne. They flinched as she attempted it and then all jumped when the cork seemed to come out of its own accord and catapulted into the room.

Chrissie had several presents, whereas she had only one, but that was to be expected. Nevertheless, she felt a pang as she undid the wrapping paper which had robins on it. She was given a pair of socks, grey, homespun, substantial socks which might be worn with wellingtons. She believed it was her punishment for not having gone home. With the taste of the champagne she felt a bit happier except that she could not stop crying and had to go out of the room twice. Chrissie was cooling off her, siding now with her mother, saying, 'Mummy, you are doing too much,' or 'Isn't Mummy's hair beautiful,' and 'What a pity that Mummy's boyfriend could not come.' His name was Rod and he was performing in a pantomime in England.

After lunch they took a walk to work off the calories as Chrissie's mother said. She walked with the stride of a young boy. Her boots came up to her thighs and she wore corduroy leggings. They parked the car up at the road and walked along a dirt road with the sea on one side churning its rage out and the fields on the opposite side with cows pitifully grouped together and looking for the sight of a human that might bring them fodder, the ground on which they stood mere ridges of grey rock with wisps of hair-thin grass.

'The farmer gives them their din-dins at night,' Chrissie's mother said, soulful, wretched.

Sometimes they walked together and sometimes they were in pairs with one or other straggling behind. Chrissie's mother did not know the new owners of a house they passed, but reckoned they were well-to-do because of the satellite dish. It lay perched like a scooped-out, whitish moon on one side of the roof, and in the garden down below there were several bags of cement as obviously renovations were about to be commenced. There was a Christmas tree the height of the house itself, decorated with tiny lights and very taut cobwebs of mock snow. Chrissie's mother's Christmas tree was made of feathers and could be put away each year in the attic. When they got back to the house Mary felt that she wanted to be alone, and believed that they wanted to be alone too.

She walked in the opposite direction, past the shops and the guest houses, the gulls coasting just above her, creatures of town as much as of sea, and seeing a sign for a factory, she headed there. To her surprise it was open and there were a few customers inside. At the back the men were busy making the instruments, one with his hands clasped around a drum while a second one was stretching the moistened skin over the barrel, and then a third man thonged it down. Finished instruments were on the shelves ready to be bought, different circumferences, their fawn-grey skins decorated with pictures, solemn and beautiful, faces in blue and indigo, redolent of Christ and the apostles. Now and then someone tapped one of the skins or picked up a musical stick and attempted a tune. Different tunes were heard until the workman at the back had the brainwave to play 'Silent Night' and everyone paused to listen, people lifting off the hoods of their anoraks to hear it more clearly, and afterwards there was clapping and the lady at the counter handed out cartons of coffee and mince pies for free. It was at that point Mary felt in her pocket, felt the key there and her mother's note – 'God grant I'll see you some time again.' She sat in a corner and read it to herself and felt a most terrible pity for her mother and pity for her father too and shame in herself for not having gone home.

They were upstairs when she arrived back; a light was on up there. She could not find the key. She felt the folded letter and a little nest of holes in her pocket but not a key. It had slipped through the lining, that was it. She ran her hand along the bottom hem, heartening each moment when she felt something hard, only to realise that it was the pennies the tailor had put in there to keep the hem from bunching up. She tried all the way in one direction and then another. It was not there. The street lights coming on were in themselves a lucky omen. If she kept exactly to the same route she must find it and so she retraced, recalling each detail, the bags of coal, the stacks of briquettes with metal bands, a freakish bow of geranium in the porch of a guest house, and the factory sign with the pictures of the instruments. The woman in the shop was very helpful, searched with her, searched all along the ledges and got a flashlamp to train into the darker corners but to no avail.

On the way back she decided that it was not enough to look and so she knelt from time to time, believing that it might have rolled into a crevice, and even mistook the sharp metallic wrapping of a champagne cork, thought it was it.

The moment when she knocked, she knew that Chrissie would shout down, tell her to let herself in, and she would have to answer and say that she was afraid she had lost the key. It was as she had imagined it, her describing the double journey, going back to the factory, even asking in a paper shop if anyone had handed in a key and Chrissie's mother's irritation magnifying at the stupidity of that, the rampant stupidity, asking did she want the whole town to know that she had lost their doorkey, inviting robbers in, then grasping the hem as she herself had done, getting tetchier, saying, 'What a pain you are ... What a pain.'

When her mother left the room to savour her anger in private, it was Chrissie's turn to be injured, to feel betrayed – 'It would be you ... Of all the girls I could have invited home ... it would be you.'

FUGI

As soon as the doctor said she would have to have tests Bridget knew.

'What's wrong with me?' she says.

'It could be your spine,' he says and then thinks to contradict himself and says, 'It could be an ulcer.'

He is a new doctor, spent most of his time training horses to jump over barrels which he had in his back yard.

'Which – spine or ulcer?'

'Or it could be a disc wearing out ... They do wear out, you know.'

'So it could be anything...'

'We'll know very soon ... They can diagnose anything now.'

'So it's not the shingles still.'

'I don't think so ... Anyhow, I'm going to give you painkillers.'

'I don't mind the pain, Doctor.'

'I would rather you didn't lift things,' he says, tearing a letter sheet to refer her to the specialist.

'Why not?'

'It could be scoliosis.'

'What's that?'

'Look, I don't want to be an alarmist.'

'I'd rather you were straight with me.'

She cannot utter the word. Once said it becomes a reality. She recalls reading an account of it once in a magazine, the malign cells, growths, like armies invading the body, and for some reason they have become the broken-off florets of cauliflower, brown and mouldy.

'It's a grey area,' he says, drying the letter on a rolling pin of blotter.

'A grey area.' She is holding her stockings and they are grey too, light grey with ladders in them. On normal occasions she wore lisle.

'Will I know straight away?'

'Oh, we better not move the posts till we start the race.'

Hunting talk, horse talk, snob talk.

'May I ask you one question?'

'Fire ahead.'

'Even as we speak, is it spreading?'

'That depends, whether it's in the primaries or the secondaries, that depends ... But the tests will tell us all.'

He gets into his coupé car, looks in the mirror, slicking his hair back, doesn't even offer her a lift. Probably thought that she had her own transport, nearly all had, young girls, collecting each other or dropping each other off, to play bridge or do yoga or go to a sun-tan parlour. Her stockings are still in her hands, but it is dark and she is the only person out.

The houses and the bungalows are full of new people, many of them foreign. In some windows the curtains are parted. She sees a mobile, a circlet of tin ponies, gaily painted, going round and round on a hoop of varnished timber. They are circus ponies. There is a child in the room, a child and a man. They are cooking something, the child holding up the big cookery book and the man whisking, then offering her the dribbles on the whisk to lick. They are foreign. She knew that house once, used to go there and visit, used to call on Mrs Phelan. They all called each other Mrs in those days, the women did. They did not make so free as to use Christian names. Mrs Phelan had no family and her husband owned a shop a few hundred yards from the house. In time he began to drink. No one knew which came first, his drinking or her oddness. She imagined things, Mrs Phelan did, took huff. That incident over the stockings, for instance. Mrs Phelan had gone upstairs and brought down a pair of silk stockings that Tim, her husband, had got from a commercial traveller. They were out of their wrapping and she held them and then ran her hand through one of them and her forearm to show the impression with flesh in them. It was after she removed her hand that the screaming started, her sighting the ladder, blaming Bridget who had merely looked on.

'Look what you've done ... These are very expensive stockings and look what you've done.'

'Mrs Phelan,' she had said in as low and as reasonable a voice as she could manage. She forbore from saying, 'It's your wedding ring or your eternity ring that has torn them,' and she held her own worn hand up in some sort of propriation but Mrs Phelan would not have it. She would not have any excuses and what she did then was drastic. She picked the kettle of boiling water off the range, slung the water along the floor and told her visitor to get out. A few months after that she was taken away. Not heard of again. That was the awful part. Once anyone went there no one asked and no one visited, only a husband or a relative.

'Can I help you.' The man had unlatched the window and leant out. 'Are you lost?' His voice so comforting; because of its being his second language, he took care with the words.

'I used to know the lady who lived here.'

'She did some strange things to the house ... She blocked up the fireplaces ... But we've opened them again.'

She had heard of this man. He had a mushroom farm, he grew mushrooms indoors and sent them as far away as Paris, or Brussels or Berlin.

'Let me show you ... Let me show you where I grow them.'

They meet outside and with a torch he guides her across a short field to a series of glasshouses covered in black plastic which gives the field a funereal look.

Inside it was like being sent underground, the atmosphere so dark and stifling, a musty smell, a feeling as if the air was full of spores, full of germs, the gloom of it seeping into the spores inside her. The last place she should be. He had begun some rigmarole about the mushrooms, how long they took to germinate, how diffi- cult it was to get them off to the cities, off to the restaurants in town, the losses incurred from blight and hearing that word she saw the black and rotting cavities of blighted potatoes.

'I am sick ... But how sick ... That is the six mark question,' she said starkly.

'I am sorry,' he said, a little thrown.

'And I am not even that old,' she said and staggered as she went out.

✠

LADYBIRD

Between Sister Aquinas and herself there are trysts, holy pictures exchanged, and sometimes in the convent grounds Sister takes from her pocket a pear or a plum, which Mary believes she has sacrificed from her own lunch. There are tiffs also, Sister belittling her in the classroom, saying she is slipping, her essays are lacklustre. But on Saturday these things are always amended when they meet to clean the cookery kitchen.

When Mary arrives a few minutes late, the Sister is sitting on the edge of the table, like a woman in a fairground, a trooper.

'Look.'

'What.'

'Can't you see it.' At that Sister Aquinas ruffles the serge of her skirt to reveal what looks to be a coral bead but is in fact a ladybird. It does not move.

'Shut your eyes.'

With a rubber spatula she gently eases it off and puts it on Mary's lap.

'You can open them now.' The bead is on the pleat of her gym frock, worming its way in and out. When she looks closely, she sees tiny whiskers, taut, prehensive, probably alarmed at being shifted from one body to another.

'We frightened it,' she says.

'Poor thing,' Sister says, lamenting a ladybird's life, prey to every kind of disease, predators searching for a weak spot in her armour, finding it, tapping a hole, and later grubs getting in there and eating the creature from within.

'What does it live on?' Mary asks.

'The juices of leaves and flowers.'

'How did it get onto you?' Mary asks.

'I don't know ... It must have mistaken me for a leaf or a flower, the silly thing.'

'We should bring it to the garden to a tree.'

'We should not ... It's lucky ... It's ours.'

'But who'll mind it ...'

'You or me ... We'll make a pet of it ...'

'We're not the juices of leaves or flowers.'

'How do you know ... You're not a ladybird.'

'It's gone ... It's not on me,' Mary says, looking down and ruffling her clothes.

They begin a search for it then, touching their own and each other's clothing, the touching quite delicate so that only the cloth is felt, shaking out pleats and big dipping sleeves, scolding each other for losing sight of it, feeling each other's nearness, each other's excitement, pausing for the moment for it to show itself, then patting one another with wooden spoons until eventually Mary sees it going slowly down her leg.

'You've got it ... You look after it for a week.'

'Suppose it dies on me.'

'I'll punish you if it does.'

'How?'

'I'll make a hole in your armour and then I'll eat you from inside,' she says and goes out, chuckling, triumphant. The stoves and pudding bowls look lonely then in the big dark kitchen and Mary did not know, could not know, that she would not see her idol again.

✠

COMPANIONS IN DEATH

Four women like effigies propped up on the raised single beds, the very white of the linen imparting a bridal thrall, bony hands saying their beads, in the eyes the nervousness and fear, like candles when they gutter. Greta's ordeal is over, she has had her operation, has had her breast removed and is looking forward to going home, recovering. Bridget does not know her fate. Hers are the ovaries, an ovarian mass. The doctor has not told her; he has told her husband, who balked at it, seemed unable to let it sink in. She's having treatment and drugs for the pain. Peggy, the third lady, is recovering, writing simple words such as Cat or Mouse into a little copybook. In a previous hospital she was given medicines which she was allergic to and which robbed her of her faculties for almost a year. Her mind is coming back, words, grammar, memory, and she is preparing a case to sue the first hospital. Patsy, the fourth, is on a drip and still blurred, but lucky not to have died, lucky that the burst appendix was caught in time.

They share the gifts they get, oranges, grapes, magazines; they read their horoscopes and make jokes about Venus being in one or the other's ninth house. They are a happy family, none of them boisterous. They have all received similar bunches of flowers, carnations lined along the windowsills in opaque hospital vases, a little flourish of white gypsophila over each one, like nurses' caps. Red and white were not lucky and no hospital should allow it, so Peggy had said. They are careful not to mention death, they keep to their chatter about their farms and how their children are doing and little sallies about that planet Venus.

Bridget was given drugs and sometimes, soon after, she floated off, told little tales, rambled, said snatches of recitation –

'A pound of tea at one and three
A pot of raspberry jam
Two new-laid eggs, a dozen of pegs
And a pound of rashers of ham.'

In a peremptory voice she called out to her hens and her little pullets, her flock. Chuck. Chuck. Chuck. Recalled their fret when they got ready to lay. The bother that came on them. Never touched an egg. A gug. No not she. Dirty, that dirty bit of snout inside the yolk and the whites smeary, sticking to one. Spoke of a caller then, a caller who came once a month, before her monthlies. Knew when to come. Sometimes wore a pair of pigskin gloves. The ugly yellow of castor oil. Peeled them off slowly. Dandled her legs. That fellow ... that fellow. Never touched an egg she.

They would hear her in the mornings when they wakened. Stories that she was telling herself, or them. Wasn't she bold, very. Oh yes. Once as a girl she was sent to buy a loaf, and so warm and so tempting did it smell that she made a hole in it and began to pick out the bits of warm dough, bit after bit, until there was nothing left, only an empty well-baked shell.

She held Nurse Boland's hand, her face white and aghast against the linen, and asked little things, little favours, if the nurse would be sure to mind her dog Shep and if Nurse would be sure to tell them not to let the crab apples rot in the autumn, to make a jelly and to strain it well.

'When is Mary coming?' she asked again.

'Tomorrow.'

'Will I last?'

'Of course you'll last.'

She drew back then, the breathing stertorous, the eyes both glittering and fading, saying it was a hard thing but she was beginning to doubt God. Then the words came out in a tumble, like food being thrown back. Tawpa. Tawpa. Whatever Tawpa meant. Her face, like a piece of blotter, soaking up the nurse's fresh, rose-petal skin.

'Hold on to your looks,' she said, her speech her own for an instant, the eyes comprehending, then not.

'You have a little rest now and I'll come back with your tea.'

'I'm off tea ... I'd like an ice.'

Towards evening she was sitting up in a chair. Their food had come, the food which the nurse had ticked off on the supper menu — mushrooms on toast and a vanilla yoghurt.

'Why don't we sing a song,' she said to her companions.

'You sing.'

'I haven't a good voice ... keep me company,' she said but they refused and so she launched into song herself, her voice quavery, a little hint of reproach in her eyes for their refusing of her. It was a song about October winds, lamenting around empty castle doors, and the picture her three friends would retain of her was of a woman smiling, pleading with them to join in and to feel the fate of the great deserted house where banquets were no more.

Suddenly water begins to issue from her, a great cataractic gush, as if the placenta has broken and a child is coming out, but they know that it augurs death, something in her colouring, the sudden cancellation of her voice, the body heaving, sinking down down onto the floor and Patsy calling the nurse. Nurse. Nurse. Then it is nurses flying into the ward, emergency signals, shouts, the curtain being drawn around her bed, the drawn curtain that last sheath between death and life. The doctor has arrived. Prayers are being said. Prayers for the dead.

'So sudden ... So sudden.'

'Singing like that and then ...'

'And then the body system just breaking down.'

This is what the women say and repeat, each one receding into her own slough of terror.

A PROMISE

All around the blended voices, low and funereal, the same doleful helpless words again and again, a tithe of sorrows. The table was not laid as nicely as if her mother had done it, and the cakes and even the sandwiches were from a shop. Lizzie and herself had taken the wrapping off the sandwiches and garnished them with parsley to pretend they were homemade.

'Your poor mother.'

'Poor Bridget.'

'She went so fast.'

'Too fast.'

'A merciful end ... Peace at last.'

But that was not true. Mary knew it from Nurse Boland, knew that her mother had died struggling, struggling to get something out, something that mattered, and even when her tongue and her speech had failed her she had tried to convey it with her gums, her spittle. What might that be. They were upstairs. At least they had found the money, notes folded and tucked into a small brown envelope with a bit of gold ribbon around it. For days her mother had been saying her name and Tawpa ... Tawpa, and eventually they traced what it was, herself and Nurse Boland getting on chairs and putting their hands into the dust and frayed cobwebs on the tops of wardrobes, eventually coming on it, marked private and confidential. Her nest egg. They counted it. Just over five hundred pounds.

'I'd like you to have half,' Mary said.

'No, it's yours, your birthright.'

'Take some of it.'

'I couldn't.'

'It would help for you to go to Boston.'

The nurse had told her about her boyfriend who was a doorman in Boston and how she was afraid that he was losing interest, that his voice was colder now when he phoned on Sundays and he admitted that he was no longer pining.

'I'll tell you what,' she said then. 'I'll take something of your mother's.'

'Take anything.'

'I'll take a handbag.' And from another drawer they hauled out an assortment of bags, cloth, leather, beaded, all with mementoes in them, loose pearls, prayers, hankies with mottoes and one lock of curly black hair that seemed to have formed itself into an inscrutable cypher. It was a man's hair, black. The nurse settled on a crocodile bag that had been scarcely worn, the grey pimply skin hard and mottled stiff as linoleum and the clasp was stiff too, from unuse.

'If I tell you something, will you promise not to tell.'

'I promise.'

'She was gasping for you ... Asking was it far where she was going, and would you go with her,' the nurse said, worry in her eyes.

'We'd better go down,' Mary said. Something too fearful about what she had just heard.

Her father stands in the dining room, tall, emaciated, a graven image of dereliction, people trying to comfort him, begging him to sit down, to eat a bit. His raincoat swings open and in the inside pocket Mary can see the nozzle of a whiskey bottle. He raises his hand to his head, scraping his scalp, then reaches for the bottle, a broken, despairing look in his eyes.

'Don't, Dad ... Don't drink,' and she rushes to him in a wild, pleading desperation.

'I won't drink if you promise me something.' His half-drunk eyes swilling up in childish expression. She knows what it will be and yet a gasp escapes her when he says it, when he pronounces it. Her death sentence.

'Will you stay at home for a few months and mind your father?'

Each and every face is looking at her now, straining, suspenseful, certain that she will not, that she could not, refuse a cry such as that. Their faces are swimming round her. She nods then, a mute assent, and in gratitude he puts one hand around her neck, lops it around her neck, then with his mouth unscrews the bottle top, drinks from it and spits it out to prove to them his resolve, then holding the bottle upside-down he empties it in fat glugs into the spare cups and slop bowl.

She ran out then through the hall door and shouted and prayed into the driving rain, and asked that it be not so, that the promise she had made she could be absolved from, that one of them would stand up and say, 'She can come to us', and kneeling on the hard gravel, she prayed for that, then thought of Gethsemane and of the Saviour having to drink of the cup of pain.

They came and lugged her in a further bathos of sentiment, saying 'Don't grieve love ... Don't grieve ... Your mammy is safe in heaven ... And you're still a family ...'

Only Lizzie knew why she was crying. Lizzie had done washing, Lizzie had seen things.

✠

UNDERTAKERS

The undertaker's wife scowled at being disturbed at that unearthly hour. Through the slit of the hall door, Mary saw only a thin nose and vexed eyes.

'I want to see my mother,' she said. She had come to say something. Something important. She did not know what. She had got up as soon as the light came through the blinds and fell upon the objects in the room, separating them so that there was a washstand, a ewer, holy pictures, objects rescued from the dark and dark's grope. She had crept out, hearing her father in the next room, his roaring, his flexing shins, and saw Lizzie in the twin bed clutching a big doll in a net gown.

'Come in,' the woman said, darting to the stove to lift a pan of fat that was about to catch fire. In the crook of her other arm there was a baby which she swung back and forth as she might a garden gate. She called her husband, called him by his nickname which was Buss.

'Buss, Mary MacNamara is out here and wants to see her mother.'

The remains were kept in rooms away from the living quarters, rooms that were not quite garages but almost. He came down in his shirtsleeves, a bright shirt, like a cowboy, reds and ochres. He led her through cold passages where there were bicycles, tricycles, then down steps and into a dim room with the bulk of one coffin. Two would have been friendlier. It was on four rung-backed chairs and the room spray which they had used smelled of lilac. It was a cloying smell.

'I'm sorry to bother you.'

'You're all right . . . You're all right,' he said.

He asked her things while he unlevered the nails, asked her how school was, how her daddy was taking it, when had she last seen her mammy, but he did not wait for the answers. The new nails positioned upright along the white paint of the mantelshelf were like a host of insects, and the coffin lid aslant against the window a tall, stern onlooker. For a moment its bulk had made the room dimmer and then her eyes adjusted and Mary let out a little shriek when she saw her mother's expression, a more alive than dead determining in it. There was a snarl at the corner of her mouth, her upper lip raised in a helpless and grotesque curl. She wanted to put her hand there and press the two lips together but she was afraid. Her mother had striven to speak unfinished words. And she, she now would not be able to say that which she had come to say.

'Her habit is lovely,' she said, to be polite. It was cream, a pleated satin, and her hair which was tucked under and folded had the soft mesh of a brown snood. Who had done it. Who had dressed it with such a tenderness.

'Don't you want to pray?' he said.

'Yes.'

'Then kneel down.'

'I'll pray later at mass.'

'Don't you want to kiss your poor mother goodbye?'

'I don't,' she said abruptly. She had loved her mother too much and not enough. Both. And in the end she had withheld love and now she was ashamed.

When she lay awake all night under mounds of blankets, trying to shut out the creaks, the slamming of the lavatory door and her father's outcries, she had resolved to get up early and go and ask her mother's permission to renege on the promise about staying at home. Her mother would grant it, she was sure of that. But now, seeing the cold and lifeless form, she could not bring herself to whisper the words. She thought that maybe it was because she did not love her mother enough and that one can only ask favours of those whom one loves unquestionably.

He picked the lid up, disgruntled, the bumping of it along the floor, his way of saying 'Young people have no nature in them now.'

He also kicked the white round wreaths of flowers, which looked so beautiful, offerings, like basins of settling milk.

Just as he had the upper corner of the lid levered down, and was walking with the rest, easing it, gauging it so as not to disturb the habit, a fly materialised out of the dust, like a piece of dust itself but with more swirl.

It slips underneath the lid and vanishes in there.

'Jesus it will go mad ... It will drive her mad,' Mary says.

'What will?'

'A fly ... I saw a fly go in there.'

He peers, listens, then slammed the lid down, tight as a drum.

FOALING

'The best friend we ever had ... We're succourless now,' James says and keeps asking his dead wife, Bridget, what they must do. They have come outside. Mary prefers it when they are outside. It is pouring with rain. He asks it of the bits of wall which he stops to lean against and of the clods of spongy moss which come away in his hand. He asks it of the outhouses into which he peers and hollers, as if something or someone harmful might be lurking. It is pelting down, the noise of it, through the trees, as of dry corn being winnowed through a crusher.

It is soaking into walls, grass, treetops and they themselves, and they drink it in, as elsewhere in the world someone is drinking in rays of sunshine. She thinks if the stones of these walls were split there would be little pools of water in them, little watery hollows telling their history. It is almost a month now since her mother died and the months-mind mass is soon to be said. The house is lonelier and dismaler and even though she's watered the plants and did some dusting, things are not the same.

They have come up to look at a mare that is due to foal, and getting Mary to hold the tilly lamp, he runs his hands up and down the mare's teeth and by the waxiness tells her that she is ready and furthermore her milk bag is full.

They walk, tracing and retracing the same bit of mucky cobble, his voice full of lamentation. Only two of the outbuildings are occupied, the one with hens and the one with the mare, who has suddenly started to go berserk, to let out repeated and crazed neighings, bounding to each of the four corners of the stall, crashing into a panel of hardboard like some circus animal.

'She'll foal soon,' he says.

'Shouldn't we watch?'

'They don't like it ... They don't like anybody watching.'

'Why is that?'

'How the hell do I know,' he says, the frazzle rising in him again, and he shouts back to the prancing animal, 'Your pins are dropped, missy ... You're ready.'

A distance away is the henhouse. For no reason he removes the splintered broom handle that holds the henhouse door fast, pushes the door in to shine the lantern on the dozen or so startled creatures, huddled on their perches, stirring now, thinking that a fox is come, their bronze-red feathers curdling, their eyes beady in the light, not fully awake, not fully asleep, letting out puny chuck-chucks, sounds that denote abject and composite terror. There is a smell of dung, old trampled dung mixed with fresh dung, and plops of rain fall through the hole in the skylight.

'Cowards,' he says and adds that he cannot stand a coward, then grapples one of them by the neck and says that it is all U.P. for her and her comrades, that he hasn't seen an egg for days, for weeks, and that he will get the butcher to come and buy the whole bloody pack.

'You'll be on hotel menus before a week is out,' he says, threateningly.

'Don't be hard on them, Mam loved them,' Mary says, to coax him back to his earlier state of reminiscence.

'They killed her,' he says and then dwells on the buckets of oats, the cauldrons of meal his wife cooked, then mashed, then carried to the various henhouses where her different broods were stationed, and he paints a wholesome picture of former times, breeds of hens from the four corners of the earth, troughs which did not tip over and which allowed hens to eat like civilised birds, not crack-aillies running and tearing after one stray gob of food while a pan of it confronts them and likewise the inverted aluminium cans which allowed for a steady flow of water into a timbal, and he praises his wife for knowing about these new fandangos and for sending away for them. It is as if the hens and nothing else hastened the woman's death.

'She could have been president of this country,' he says, while Mary thinks of her mother combating their poverty with the eggs she sold, or the brace of cockerels she gave away as gifts to people they were in debt to, and in her mind's eye and even on her tongue there comes the sudden mild taste of boiled chicken and warm parsley sauce, boiled because it went further than roast, and she even sees the shreds of meat kept for his snack on Mondays. Her mother is present for an instant, wiping the eggs with a pinch of bicarbonate before selling them, estimating how much she will get, in her always the growing dread of destitution, the memory of the evictions that had befallen her poor forebears.

'The best friend I ever had,' is what he is saying. Can that be true. Was there between them a nearness, that knowing, when people meet and dissolve into one another.

Was it her and her little sister that put a shadow on things. Her sister who only survived a few days and was buried in a grave a long way off, as if there were some disgrace attached to her. If only she were alive now they could manage their father together; they could be the parents and allow him to be the child, swaddle him, keep his temper from flaring.

They are heading back to the house and a bit of supper when they hear it, a series of neighings, urgent, pleading, primordial.

'She's started,' he says and runs to find her, in a last crazed swirl, navy eyes, like big marbles, whirling inside sockets of blood as she tries to climb the half door, almost scaling it, then missing, crashing and trampling on the partition which she has made smithereens of.

'Whoa ... Whoa,' he says and undoes the bolt and she comes out like a substance of lightning, hot, sable, electrified, determined to escape the violence within her.

'Catch her ... Catch her,' he shouts, losing his grip on her forelock and ducking as she makes a vicious lunge, slashing his coat sleeve, and then with that unerring fleeing instinct heads towards the gateway. He catches up with her as she tries to breach the gate, mounts her, half riding her, half clutching her, her body meteoric, trying to offload him.

'I'll get the vet ... I'll get the vet,' Mary says, but he does not hear her because of the bedlam, a metallic madness as the loose rungs and hasp of the gate keep jarring. Finally as he lifts her back, kicking and snorting she caves onto the ground in an equal mixture of outrage and capitulation. On the ground she is writhing and her face in the light is like a turd of pink rubber, and the holes in her nostrils orifices of fear.

'I better get the vet,' Mary says again.

'You'll stay here . . . This is a two man job,' he says and kneels to quiet the animal, to still her, repeating the same words, non-words, horse words, almost one with her now as he lies within the striking radius of her raised and gyreing legs, telling her to get it over, to get it out, occasionally putting the palm of his hand on the long perspiring trowel of her forehead.

'Oh feck,' he says as the light catches the metal glints of one hoof, a sign that the foal is cock-eyed inside her.

'I'll get Peadar,' Mary says again, fearing carnage and worse.

'I told you, stay where you are,' he says, shouting at her to train the light so that he can get a grip on the fetlocks and push them back in. Each time he fails. What they see are hooves and little fetlocks jutting out, then receding, then edging out that bit further and the groans of the mare so pitiful it is as if she is being carved within. Eventually he gets a grip on one hoof, holding it quite still for a second, waiting, then pushes it a fraction, pauses, allowing the mare to breathe, to breathe into the spasms of pain and then, freeing himself of his jacket, he raises his shirtsleeves up to his elbow, then his hand, wrist and lower arm disappear into her. She can feel the fear in him and the matching fear in the animal and her own fear, the fear of all three inextricable in the miry dark.

He is talking to the animal again, the half words, the horse words, his arm both a hearing and a listening implement, and from the mare now an almost human plaint, no longer frenzied, crouched, abject, her gasps no louder than a stutter, the occasional weak purposeless surge to rise a mere parody of her earlier zaniness. Then she stops breathing as if it is all too much, as if she will die. Mare and foal, though of the same flesh, are warring, two warring things, not like a mother and its young, each fighting the other, except that the foal is the stronger, her energy and her thrusting prodigal now. With his free hand he massages the mare's rump to rally her, to put life back into her, for one last supreme effort, while inside something is heard, a clatter like a chair being thrown, and he waits a moment longer, all of him listening, then withdraws his hand and says, 'She'll fly out, she'll fly out now.' But that does not happen. Not yet.

In her hastiness the mare has managed to cause the head inside to twist and what they hear are the legs, bunched up and battering on the chest. Hearing it, he becomes alarmed, shouts to the mother to muster herself or the thing will have to be cut out of her. Dead.

With a taut and terrible delicacy, as if it is a child that he is assisting into the world, he puts his hand inside again, using his palm then as a font, for the foal to put its chin on, and with his two fingers he tries to keep the nostrils open, saying the words, the same animal words, a Morse. They wait, completely silent, then it is as if a feat of nature has commenced, and in complete contrast to the obduracy of almost an hour, the foal begins to flow out, a long and tender swathe of wet flesh, fluid, dimensionless, with the beauty of a stream or a river, and behind it the after-birth in a flurried and spongy mess and the mare's breathing starting to be normal again and his exhilaration as he tells Mary to run to the house, love, for the scissors, so that he can cut the cord.

When she comes back she sees the mare starting to lick the animal, quietly and meditatively, her whinny so soft, so calm, like the rustle of birds in the trees at dusk. Everything is changed, the animals, her father, herself. She is crying with a kind of relief.

'Villain,' he is saying to the foal as he tries and fails to get her up. She is like some painted puppet, richly burnished, her various limbs and ligaments not affixed to her, merely placed side by side, useless, because each time as she rises, she stumbles again and decides to fall. Her legs little tapers. When she does at last stand she staggers and he holds her, murmuring the same kind of talk, and she begins with her eyes and her exhalations to absorb her new world, a yard, the after-birth, a bit of moon, the dark silhouette of her mother standing nearly inert, waiting to be suckled, the rain cooling the sweat on her haunches.

'I've been around horses all my life and I never had to do that before.'

'You did it.'

'Did I, darling,' he says and patting the foal again he pronounces her villain and says, 'You nearly killed your mother, only for me.'

The absolute and instantaneous rapport with the animal, so tender and true such as he had never shown her or her mother or possibly anyone. She thinks then that if she could be a child, maybe if she can be truly a child and make her needs known, he can feel as a father, and then in a lunatic impulse to make that come true she throws away the one thing in the world that might have been her independence.

'You know you said that you wanted to get a tombstone for Mam ... Well, I have a bit of money.'

'I want your mother to have as good a grave as anyone, a better grave,' he says.

'I'll give you the money,' she says.

'You're the best girl,' he says and pats her as a moment before he had patted the animal.

Deciding on a tomb took an age. They walked around the factory which had second-hand furniture in one wing and an assortment of different type tombs in the other. The plain functional furniture and solemn sofas, a prelude to life, and the numerous tombstones awaiting their quota of dead. They decided on a black slab onto which letters could be stencilled in gold. From time to time he took the money out of his pocket, a humble wad folded and crumpled. The stonemason had taken a liking to them and had given them bread and tea. Her father mused over what he wanted written: comfort words – love and loving and beloved. Where was her mother now. Were her first wanderings over and was she in some interim place, the dried fly stuck to her, with other dead souls, doing penances. Was there a communication between the living and the dead, the dead maybe having more mercy because of what they had been through. She had read that in a school book.

The stonemason threw in some marble chips at half price, the lumps the off-white and brown of coffee sugar. They had the tombstone wrapped and re-wrapped in sacking, and late that night under the light of the moon, Ned, a young workman, dug and dug, until the cavity was deep enough to hold the base and allow it to balance there without wobbling, and then for good measure he dug a few more sods. The clay looked grim and unfriendly. The moon was making zany patterns, fastening on anything it could, framing the young man's brow, and her father's cigarette, which somehow seemed profane. Her father was in his element. He said then that they should kneel and pray, and they did. The two men with their heads uncovered, half-kneeling, praying, and she too asking that when she asked her father if she could go back to the convent he would say yes. Yes. The patterns of the moon were light and glancing in contrast with the austerity of the full moon itself.

ROOSTING

The hens were already in and on their perches, huddled together, feathers pleached tight. The place was cold and clammy at one and the same time. She had been sent home from school with a temperature. It was cold near the door and warm over in the far corner, a stifling smell of dung. It was almost dark.

Up at home she saw the blinds drawn which meant that her father was in bed. She did not want to go in then. She would go in when he got up. In the meantime she could tell the time by the sky. She watched the sun slant down and veer far out into rosy tributaries of reds, then copper coloured, then last of all, a beaded lilac. The songbirds were in droves, rather than separate, whirling and somer-saulting, exercising themselves before going in for the night.

The teacher had called her aside and asked her why she was not well. He was the head teacher, a nice man, said he wanted her to know that he was there for her, to think of him as a shepherd on the mountain. He had felt her forehead. Had asked her if she would like him to call the public nurse. She said no. Again, he had asked her if there were any problems. Again she said no. It was the only thing to say. He was a big man with a big appetite and she smiled when he said that her visits reminded him of a robin redbreast landing on his doorstep. He asked then if there was anything in particular she wanted to talk about. She said no. He asked if she would prefer a female to discuss her problem. She said no and felt tears welling up. He went out of the room to the little pantry and came back with a doughnut. Gave it to her to take home. He said he wanted her to trust him and he wanted her to know something. She flinched at that. He wanted her to give her all to her studies, because by his reckoning she could go far, she could sweep the country, she could make a name for the county.

'What in Christ's name!' Her father leapt when he saw the shadowed form in the henhouse, then bristled at being made to seem so foolish as to show alarm. He had come out to collect an egg or two. He wore a raincoat over his pyjamas.

'What are you doing here?'

'I was sent home sick.'

'Why didn't you come up home?'

'Because I'm waiting for Tara ... She said to wait here.'

'Get on up home.'

'She'll be here in a jif ... We're doing French together ... The teacher said we have to talk it to each other ... We have to talk French.'

'C'mon up home.'

Even in the draining light she could read his face, the expression in it not cross but melting, and his eyes getting that bit softer, liquidy, as if the pupils had burst and overflowed. He searched the various nests and cheered at his find. Five eggs. A windfall. Told her to lift her gym frock then, for it to be a basket, an egg basket.

'Are they all in?' he asked.

'I don't know ... I don't think so.'

'Is Mr Cock-a-Doodle-Dandy in ... He better be ... He has jobs to do with his buxom family.'

'I think there's some still out,' she said, moving to go, and he pushed her then into the shadows, saying that all he wanted was a little lady to cook him his tea.

'You can't,' she said, hearing the eggs with a feeble plash drop onto the straw.

'What can't ... What are you saying?' and he stumbled on one of the feeding troughs and she runs out as if guided by a certainty, as if she knew exactly what was to materialise, knew exactly that which was to become true, Lizzie crossing the fields with their washing, a big bundle, like a linen baby in her arms.

She ran to her until their faces were quite close and then said, 'Lizzie,' but in a voice which conveyed everything.

'The divil ... The ringing divil,' Lizzie said, then mashed her lips because of the words which had escaped her.

✠

SHRINE

The driver was late. Hock was his name. First a funeral and then a puncture, Lizzie and herself having to sit on a strange wall while he changed the tyre. The countryside was very different, very bleak, not many trees and no hedges, just vistas of stony field with young calves, delicate as fawns, munching but quite unsteady on their legs.

When they passed a golf links Lizzie asked him to slow down so that they could look at it, admire the little elevations of green with the flags on them and the golf balls which were like freak skulls. They were going to a shrine to pray for their special intentions. It was a famous shrine, known for its miracles and for the relief it brought to sick people.

It was dusk when they found it. They had passed it two or three times and eventually Hock had to wind the window down and shout out, 'Where's the holy shrine?' In the path which led to it garments hung from a bush and looked spooky in the light. What met them inside was the rapid sound of running water, water pouring through a wall of stone, and forming a kind of waterfall before it reached the well proper. The well was known never to have dried up, not even in a drought. Another proof of its holiness. The atmosphere felt damp, damp spaces between the stones crammed with statues and requests as well as gifts and offerings. People had left their crutches and walking sticks. There were hundreds of rosary beads. Beside the well itself there was a cracked cup for the faithful to drink from. Lizzie whispered that it might give them the runs but that they would have to do it all the same so as not to be heathens.

The well water was very brown with foam on it. The painted

Virgin above was in blue and perched on cloud, pillows of blue vapour holding her up.

> 'Sweet St Bridget of the kine
> Bless these little fields of mine
> The pasture and the shady trees
> Bless the butter and the cheese.'

Lizzie read it out. She said then that they should kneel down but in God's name to be careful not to fall in. She told Mary to implore, to repeat her request again and again, to make sure that God heard. She said that before they drank of the water they should dip their hands in it and dampen their mouths and dampen their lids, in order to make themselves worthy. When they had done that she asked Mary to hold her coat while she leant in to peer down. She was looking for an eel. If they were to see an eel, everything would come out all right. A lame man had seen three eels one morning and was cured. It was Hock who told them that. Lizzie pointed then to the big horn rosary suspended in a niche and said that they were probably meant to finger the beads as a mark of devotion.

When they had done that she said that there was only one last thing and that it was very private and they would each have to put their coats over their heads while they did it. They were to touch the private part of their bodies with the water to banish all stain of past or future sin. They did it at the same moment, then pulled their coats down, smoothed them and knelt for a moment while they asked for guidance on how to word their requests. The most important thing of all was the wording. They had read some things other people had written – 'God save my aunt and uncle and all the family and the cattle' and above it a different request, 'Oh Jesus, please get me the fare to go to America as I am wasted here'. There were prayers for peace and prayers from women who had had trouble with their husbands, whose husbands beat them. Lizzie had brought pencils and a little notebook and carefully she tore out a middle page, then another and warned Mary to make sure that she wrote the right thing, that she did not write something fanciful about clouds or scenery, that she wrote the thing they had come for, the special intention.

'Is that what you're going to write?' Mary asked her.

'Mind your own business,' she said, getting huffy then and crossing to the open doorway to get the last of the light. They took an age over it. She crossed out words and she could see Lizzie crossing out words too. She had to have a second piece of paper. Eventually it was done, and folding it she looked for a place close up to the statue of the Virgin, believing the closer it was the more likelihood she had of being heard. Lizzie snatched it from her then and went to the door to read.

'Please cure my father's epilepsy,' Lizzie read aloud, thought about it, then nodded, said that God would understand, that it was in code, and that it meant something else. They put their folded notes side by side, dipped their hands once again in the brown water and went out.

Hock was nowhere to be seen. Lizzie stamped her foot when he came back, saying he had had plenty of time to do what he was away doing, and why leave it to the last minute. They were all hungry. They drove for three miles to a town and he stopped the car outside a chip shop, but they were not in luck. The long aluminium windows were pulled down and there was no smell of frying fat. Lizzie said that they mustn't mind, they must offer it up to God and their prayers would be answered all the quicker.

'Did you see any eels?' he asked.

'You have eels on the brain,' she said then, and turning to Mary she said that she would come up and sleep in their house that night and that when nine days had passed they need never worry again.

JACKO

James covers his face with his hands while he is seated and howls to the brooding emptiness, lets a swipe at a fly, misses it, curses, gets up and says, 'Where the feck are you, Jacko?'

The man has been due since four o'clock and it is now almost dark. He is edgy. That social worker calling to the house except that she got no answer, her big mopey face pressed to one window and then another, calling, peering and then a note – 'My name is Lorna, I am the social worker and would like a little chat.' A little chat. Every last tattle pulled out.

'Where the feck are you, Jacko.' He sits, then paces, going through the unlit rooms, an on and off wheeze from the telephone which he has taken off the hook.

Eventually he hears the knocker and jumps up. They meet on the back step and he modifies his temper, because he needs this man, he needs a place of refuge.

'I was nearly giving up on you,' he says.

'I'm out there for the last half hour.'

'You can't be out there for the last half hour, I've been scouting.'

'Well, I rang the bell . . . But maybe you're deaf. Wha,' the older man says, slack-mouthed, a cackle in his laugh.

'What deaf! I can hear a blade of grass growing.'

'A young lad said that you wanted me to call over.'

'How many rooms have you got in the mountains, Jacko?'

'Plenty of rooms, rooms en suite, no one in them . . . I have a daughter in Yorkshire, she's a Yorkie . . . I could open a B and B except they'd want breakfast.'

'Could you put me up for a day or two?'

'Why wouldn't I ... You and I friends for thirty years ... Mind you, you were the big toff and I was the scutty little sheep farmer.'

'It'll be a week at the most.'

'Are you on the run, Jamesie?' and again the mirthful laugh.

'I'll tell you what it is, Jacko ... It's loneliness ... I find it worse in the fine weather ... In the winter you can light a fire and look in at it.'

'It's a divil ... Loneliness is a divil.'

'My wife died, you know.'

'Sure, wasn't I there ... I shook your hand ... Lovely woman ... A great homemaker. You have a little girl.'

'She might as well be in Yorkshire ... I never see her.'

'They have no nature ... When you think how you bring them into this world and the way they turn out ... Sharper than a serpent's tooth.'

From habit he leaves the big key at the side of the sewage in a bit of ripped spouting. Herself and Lizzie gone to a shrine, a shrine.

From the seats of the van wadding and wire prongs gape up at him and in the back are three greyhounds, eyes moist and ravenous-looking.

'Fine dogs.'

'They have me broke.'

'They're good dogs.'

'Would you care to bet what it costs to feed a greyhound.'

'A nice penny.'

'You always preferred the horses.'

'How's that horse I advised you to buy?'

'RIP ... A wind sucker ... She had to have the bullet.'

'You're no good with horses,' James says.

'I'm finished with them,' Jacko says bitterly. 'And I'll tell you something ... I'll tell you where the money is now ... Being a woman, lying on your back and having kids, kids galore ... Unmarried mothers fleecing this country ... The more they have the more dole they're given ... Up near me there's a Dutch woman in a mobile home ... Six kids ... Two live-in men ... Both of them hammering her.'

'Now who can this be,' James says as they see a car slowing down then swerving into the wide gravelled sweep which leads to the gate.

'Did you shut the gate?'

'You can see I did.'

'Feck you.'

'I thought you might have thoroughbreds in the field.'

'Beat her to it.'

'I can't beat her to it,' Jacko says as the headlights come flush with the worn silver paint of the gate and a woman gets out to open it.

'Ram her.'

'I can't ram her,' Jacko says and dilates on the necessity of having a car; even if it is a crock, it is his only link to civilisation. He is enlisted to get out and talk to her.

'Ask her her business and send her packing.'

While they are talking James chain-smokes, the cigarette never leaving his lips, the feathers of ash dropping off.

'She wants to ask about your daughter ... Your daughter's schooling,' Jacko says through the opened window.

'Tell her to make herself scarce ... Wait ... Tell her nothing ... Sit in.'

'You're plotting something, Mac.'

The two cars and their occupants stare it out, two warring encampments, each waiting for the other to strike. The men smoke, the girl consults her notes and thinks of the anonymous caller, a woman's voice, frightened, saying that something funny was going on in that house, a man and his daughter alone, things not quite right. If she goes back without seeing him she will be in trouble with her supervisor. She tries one last strategy, she gets out and waves her notes at them, an officious look on her face. She can feel them laughing at her, at her long skirt and her wellingtons.

'I'll tell you one thing, Mac ... We won't be taking her up to the Congo ... Oh no boy.'

'You should have rammed her . . . They have no right poking into people's lives.'

'Wouldn't care to see her in shorts.'

'What the hell would you know about a woman in shorts.'

'What would I know . . . What wouldn't I know . . . A woman on my own doorstep a few weeks back . . . German woman . . . Shorts . . . Two crooked eyes in her and divilment in both of them . . . Hopping mad for it . . . Making a noise with her swallow . . . Every other word was gut . . . Was I gut . . . Did I have gut wife . . . A gut *frau* . . . One eye sizing me up and the other eye sizing me down . . . They're fresh air fiends . . . I declare to God I discovered in the end what she wanted . . . She made it with sign language . . . She wanted me to top her . . . Up there on the mountain . . . Holy Christ I could catch pneumonia, or a guard come on us or a mad dog . . . *Auf Wiedersehen*, I says to her.'

'Wait a minute,' James says. He has been thinking while watching this mope. He has a plan of campaign. Jacko is to get out and tell her to back her car out of the way and they will repair to the hotel. While they are conflabbing he will drive the vehicle out.

'Sound.'

'How do I work this thing?' he says, sliding over to the driver's seat.

'How do you work it . . . Christ, man, you must know how to work it . . . You put it in gear . . . It's in gear . . . You put the clutch down . . . Put the handbrake up . . . Put your foot on the accelerator and once you feel you have juice, go . . . But for Christ's sake give me a chance to jump back in.'

He watches them talk, watches them nod, cannot in Christ's name figure out why they are laughing or what there is to laugh about, and in a moment unpreconceived, he lifts the handbrake, puts his foot down and finds himself and the yelping hounds hurtling through the gateway, grazing one of the piers and scraping the Snowcemmed wall while Jacko rears in front of him, his arms up and out like oars. He manages to jump on.

'Jesus Almighty . . . when did you last drive a car?'

'Never.'

'Never?'

'I only ride horses ... Horseflesh ... Did you fool her?'

'I gave her a bit of the old gab ... Then I told her that your daughter is at a convent ... She is, isn't she ... And as for you, you're an outlaw who keeps pistols under his pillow. Pull in at the crossroads and I'll take over ... Somehow I'd like to get home alive.'

'Where's the horn on this thing?'

'There isn't one ... For Jesus' sake, pull in before we're arrested.'

There were no trees around the house, only a wall, a hay shed, tar barrels and a great heap of stones. A gale of wind met them and the freed hounds moved like muscular wraiths across a field that was itself a low-lying ocean of mist.

'Great air,' Jacko said and swallowed it lustily.

'You're very high up ...'

'Four seasons in any one day and no traffic jams.'

'I don't think I'll stay.'

'Whist man ... You're all hyper ... You're psyched up.'

'Have you drink in the house?'

'Drink will only make you worse.'

'I have to have a drink ... A pick-me-up,' he says and links his companion's arm as they make their way over cairns of heaped stone.

As he crosses the kitchen Jacko kicks things out of the way in some housewifely gesture of welcome. Switching on the naked bulb, James is greeted by clutter, a table strewn with dishes, farm implements, two set mouse traps with rinds of bacon and, above the fireplace, his Holiness the Pope in a white free-flowing outfit, his hands and sleeves a grail for swarms of worshipping women.

'Great man ... Great man,' Jacko says, going close to it, 'An ambassador ... He's everywhere ... He's in Crumlin one day ... Buenos Aires the next ... Gambia the day after.'

*

The dogs sniff at their tin plates, step cautiously over the mouse traps and make for the table, one of them reaching for a gnawed chop bone, puts her forepaws up and causes a carton of milk to overflow.

'Divil . . . Dealáin,' he says, hitting her, then turning to his visitor says, 'You must be hungry . . . Would you like a steak?'

'I'd sooner a drink.'

'There's nothing to beat a good steak.'

'Have you a drop of whiskey?'

'Now look here, Mac . . . The man that goes to the pub belongs to a pub.'

'I never go to a pub . . . I detest them . . . I haven't had a drink since my wife died.'

'Sit down man, relax.'

'You must have something . . . Hooch . . . Hidden away in your sideboard.'

'Something is telling me we shouldn't . . . Something is telling me we'll regret it . . . We'll come to blows.'

They sit and smoke and the shell which serves as an ashtray is passed between them. From around a vast bandaging of newspapers Jacko produces a litre bottle of the homemade stuff and at first they drink slowly on account of its being so lethal but in time they become used to the taste which is like fire on the tongue, filling them with bravado. They are reminiscing. The old days . . . The great days. The batters they went on for weeks.

'Will you ever forget when we went on a safari to that island?' Jacko says.

'Nothing but stones,' James says, ridiculing the islanders, a rough breed with different caps and different teeth; food that would disgust you, molluscs and snails and things.

'You asking that woman for a drink,' Jacko recalls.

'She didn't want to serve us.'

'You said, I'll shoot you if you don't open up that bar.'

'I would have.'

'Big storm on the way back ... I couldn't swim ... I can't swim, says I ... Well, if you can't swim, says you, I'll have to conk you out and you'll float on the water like a log.'

'I would have.'

For no reason then James is up and infuriated, calling his friend a windbag, nothing but a windbag ... Woman in shorts with two crooked eyes ... Bluffing.

'What's up, man?'

'Every horse you had died ... You were an idiot above on a horse ... Never knew how to use your backside.'

'I knew how to use my backside in other ways. Mighty ways.'

'No horse would trust you and no friend either.'

'Now that's not a nice thing to say ... That's not a sporting thing ...'

'You'd go to the guards if you thought there was money in it.'

'I never went to the guards ... I never betrayed a friend ... Never.'

'Someone is out to get me.'

'Christ, not me, man, I'm no informer.'

'How do I know what you said to that social worker ... How do I know.'

'You're out of order there, Mac ... I could tell you some things this very minute that you wouldn't like ...'

'Say them.'

'I will not say them.'

'Yellow. You're yellow.'

'I'll say one thing ... Drink does not suit you ... You're laughing one minute and crying the next ... You're like one of them schizo-phrenics.'

'Schizophrenic ... Get up, and I'll fight you.' He's tugging at his coat, to pull him from the chair.

'I won't fight you, Mac ... You're too tall for me.'

'You will fight me ... We'll go out in the yard and fight,' he says and kicks one of the dogs who tries to protect his master.

'We'll go out in no yard ... Because I tell you now, you'd win.'

'You were never a man ... Never a man.'

'Ah, look ... We shouldn't be arguing ... Now you have a great singing voice ... Why don't we have a song,' Jacko says then leafs through a torn song book and chances on a song about a hanged man, half singing, half speaking the words.

> 'De night before Larry was stretched,
> De boys dey all paid him a visit;
> A bit in deir sacks, too, they fetch'd;
> Dey sweated deir duds till dey riz it ...'

'That's not a fecking song,' James says.
'It is a song ... It's here in a song book.'

> 'And I'll be cut up like a pie,
> And my nob from my body be parted.
> You're in de wrong box, den, says I,
> For blast me if dey're so hard-hearted.'

When he looks up he sees that his friend is crying, a man who wanted to box him, a Cassius Clay seconds before, crying like a child.

'Are you in trouble, Mac?'
'I might be.'
'Is it the tax man?'
'It's not.'
'I don't want to pry into your business, but if you're in trouble you had better be smart about it ... The law is savage now ... You're brought in to a barracks, all sorts of truth drugs, forensic tests ... They can concoct evidence as they go along ... A fellow is charged ... Clink man ... Clink ... In with the riffest of the raffest ... Bank robbers, murderers, having to use the same drinking mugs and the same bars of soap ... Having to play tennis and handball with sickos.'
'Would you come away with me?' James asks.
'I would only for them dogs.'
'I have to go somewhere.'
'I think I know ... I think I've clicked ... It's a lady of the night ... It is ... By cripes but aren't you the scamp ... And now she's holding you to something ... She has something over you ... If she says she's pregnant don't listen to her ... None of them need get

pregnant now ... They're on the pill ... They're on the patch ...
All they're after is your lucre.'

'Where could I go, Jack?'

'You could go to Agadir.'

'Where's that?'

'Look ... We'll ring Mabel ... We'll get all the gen from Mabel
... She'll sort you out. East of Eden Tours.'

From the drawer of the table he hauls out a cordless phone,
grimed and nicotined, holds it to his ear, lifts the steel aerial up,
shakes it and smiles when he hears the pulses within.

'Here you are man ... Take my advice ... Leave town.'

✠

DISCO NIGHT

'Our toilette … Our toilette.' Tara has been prodigal all day. They have pumiced, pummelled, plucked, bickered, made up, and now Tara is seated by her dressing table reading the lore about contouring make-up. Also they have fasted. Tara is convinced that the fasting has made her giddy and she cannot refrain from using the same two words – mainstream and couture. Their conversation at the disco must be mainstream, not wretched drivel like 'Would you like to go out with me' or 'May I give you a snog', but mainstream, such as 'why River Phoenix could not take the heat', that sort of thing. The make-up bought with her birthday money is couture and the powder a silky silicon pearl. She is allaying Mary's fears about the disco, the type of dancing, explaining how once you get under the lasers the lasers do it, the body is one fab rainbow that can bend or be bent, suck up to him or play ice-maiden.

Tara has been given leggings and what she dreams of wearing with them is a three-quarter jacket which she once saw on Mary's mother, the day of the carnival. It is the brown velvet jacket with little pepper and salt spatters in cream and buttons chunky as conkers. Her thinking is this: If she arrives at the disco and hangs around the bar in it, both men will look her up and down and that will be it.

'Oh please … Please.' She is kneeling now, interceding, and in the smoky swirls from the joss-stick her eyes are an Eastern princess's, tearful.

'I can't … My father would go mad.'

'Don't tell him what you've come for.'

'He'll follow me upstairs.'

'He follows you upstairs! Crikey.'

'He might not even let me go.'

'He'll be out the fields or in the pub,' Tara says, determined.

'You'll have to come with me,' Mary says.

'I can't,' Tara says, tapping on the mask which has crusted her face and made her eyes seem like gentians but with devilment in them.

'I'm afraid to go.'

'Oh please ... You're my best friend ... It can be my birthday present. You said yourself how awful you feel not giving me a birthday present.'

'Oh Tara!'

'Did you see any sign of my father?' Mary asks Paud who is tackling a donkey in the front field.

'He went off in a car.'

'Whose car?'

'That friend of his from up the mountain.'

So now she is safe. The rain had stopped, the clouds with densities of gold, birds scudding over the wet fields, thrushes and crows pecking and squabbling over worms and grubs, the victorious ones swooping off up to the telegraph wires to gobble. The ragwort which had sagged under the weight of the rain starting up again as if newly blooming, their very yellow pom-poms giving the green fields a yellow bravura. Even the trees seemed refreshed. Leaves and branches weaving and dancing, the dance repeated in the pools of lodged rainwater, merriment. She touched the trunks of the trees as she always touched them in a talismanic pact, saying different words, using a different finger for each bole and each bit of grainy bark, making wishes, or rather making only the one wish now. The loose stones were wet on top but dry underneath and worm clogged. She touched them too. Shep met her half-way, chewed and licked her coat as they walked along, then licked her face when she knelt to get the key from the spout and followed her inside for bread or attention or anything.

'Only you and me,' she said, lifting the lid of the range to give out a bit of heat. She would take a few things, each time she came she would take a few things so that it would not be too noticeable. Also a few ornaments for Tara's mother. She'd spent a week in Tara's house and Tara's mother kept remarking on the price of food and the extra washing.

She would bring something so as not to be under a compliment. The nicest things were the plaster busts of two ladies, one on either side of the marble mantelpiece, creatures with bare pink-tinted necks, morning gowns and auburn hair piled into a cone. But they were too heavy.

Upstairs, the Hoover and its attachments were in the middle of the floor where her father must have had some notion to tidy up but then abandoned it. Under the glass of the washstand was that picture of her mother and father on their honeymoon on a seafront, her mother's accordion-pleated skirt billowed as if it was going to blow out and upwards and disgrace her. For some reason it was a sad looking picture. She got a fright when she went into her own room. There were clothes of hers all over the floor as if her father had been looking through her things, looking for her diary maybe. Also the head of the Sacred Heart had come off. The fallen head with its chalky root lay beside the body that was blood-spattered: the very red life-like heart looked pained. She got sticking plasters and rubber bands to put it together again but each time the head just lopped off and in the end she put the two parts side by side on the ticking of her pillow.

'You,' she said to the cloth swan in the fire-screen which her mother had embroidered. It was a very malcontent swan, not like the couples who glided suavely up and down the river, revelling in their stately passage and going into the reeds to sleep and to nest. This was a cross swan with styes on its red-rimmed eyes.

The wardrobe is stuffed with things, linen, bolsters, old clothes, her mother's and her father's together, three or four garments to each metal hanger. She has found the jacket for Tara and is debating with herself whether she too shouldn't put on a good dress, the one her mother had promised her when she came of age. 'Go on ... Go on,' she's telling herself, still feeling that there is some wrongdoing in it but putting it on all the same. It is a black grosgrain dress with pleats which swirl around the calf. Just as her mother did, she will. She will brighten it with that brooch, the one with the dun stone which, when shaken, transmuted and burst into a firmament of stardust. She looks first in the bone bowl, the knob of which is a Bakelite figurine of a baby's head and which she used to be afraid of when she was little, feared it would bawl. Then next in the empty powder bowl, which carried the faint and delicate smell of talcum powder. Then under the steel crucifix. Failing to find it she remembers that her mother kept her favourite things downstairs, within easy reach, when rushing out to mass on Sundays.

She is standing on the kerb of the tiled fireplace, rummaging, when she hears a footstep, thinks it must be Tara and runs to show her.

Her father seems to materialise as from nowhere, like a fork of fire and so heartened is he to see that she has come home he salutes her as he would a special visitor.

'My darling ... My little darling Clementine.' He is drunk, that drunkenness that allows for expansion, affability, a hint of the theatrics. He talks rapidly, schemes for improvements in the house, the outhouses, outlandish plans such as he might have read somewhere. He says that they must go out more, that they have mourned but now is a time to stop all that, and he quotes from a sermon that the Missioner gave about there being a time to plant and a time to root up what is planted, a time to wreck and a time to build, a time to mourn and a time to dance. He grasps her arm as she goes towards the door. Looking closely then, he says what a young lady she has become, what a madam in her mother's dress, and who said she could wear lipstick.

'Tara and I are going to a disco,' she says, her voice high pitched.

'I'll come with ye.'

'It's for young people...'

'Aren't I young, Clemmy ... Clementine.' And he allows himself now to advance into a charade that she is not she, she is a stranger in her black dress and her little beaded evening purse.

'Care for a dance?' Without waiting he leads her into a movement that is half dance half gallop, a charge around the room, knocking things, coins shedding from his pocket, starting up different bits of song and deciding on 'She'll be coming 'round the mountain when she comes'.

He touches her forehead with his, bumping it smartly, making her do return bumps and repeat the refrain – 'When she comes, when she comes.' He is talking, telling imaginary swains to keep off, that it is not an excuse-me dance, it is his dance; they can ride the hacks, he rides the hunter. The temperature of her body goes from hot to freezing and back to hot again and her limbs, especially her legs, seem substanceless. In the whirling daze she sees ornaments as if flying and in the blotched mirrors of the swinging sideboard door she sees their feet, his fawn jodhpurs, the buckles of her shoes, and the ground becomes mercury under her.

'I'm dizzy ... We're going to have to stop now, Dad.' She is shouting it. Shouting it.

'As you will ... We can pause for a little refreshment.' And from the sideboard where he has kept a spare bottle, he helps himself to a drink, pours it into one of the gold glasses and remarks on how well he can hold his drink now.

'Ladies and gentleman, will you take your partners for the next dance ... Which is ... Which is the Military Twostep.'

'I'll be late, Dad ... I have to go.'

'What late ... Aren't we dancing ... Isn't this a disco?'

'It's not right.'

'Do you love your father?'

'Let me go, Dad ... Let me go.'

'You've shown your love.' By that he is alluding to the night, the two nights, his turning the knob of her bedroom door with an impatience which said 'Open it, or I'll break it down,' and finding her where she had gone behind a screen, her body no more than a pillar or a bit of galvanise to thresh against.

'They're down at the gate ... Tara is ... They're waiting,' she says, breaking from him.

'Give your father a kiss.' When she offers her cheek he smacks it aside, and with his two fingers purses her lips until they are full. Sugar plums, sugar puss, givvus a kiss.

The voices inside her are hectic now, one saying 'Don't panic ... Keep him talking then it won't happen,' and a shakier voice saying 'Tara will come ... She is in the taxi now ... They are passing the pillar-box ... They are coming near the gate ... They are coming up.' Then no voice because it has begun and no one is coming to prevent it.

Outside the window, under the bony roots of the old creeper, Shep probably lay, Shep who would jump up and bark if she were to shout, but if she shouted now it would only worsen things, the unreason, the gloating energy, that almost independent of himself is informing every swerve, every bit of stroking, hands smoothly thrusting, into the soft cool glade of unknownness. And words. The words said make no difference, they are different words, opposing words – 'It will hurt ... It will hurt,' and 'It won't hurt ... It won't,' mere syllables, clashing, passing one another by and dissolving in the maddened air. The hard spring of the chaise like a plank, then a spume of murmurs, maudlin, breathy, her dress and things gone and decrazing herself by thinking that in a given number of minutes it would be over. How many minutes she could not tell.

All became stiller, in some kind of laxed hiatus, cornices and ornaments to fasten on and then it was not that, the raw instancing, the tearing of flesh, like cloth, but with terror and cognition in it and that which tore was flesh too but devoid of thought, the same bit of air passing between them; a rank sluice, then the mad acceleration of limbs and joints with scarce an interval for breath, a peal of sound, high and scintillant and just beneath it and deafened out by it her own wail, begun but unfinished, left there – for where else could it go – left there between the folds and cavernous places called home.

Silence. Suspended. Coming back to the room and the scarcely swinging sideboard door. The disentangling itself another brutal breach. He was weak, needing, a tender baleful plaint in contrast to the moments before, and she felt that she would always feel this shame, a shame lurching into sorrow for being witness to the outcast's forlornness of him, to the wailing which followed fast upon the wild and tautened notes of yeah and she felt that he knew it too, for just a second before it passed into the all-mother of obscurity, defeat and forgetting.

The hooting of the car from down at the gate seems so far away it could be another world. It is another world. Her mind cold. Like a little skull. And like a skull, empty of everything. 'I will not put myself together again. It is broken now. That which was is gone.' She lay on her face and bit. And bit.

'Go to your disco,' he says, and reaches for his trousers, misses, then clutching the braces he takes money out. She does not move. She is not able.

'Go to your disco,' he says, throwing a note and coins along the floor, then picks his clothes up and goes out.

In the morning what the sun caught were the score marks of her teeth, and the little pink pulpings of sawdust on the rosewood rungs of the chaise.

✠

CATTLE

The sight of the animals, dazed, sliding, myopic, is pitiful, their thin khaki scutters sprawled over the concrete floor. She has come to the mart to ask her father for money, to ask in front of people. From time to time a jobber belts the beasts so that they huddle and in concert whisk their tails on their clotted croups, letting out moans of desolation. The auction is in an inner room.

A man in a white coat is leading a bull on a blue rope, and inside, another man in a white coat conducts the sales, his voice warbly, like a talking turkey, and at other times as if he is gargling as well as speaking. The price of the bull escalates by the second. The figures were hundreds, then suddenly a thousand. Her father does not have anything to sell but he goes anyhow, he likes to be among the men. When she stands inside the doorway she cannot see him at first. What she sees is barricades of men in caps and hats, smoking and occasionally confabbing with each other. By going back and forth along each row, she eventually finds her father, up near the back, his hat at a jaunty angle, his expression animated. He scowls when he sees her. She has no right to come there, into that man's world. She has never seen so many men herded in together. Weathered faces, not talking, not laughing, just smoking and studying the form of the animals with cold, gauging eyes.

As she goes up the steps she sees him come to the end of a row of men, to tackle her.

'I have to give in money at school.'

'What for?'

'Some of us are going to France for a week in September.'

'France.'

'The head teacher is going to talk to you yourself about it.'

He hesitates but she knows that he is cornered. From his top pocket he takes two very new, very crisp notes which are stuck together and blasts them for their not wanting to be separated but in reality the blasting is for her, for her audacity.

'I'll be home in an hour,' he says, his voice hard.

Outside there is a boy selling shoes from a lorry. New shoes and old shoes, all men's. There are two smells, the smell of boot polish and the after smell of feet. She asks him if she can have a lift to the town. He says he will have to ask his father. He has an earring, a metal earring, and the gentlest hazel eyes. They are like hazel leaf in the spring. He whispers to his father and then says, 'No problem.'

At home she packed in a frenzy – another pair of shoes, tights, a jumper, a bath towel and a face cloth, and when she heard the engine below at the gate, stopping and starting and the hooter loud as a trumpet, she ran through the kitchen and did something she knew to be a betrayal. She locked Shep in because she knew that he would follow. Her things were in a basket with books over them so that the men would not realise that she was running away. She was squeezed in between father and son.

'Where in the town do you want to be dropped?' the father asked.

'It's a knitwear shop ... I'll know it,' she said and prayed that there would be some shop that sold balls of wool and knitting needles, there was bound to be.

Glints of setting sun on the young man's cheeks emphasised his short blond hairs and his sweepy eyelashes which were very delicate and also blond like the lashes of the beasts, which in some sad way contradicted their dunged clotted rumps.

'A bull went for two thousand pounds,' she said, to be grown up.

'Bulls are a fortune now,' the father said, then asked his son what they had taken and grunted at the miserliness of it. His son lit him a cigarette then and said they would do better on the following day as it was a bigger mart.

The cigarette smoke was roamy and level between their three faces and it was like being at a party or in a pub and she was going away and would not have to live with her father again.

✠

THE BOHRÁIN

'There's a wee shortcut here,' Luke was saying as he led the way through a series of stone passages, past the ruin of a church which fronted onto a floodlit lawn. He had a pale, slightly gnawed face and a huge mass of hair, like a zodiac, spoking out, bronze and gold-flecked, his bright blue shirt swelling and deflating as he walked in the light, the round marks on it where he had sweated seeming like the traces of big soft damp flowers and his shoulder blades thin and jutting.

When they came out onto the main street they had to stand to let a procession go by, mostly women carrying banners and reciting the rosary. She ducked behind him in case any one of them should look in their direction and see the stark fear in her eyes. He noticed this and lifted his music case to form a shield between them and her.

He had found her on a bench along the river, the bench where he went each evening when he had finished his gig, went to slow down, to stop the humming in his head and in his heart and think of the songs he had played, the times when his knuckles on the bohráin rung from it some surprise, epiphany, and then the flat times when it was just heavy, dead. She told him that she had nowhere to go. She'd been in a guest house but her money ran out. She bluffed then, said she would be getting more money and that she would go to a hostel. He didn't doubt her. He never doubted people who were as stranded as that. She recognised him because she had stood and listened to his playing, stood for a long time, then gone on to the next street and listened to the penny-whistle and then to the main street where a blind man played the accordion, a pouch attached to the instrument, a deep oblong of leather so that money could not easily be filched. All day and half-way into the night, music filled the streets and people strolled about in a kind of exhilaration because of so much entertainment. A juggler with a painted face threw balls into the air, three girls in short plaid skirts did step-dancing and a man who claimed to have been a water diviner until the Blackthorns blinded him said, 'God bless you all,' or 'God feck you all,' depending on his humour.

She knew the streets well, very well, after the two days of moping about. Sometimes she sat in the square and looked at a statue of a man on a donkey and a big mural which had been defaced, a mous-tache added to a woman and the eyes plucked out of a man so that there remained only the gory sockets. She listened to people talking, an oldish woman telling another oldish woman how lucky she was because she had got a good night's sleep and the pain had eased. She never stayed too long in one place, in case ... The future was like a big hole, but if said, if those six letters were said, she would be sucked into it, like into a vortex. She was waiting for only one thing, she was waiting to know for sure. Except that she knew for sure. She was sick in the morning and then later had longings, longings so that she was able to stand outside the cake shop and in her mind taste the custards and the mock cream and the tarts and last of all the chocolate Swiss roll filled with oozy chocolate and dusted with caster sugar. Each day she bought two pancakes, lemon flavoured, and ate them in the square, then off again, traipsing. She knew every blouse, every jumper, every suit, every pair of shoes and every pair of jogging shoes in all the windows, and she knew when an engagement ring had been sold because of the absence of that diamond-hard sparkle on a plinth of velvet and she felt jealous.

'I heard you playing,' she said to Luke.

'Was it OK?'

'It was great.'

'What was I playing ...'

' "Enniskillin" ... And ... I didn't know the others.'

He ran through the tunes he had done, connecting how one followed another unless a mate shouted out a request.

'I'd remember better if it was songs.'

'I don't do the songs much ... I find the songs grating ... I prefer the tunes.' And he holds up the music case to show her the picture which an artist has painted, two figures, male and female, entwined around a tree which he had called the Tree of Life.

'You can kip down on my floor if you like.'

'Can I.'

The street was no longer a sea of lonely journeying faces, but a boulevard of lights and excitements, and she walking next to him, walking home.

His room was small, a mattress in one corner, the heaped purple duvet like a figurine, articles of clothing, a tiny television, stones and a wine bottle crusted with thick blisters of grey candle-grease. He pointed to his Buddha, a female Buddha who protected him.

'From what?'

'Everything ... Hunger, the civic guards.' And then glancing about the room he said it needed furniture, it needed bits and pieces, it was more homely when Omar was there, cushions and candles and things. Omar was his friend in Morocco who had come to collect the tunes and the words, in all had collected sixty songs which he was now playing in towns all over Morocco and in the desert itself. He held the Buddha for her to see and said that the wood it was carved from, sandalwood, was the most expensive in the world, it and eaglewood. He took the bohráin from its case then so that she could touch it. She looked down at it, shy, the grey-white skin stretched to such an extremity as if it hurt. He gave her the stick and said to make a sound, any sound, but she refused because of feeling stupid. With his knuckles then he went tee-tum tee-tum tee-tum tee-tum, his head lowered towards it, his hair and his torso moving with the beats, body and sound resolving into one another, oblivious of everything else. That was how she had seen him in the street before she knew him, before she ever dreamed that she would come to know him. He was telling her that he could not remember how he got stuck into it, coming from God-fearing parents and all that, but that he did and now it was his life, his whole life, out every morning, lateish, two or three cups of coffee, depending on which waitress was on duty, starting off real quiet and then building, building, and by nightfall all the pulses beating together, his own and the other buskers, the streets awash with music.

'How many hours do you play?'

'I'm doing twelve or thirteen at the moment ... Saving to go to Morocco.'

He and Omar were going to do sessions, mix the songs of the two countries, but he would not stay long, he liked home too much, not the crowds, not the messing, not the people talking their heads off, but the music that was there, somewhere, dormant in the soil, never yet heard, unheard, music that was the true scripture of the land. Then he played a little tune on the penny-whistle, a jig so that she would not feel constrained, and he said that if she liked they would give her a wee book and she could learn from it, learn which fingers to put on each hole and make a sound, alalalalalalalalalala.

'Take your coat off,' he said then. He said it very gently and with a down-slanting look of his smoky eyes which was also saying, 'Don't worry ... You won't come to no harm.'

They sat then and he took tobacco, mixing it with little shavings which he sliced off a brown stick, that was like a stick of sealing wax, and tucked it delicately into the funnel of white cigarette paper.

After he had been smoking for a bit he began to thaw, laughed, said she was very welcome, said he was not used to visitors and that yes, the smoking helped, it changed the loneliness, made it a more satisfied loneliness, laughed more, said oh yes, a person did fall in love four, five times a day, but had to be restrained about it, had to resist it.

'Why?'

'It gets heavy ... Owning people ... Being owned ... Tears and stuff.'

He thought for a moment and said there was that one time when he wasn't in the least bit lonely, the opposite, flush; it was in a forest after having eaten the mushroom, himself and a friend, the wind, the leaves, them, all in tune, sound within colour and vice versa, being wafted along.

'Crikey.'

'Only the once, mark you.'

He said then the love of music was a bigger love and more long-lasting. It never deceived. A woman could, a woman could dance rings around a person and he not to know it.

'Do you not talk to the girls you take a shine to?'

'Hardly ever ... I tried ... But it came out wrong ... It came out falsetto.'

'Are you back?' She whispers it across to where he is unfolding a sleeping bag. He had gone out onto the landing for her to undress but he had stayed outside a long time and his whistling had ceased and she thought that maybe he was gone off.

'Oh, I'm here.'

'I'm sorry to ...'

'You're no bother.'

'Is that you in the photo on the mantelpiece?'

'The very one.'

'Why did you shave your beard?'

'Didn't like the itchiness ... It got so long I used to chew it.'

'Did it taste nice?'

'Awful.'

'If you could eat anything now what would it be?'

'Fried black pudding and fried bread – You?'

'Cabbage.'

'Are you hungry ... I should have brought stuff ... I've no cooker so I bring in stuff.'

'I would have taken the sleeping bag.'

'You're all right. You're no bother.'

'Do you live alone?'

'I do now.'

'What happened?'

'Hard to say ... She wasn't over her other boyfriend.'

Although she cannot see him she knows that he is sad and thoughtful, but not bitter, because he likes the memory of this girl, her remembered lilt in the room.

'I'll tell you what . . . Tomorrow's Friday, I always make a jackpot so I'll bring home provisions.' That means she does not have to leave, not yet. He talks while drifting into sleep; the words, scattered around the room, tender, nonsensical, glow-worm's darting fire.

They hear the letterbox flap, one, two, three tetchy thuds, then getting louder, stroppier, more urgent, then stopping for a moment, then the rapping on the window, the sound hollower and more menacing as if the intruder is about to break in. They lie, utterly still, accomplices in some unspeakable dread, fearful of some terrible eventuality. Each knows that the other is awake, every nerve, every hair follicle on end. She believes that it is for her, that they have come for her. They wait in a pending silence and then suddenly it stops and they hear the footsteps stomp away.

'Who do you think it was?' she asks after a while.

'Could it be someone for you?'

'Nobody knows where I am.'

'I hope it wasn't the civic guards.'

'Do they come here?'

'I've been in a cell nights.'

'Here?'

'Not here . . . In Glasgow . . . The last people I want to meet are the civic guards.'

They lie silent then, short grateful breaths giving thanks and asking let it not return, when suddenly they both start up and he says, 'J'sus.' A light almost airy tune wanders through the room, a tinkling as from the ether, non-caused, and collecting himself then he remembered the little music box which someone had left but which was not supposed to play until the key was turned in it. It had come on for no reason, and bunching himself in the sleeping bag he moved clumsily to find it, silencing it with a kind of ongoing caress.

'Will you sleep,' he asked as he stood above her.

She thought that if he were to kiss her it would be like an enchantment or that even if he were to bend down and she were to feel the condensation from his lips falling onto hers that it would be a transport from the old and awful life, like the moment in a fairy tale when a person is released from damnation.

✠

CITY

The chemist shop was the brightest in the row because of the tubes of fluorescent lighting. She studied each and every thing in the windows – the ugly things and the tempting things. Tortoiseshell powder boxes, with their lids half off and little filters of net, to keep the powder from spilling. Beside them, companions to them, velour powder puffs, the frail pink of flamingoes. The various creams and lotions had posters of waterfalls and seaweed and sea salt affixed to them to show the natural ingredients they were made from. Another poster featured a bronzed girl, Bianca, fishnet down one half of her body and nothing along the other. The ugly things were the baby tins with baby faces, a baby scales and special lumpen sandals for women with foot ailments. She would go in, in a minute.

Two streets away she could hear the tin whistle being played, sweet and rousing, coming near and far, as if whoever played it was moving from street to street. Luke would not have started yet, not until he had had the three cups of coffee which the friendly waitress gave him. She wouldn't disturb him. He had given her a spare key. All she had to do now was go into the chemist shop and ask for it. Still she was hesitating, weighing herself on the big scales that was chained to the handle of the door. She read her weight on a blue screen. She did not weigh any more or any less, there was no alteration in her body. The assistant inside the counter looked haughty. She had the same sort of pout as Bianca, and her hair half up and half down looked as if it might cascade any minute, as if she wanted it to cascade.

At the next chemist shop there were the very same lotions and creams and waterfalls and a Bianca, while inside, two assistants were talking and pointing to their chins, to their pimples maybe.

She stood outside four chemists in all and each time found a reason not to go in. She was ashamed to ask for it, and also once she had it and did the test she would know for sure, there would be no room for faith or hesitation or anything. When she got it she would have to study the instructions very carefully, so as not to botch it. She would have to go somewhere private, maybe a few miles out of the town to the seashore. She knew about it from Tara. Tara's other best friend, Virginia, had been three weeks late and panicked.

People were milling out of the hotel. Their suitcases were already out and lined up on the pavement for a bus. There was something very practical about them, the way they were stamped and labelled, as if they would find their way back of their own accord to their owners. The owners were waving coupons and vouchers and asking where the hell the bus was as they were hungry. She knew the lobby, she had looked in there before and had seen how friendly it was with the big fire and armchairs and a carafe of sherry with small sherry glasses stacked beside it, for guests. She went in quietly and pretended to be looking for someone. Then she studied the picture which she already knew, women in red shawls, with their skirts up, wading into the water to pick cockles. She would help herself to the sherry, the way she did the other day, do it when everything got a bit bustly, when the bus came and people were shouting last minute things to the girl behind the desk.

She would go down into the ladies' and she would look and she would keep looking and she would keep willing it, keep asking it and it would come, one berry of red on a mesh of hair, like a holly berry, heraldic.

✠

DEAR LUKE

Dear Luke,

I have something huge to ask you. I know it's awful but I think I am going to be a mother and I am afraid. Could I stay here for a little while. I won't be in your way. I promise. Probably you have a girlfriend in some other county, up north maybe or in Glasgow or in London, so it is not that I am asking. It's just to be let hide. Every person has to have one best friend and once they have that they are flying it. I love that you don't get cross with people, the people who come up to you when you're playing and ask you the way. I lied about my age. I told you I was older because I would like to be. It would be better if I was. I never felt young. Never. You said you would like a dog. I have a wonderful dog. Even if you belt him or kick him he'll still nuzzle you and haw on you and talk to you with his eyes. I nearly died when you gave me that jumper. You shouldn't have. Turquoise is my favourite colour. There are two kinds of alone, there's the kind which you are and the kind which I am. Your alone is beautiful, it's rich. I will go to a doctor soon. The person whose it is is the last person's it should be. I would rather not say, ever. Out in the country things get very murky. I would like to live in a city because if you scream someone can hear you. I would like, of course, to go to the country for the fresh air and the blasts of wind. I will go to the hostel anyway and when you read this please do not feel bad if you can't have me here. We will always be friends.

Mary

BONE DISEASE

'Hi,' she said, 'I'm Mary-Lou.' The door was open for a bit of fresh air and she came in giving the merest swivel to her wrist on which there was a bracelet as big as a napkin ring with a scarab on it. She wore extra pale make-up, and carried a walking stick which she also held up by way of greeting. It was the way she sat down which gave her such an imperial quality, the way she dragged the chair to the centre of the floor, turned on the television and got out her little stock of goodies as she called them. She had brought soft drinks, straws, a candle and some joss-sticks for her little tête-à-tête with Luke.

'He said he'd be home early,' she said and pulled down one side of her black satin blouse, then secured it with a marcasite brooch.

'Can you draw the curtains, honey . . . I prefer it dark.'

Her eyes were soft but they were also not soft, they had two expressions in them and they were a pale green.

'I'm between jobs,' she said and lifted the baseball cap which she was wearing in order to be matey. Then she held up two mandarins that were joined together on a green stem and had leaves around them as if she had just plucked them in an orchard. They were his surprise.

'Are you his sister?' she asked.

'No . . . A friend.'

'Don't you love him . . . I love him . . . Other men just talk talk talk, not Luke, not my Luke. The first time I saw him . . . My God . . . Couldn't take my eyes off him . . . Still can't . . . He was beating out this tune . . . Real slow . . . I was on the opposite side . . . I was sitting down . . . I have this disease . . . Sometimes I just have to sit down ... I have had it since I was seven ... A bone disease ... He looked up and he came across and he brought me to that pub ... You know, the one with the little nooks ... Real neat ... He sat me down and he asked me what I wanted ... I wanted a Coke with rum in it ... Then he asked me if I was sick and I said I want to see all I can of life, I want to do all the wrong things, and he knew, he knew ... Guess what I did then. I said to him, feel how cold I am, and he did ... He just touched me ... It was the most ... It was the most ... You know, other guys, forget them ... It was the most reserved touch ... He left his hand there and told me about his music and I thought, I'm going to learn all about his music because that's his baby, that's how I'll get him to love me ... We have the same birthday ... Isn't that weird ... Guys that come up to me and want it, they just want it, but this guy holds my hand and tells me the story of the music, the history of the bohráin and how he got started ... I mean, it's a fairy tale ... Basically, men are OK, they take care of me and stuff, but Luke, Luke, he's different ... He's way up front ... Have you looked into his eyes ... They're green and they're brown and they're mauve ... You could drown in them ... I have drowned in them ... So I began to read this stuff ... To get on his wavelength ... By the way, what's your name?'

'Mary.'

'Mary. That's nice. That's a nice name. You don't meet many Marys now ... You meet every other God-damned name but you don't meet Marys ... Do you mind if I ask you something?'

'No.'

'Something really big ... A favour ... A big favour.'

'No.'

'Are you sick too?'

'No.'

'You look sick. You're not sick, good ... So I can ask it; you see, I want to talk to Luke alone ... It's about my being sick ... It's about my disease ... I can't talk to him out there on the street ... It has to be in this room with the lights out and the candle ... Are you getting me?'

'Yes.'

'So maybe, chérie, you could go to the movies ... There's one about a shark ... Supposed to be terrific.'

'How long have I to stay out for?'

'Oh, honey,' Mary-Lou said and looked at her with a scorn as if she should know better, then coated her lips with salve and puckered them.

'Could you give him this,' Mary says, handing her the letter she had written all morning.

'Oh, honey ... I hope you're not getting any ideas,' she says, takes it, looks at it, then tosses it onto a nearby chair.

✠

STRATOSPHERE GIRL

A voice, some voice, told her to keep indoors, to go up and down the escalators and hide in the back corners of the shopping centre.

It was 'antiques' day and on different tables there were candlesticks, clocks, ermine coatees, cutlery cases; the owners chatting to one another, not bothering whether they had a sale or not, then one crossing to the canteen to fetch tea and buns. What took her fancy most was a series of photographs, which opened out like accordion pleats and told the story of the stratosphere girl. This beautiful young girl, it said, had fallen from her steel mat which was one hundred and twelve feet high. It happened in Berlin. It said that she was the greatest aerial acrobat ever and that she had loved her mother and her sister dearly. Then she saw a lady come up close to her, look at her and go off and converse with another, and then both were looking and about to come across and question her.

The food hall was much more crowded, people doing their week's shopping, pushing avalanches of food from counter to counter and children queuing to go into the ghost train. It was next to the butcher's that she stood to look in at a tank of pet fish, little tittlings, gaily coloured, gliding through their universe of water, feathered trees like so many curtains, and rockeries to shelter under. A wheel turned the water and in the bubbles they glided like tapers crusted in jewel. Some were languid, others were moving with a purpose, thrilling to it while one courting pair lay prone, their mouths adhered. They were of every colour, silver and striped and pale yellow and jet black, the bodies like neon, allowing her to see the intestines within. A boy from the butcher's came then and sprinkled

food for them and it scattered through the water like confetti.
Depending on the movements she would think that Luke would get
her letter and would come to the hostel for her. She made little bets
as to which fish would reach a certain point first and sometimes
she won and sometimes she lost.

It was a large hand and it encompassed the back of her neck
while also tugging on her hair. She was certain that it was her
father, jumped, then turned and saw that it was a guard, repeating
her name.

'Mary MacNamara...'

She did not reply, she smiled, a vacant smile. She was the stratosphere girl, and she was climbing up onto her steel mat where she
could fall from one hundred and twelve feet high.

'I'm right...You are Mary MacNamara...You answer to all the
descriptions,' and he looked at her eyes, her hair, the plaid of her
coat, then turned the collar inside out to check the maker's name.

'I'm with friends,' she said, trying to sound grown-up.

'Jesus Christ, the whole country searching for you ... Every
station in the west ... Searching for you ... Your poor father gone
out of his mind,' and he caught the sleeve of her coat then and
dragged her shamefully, as he might a yelping cur.

Outside the ghost train two children watched and stuck their
tongues out at her.

BROOMSTICK

They take their leave, speaking the usual platitudes about her being safe, how you can't put an old head on young shoulders and of her daddy's three days and three nights of agony. On the step as she sees them out she looks at the woman guard, makes a sign, which is then extinguished, and there passes between them a look of fumbling and helpless baulk. That is all. That is all. The sky is pale pewter, the colour draining out of things, the thick shadows around the hedge bellying out to the bulk of ogres and animals. She calls their dog but he does not come. Shep. Shep. She calls and calls. He has not forgiven her for going away.

'I know you're there,' she says to him.

Inside she starts to prepare her father's tea. There are mashed turnips on a plate and she begins to re-mash them with a fork where they are lumpy. She sprinkles pepper and salt, does it repeatedly, merely biding her time to assuage things. He is standing by the range warming himself and asking again if she needs a doctor. She does not answer him.

'I asked you a question.'

'I heard it.' She feels him move and then feels behind her the palpable frame of rage. Why did she run away. Answer. Answer. Nothing to run away from. Disgracing her father like that. This hobo, this tinker with his tinker's instrument, he would have him put behind bars. He would have this tinker prosecuted for abducting her.

'Nothing happened . . . Nothing bad happened.'

'Oh, Miss Sugar Wouldn't Melt,' he says and asks where she got the money for that new cardigan.

'I won it,' she says brazenly, the tone now too flagrant by far for him so that he lifts his boot and starts to kick her, recklessly, as if only lewd and obscene gesture will wring the truth from her. She remains glued to the ledge thinking that she once saw her mother in this very spot, subject to the same exact succession of kicking, and that it was a Christmas Day and everything got ruined, the shallots and sprouts like black knobs of anthracite and the goose burnt to a cinder. Much later, her father sat by the fire scratching his head and crying.

'Bought you goodies, did he?'

'I won it.'

'What did you have to do for him ... You strumpet.'

'Nothing ... Nothing.'

'I'll kick the shite out of you,' he says, turning her round, and she meets him with a raised fork and sees a man in a charging rage, then hears the clang of the fork, short-lived, on the tiled floor and his telling her to get upstairs to the bedroom and he will de-fuck that bastard out of her.

'I will not,' she says.

'You'll do what I say,' and as he pulls the cardigan from her she hears herself shouting crazily, zanily, incriminatingly, that she is having a baby, and she knows when it happened.

'Liar,' he says and refers to the sanitary yokes in her locker, ones that she bought and wore, thinking that by some divination they would bring on her period and, even when they didn't, putting them back in the packet in anticipation, some sort of invocation that it would come.

'You were having no baby when you ran away and if you're having one now it's that tinker's.'

'It's not that tinker's,' she says, and threatens the guards on him. It is as if up to then he had succeeded in walling up what had happened and now he is seeing it, made to see it, like a man awakening from a dream and finding the monster he has dreamed, agape, beside him on the pillow. His mouth opened, stricken with terror, and as he ran she thought, the terror has got to him, but no. He met it with madness, a madman's frenzy to obliterate the substance of what she had just said.

'I'll make short work of it,' he said, grabbing the broken and splintered broom handle which might have been waiting for this grotesque rite.

She lands in a basket of turf mould, his legs the stirrups that hold her out. Thrusting it inside her, the whirling of it in exact ratio to his crazed words, his intent far exceeding anything the implement could do, because in truth he did not know what he was doing, fear and delirium having engulfed him. He was simply making certain to push it inside and wind and re-wind it, and almost at once she could hear her insides slushing, like an over-full bucket. She could not tell how deeply it had plunged, all she felt was the wooden teeth cutting and the splinters snagging, and the madness passed from him then and into her, for while it could not be so, she believed that the implement was going right through her and out the crown of her head, like the chimney sweeper's brush but bloodied instead of sooted. The pain was being converted into something other, so that she was all wound, only wound, and she could shout a wound sound and did so and he heard it.

'It's happening ... It's happening,' she said and by the way she repeated it he ceased, pulled the thing out and holding it at arm's length like some poisonous totem he went off to bury it.

She lay there, half gone, her mind a semi-nothingness, and saw the soft moonlight splash and dapple onto the table and across the floor and make bright stripes on Shep's black coat, Shep a few feet from her, like a person, feeling it all, sensing it all, prehensile, there for her. There.

✠

RIVER

High up in the mountain the river rose, a narrow noisy trickle that twined and wove its way through rock and gorge, gaining as it came down, swelling to form eddies and silver cold currents and widening into a broad and picturesque sweep as it approached the town, the town's principal attraction and also that which gave it its name.

With each swig the surface of the water looked different to Mary. The stuff she drank was potent but tasted sweet and was thick like whisked condensed milk. It had a picture on the label of sun-drenched fields, not a bit like the field where she stood, the high tussocks of grass damp around her legs and the ground beneath frozen solid from the ice which had not thawed for five days. It was the best thing, the only thing. It had not gone. It had outlived his scourging, clung, clinging, limpet-like. The drink was to give her courage.

In places the water meandered, then again it galloped, troughs of it like herds of water-beasts, humping over the boulders, giving to the bouclés of moss a fresh pulsing greenness. In the very centre the dark coils were hungry and sinister. Did one go straight to the bottom where river-life strove and warred just like all other life or did one drift as an Ophelia entwined in a corsage of reeds and trailing weeds. How fast was it?

The pair of swans were not to be seen but from somewhere there was a shuffle of feathers or wings, or maybe it was clot weed and sedge, sucking in the moistures. Tara would cry. Tara could have all the clothes now and the tortoiseshell box with her mother's trinkets. She did not want to meet her mother in the other world.

'I do not want to meet my mother,' she said brazenly to the round tower which looked like a big grey man on stilts moving across to impede her the way the guard did the day she was standing looking in at the iridescent fish in the tank.

Smoke was rising from the town chimneys, different plumes, tapers at first, then getting fatter and fatter as they went up, then breaking apart, fragmenting into nothing. Nothing. In her school-bag were her books and her diary. Yes, Tara would cry. There was a chatter to the water like scolding old women, then slipslop at the edges where it was being sucked in and drunk by the tubers and roots of the golden reeds. Somewhere on the street near where the fish manoeuvred Luke would be playing, playing to the heedless people who went by and filled with that lamp-like evening exhil-aration. Goodbye Luke. The river rushed and purled along as if it was expected somewhere, each new swathe of water following upon the preceding one to its destination. The sky which had been a blaze of resiny life a while before was paling now, woolly grey clouds, and very soon it would be dark.

She had been in that river once before, wading with her mother, summertime, running away, always running away, crossing to the big house to ask Betty the owner for help. The tide was low then, it being summer, and the sharp blue stones were like ones she read of where pilgrims walked barefoot to wound their feet.

What lay down there in the depth of the water – pebbles and plankton and fish, several kinds of fish all preying off one another. But she would be dead and would not feel those clawings and pickings.

When she and her mother got to the big house her mother was too ashamed to say why they had come. Mary thought she should and so put on a funny accent and said, 'My daddy took a hatchet to my mummy and my mummy said, "There's a place where you will be sent and you will never come back,"' and her mother glared at her to shut up and she cried, and then they had tea and white scones that were square shaped, whereas her mother's scones were round. She got money going home.

The way to do it was not to jump but to sit on the steepest bit of bank and slide down, to think of it as being plunged into a big bath of water, or a font, a baptism font with no floor to it. She'd left only her beads, the mother-of-pearl ones, under a bit of loose concrete curbing on her mother's grave. It was supposed to mean something. If they found her in days to come and opened her up they might know. Some might even feel sorry for her then.

It was not like being on the brink of death, it was like wandering elsewhere, drifting off. She took another slug. It was a nice feeling, the muzziness, and even her father was not her father, she was waving to him or a him in his stiff off-white raincoat with perforations across the shoulders. What was keeping her. One minute it was to run along and hide her black buckled shoes in a different spot as if that mattered, then it was the round tower, how she would not see it again and so an elaborate charade of saying goodbye to it and to the saint it was named after. He had fasted in there and died there and his crumbling bones were powdered to make relics. The damp grass made her shiver when she lay down on it and she began to doubt that she would have the courage to get in.

It was the hour of evening when Betty walks, could walk in peace with her wolfhound without timorous people dreading that he was going to take a swipe out of them. Angus had never bitten anyone but the story went that he had mauled children, tinkers, postmen, a poultry instructress and anyone intrepid enough to have gone up the drive without first telephoning to have him put on his chain.

When Angus races into the reeds, chafing and slobbering, he senses something living, maybe a sheep, or a bullock. Betty runs to stop him and coming level with the body she thinks at first it is a corpse, then jumps in fright at hearing the frantic succession of screams which the girl lets out.

'He won't hurt you, he won't hurt you,' Betty says and tries to lift her up but each time her weight drops back as if she is under some hallucination. Her hair and her clothes are soaking wet. Betty hoists her up by the armpits and drags her along the grass with Angus soused now from having gone into the water, yelping with excitement, the rag of his tongue eager for play. By the stile that leads to the road Betty hesitates, irresolute, wishing a passing car would come and take the girl away and maybe, maybe dimly half-guessing the fatalities to come.

In the warm kitchen, wrapped in a fawn dressing gown, her feet in a basin of water, Mary will commit herself to two words – 'Thanks' and 'Sorry'.

'Why don't you call me Betty?'

'Sorry.'

'You came here as a little girl ... Don't you remember?'

'I remember coming with my mother once.'

'Oh, you came long before that, your father brought you and my poor husband picked you up and you said to him, "You have two crooked eyes." He had.'

'Sorry.'

'He thought it was a scream ... You weren't going to do anything silly, were you, Mary?'

'No ... I was tired.' Every other minute she lowers her eyes, in a constant expression of listening, as if someone is passing the window outside.

'Angus would fly at them,' Betty tells her and says that when her husband died she came again with her mother and father carrying a bunch of narcissi.

'We should try your daddy again.'

They could both hear the ringing in the house on the far side of the river, a ringing that was at once urgent and plaintive, a last summons to a house where things were coming to a reckoning.

'He must be gone out ... He goes to drink with Jacko,' Mary says, the voice far off, insensible.

'It would have been an awful thing ... Terrible for your poor father ... For your teacher, for the nuns.'

'Sorry.'

'Thank God I went in that direction and not the opposite.'

'There's someone out there.'

'There's no one out there, Mary, and I'll tell you something, I've walked there every evening since my husband died ... I've asked him ... I've spoken to him ... I've prayed to him for a sign ... Because you see they, some of the people, said he drowned himself and I knew he didn't. I knew he wouldn't do that to me. It was an accident and for fifteen years I've prayed for a sign and now it has come, you are that sign tonight.'

Between four and five Betty always wakens. She dreads it, dreads the blankness inside and out, all human intercourse suspended, the countryside de-peopled, even stray dogs gone home to their own holes to sulk, the pipes and the cistern utterly still, but on this morning a sound of running water, a tap being run and coughing, hard ceaseless coughs like that of an animal, a rabbit. Moving to the door, she listens and the hunch which had occurred to her the previous night at seeing such agitation is confirmed now and she guesses that the child, herself a child, is expecting. For a moment, but it is only a moment, she freezes, the retching making her recall her own short-lived pregnancies, feeling so sad and useless, telling her husband that her insides were barren, a curse had been put on them, and his saying he loved her and that they would try again, the words so sweet and brotherly, and she gasps aloud at the two periods of her life, knitted so strangely together and across such a bitter wasteland of time. Gaunt, almost reclusive, vetting callers from an upstairs window, venturing out only at evening time, going down to the river to talk to him, to ask his forgiveness for a sin he did not even know of and now this. This.

'Is there something wrong with you?' She stands just outside the bathroom door trying not to sound too strained.

'I don't know.'

'Could there be?'

'I don't know.'

'Mary, you have no mother, think of me as a mother over this.'

'She'd kill me, she would.'

'Have you had a period?'

'Yes.'

'When?'

'A while back.'

'How long back?'

'I'm not sure.'

'Oh Mary ... We have to do something ... Fast.'

'What ... What can we do fast?' and the terror in the face reflected in the mirror is not that of a little girl at all but of an animal, animal eyes staring out from the prongs of an iron trap.

✠

DR TOM

Betty has chosen back roads. The little sports car is squeezed in between two ranges of high mountain, the peaks a mustard yellow in the sunlight. There is something precarious about it. The car keeps skidding because of the ice puddles and because of having to come to sudden halts what with animals grazing on the roadside, cattle who stare at them with sullen, lumpen, immobile expressions. The houses, cottages mostly, are set far away from one another, farmyards a conglomeration of shacks, haysheds, old tyres, and ricks of turf with bags flung over them. In a gateway a caravan with two little girls in bright red tablecloths standing on the top step, waving and saying something. Then it is mile after mile of burnt and scorched furze and Betty saying she is not sure where the road will come out.

'Is it wild enough for you, Mary?'

'It's very lonely.'

'Oh they have great times up here in summer ... This is where all the traditional music springs from ... And they drink Potheen.'

'My mother had a bottle of that for years ... She used to pretend it was holy water.'

'Do you miss your mother, Mary?'

'It's better she's dead.'

'That's an awful thing to say.'

'I miss the convent.'

'We'll have to get you back.'

'That won't happen.' A finality in the voice and inside thinking that by lunchtime they will know except that she already knows, she knows about her body, the sickness then the cravings, wanting to sleep forever.

A few miles on, they come on a less bumpy road with forestry on one side, thick clumps of dark green huddled together, the leaves rustling in all weathers, like an endless sea, the half-shorn tops thrusting up like bits of plaited crucifix. It is an unlucky wood and people have met their deaths there. Instinctively they bless themselves. It is where Mary's father threatened to take her if ever she told the guards.

Black Wood it came to be called.

'We don't know how lucky we are,' Betty says.

'No,' Mary says, vacantly.

The surgery is packed, people as close together as the forestry trees, a mother trying to lull a baby, hitting its back in order for it to burp, older people too awkward to even look up and children on the floor playing with bricks. The rocking horse has had most of its paint scratched and scraped and at each oscillation it gives out a stiff angry creak.

'God save all here,' Dr Fogarty says. He stands in the doorway surveying his morning flock. She tightens when she sees him, thinks how rough he looks, dreads the power of his hands. He is a big man with a red complexion and he is holding a jug of flowers, roses, wide-open roses in a squat jug with a belly on it. He waves the flowers censor-like and then nods to Betty who follows him inside.

When they call her in Betty tells her that she is to tell the doctor everything, to leave nothing unsaid. Seeing the waiting couch with its white paper and a bolster of white paper above it, the plastic gloves faintly dusted with talc, she jumps and says she wants to go home.

'For Christ's sake,' he says, quick-tempered, and tells her to sit down and open that jumper so that he can listen to her heart. The cold of the stethoscope is like a muzzle and like a verdict too, and so is the expression in his bloodshot, weary eyes.

'Why haven't you had a period?'

'I don't know.'

'Why are you vomiting?'

'Something I ate.'

'Is that why you went down to the river?'

'No, I wanted to be dead.'

'Does your daddy beat you?'

'No.'

'Do you love your daddy?'

'I don't think I do.'

Seeing him go towards the sink she screams again. Screams, 'Don't examine me,' and he turns as if he might strike her and then something so broken and aghast in her makes him soften and he tells her to calm down, all he is going to do is feel her tummy and ask her to pass water.

'Now that's not too terrible, is it,' he says, and dispatches her behind the screen, one panel of which has come unhinged.

'Who are your friends, Mary?' He shouts it to cover up her embarrassment.

'I have no friends.'

'Everyone has to have friends,' he says and lifts the jug of flowers to inhale the dew and beauty of untouched morning. Without the mornings and the mountains he'd go mad, stark raving mad.

He whistles as he unwraps the plastic kit and invites her to look with him. Then he pours the drops of urine with a delicacy which belies the bulkiness of his raw chapped hands. Everything is compressed into that instant of time, made longer because of his having to take two phone calls and tell importune people at the other end that no, he has not forgotten, and yes he will be there and that there is only one him, no little leprechauns to bogtrot with bottles of cure, that only Biddy Early could have done that and that she was sprouting daisies. He puts the phone on its side then.

'Okey dokey,' he says and together they watch the needle of white and the patches at opposite ends waiting for the first trace of blue.

'Blue is our lucky dip,' he says and they see it, they both see it and instantly it turns white again.

'You often get that,' he says, reaching for a second kit.

'I'm costing you a lot,' she says.

'Government money,' he says and this time when they lean in they see only white, glaring white, and his saying, 'It's a bugger ... There's a poltergeist in it.'

'Don't examine me,' she says again.

'I can't examine you without your father's permission,' he says flatly and thinks the next unwelcome task will be getting her father in and having to endure the irrationality of a father who, when he learns of it, always thinks the doctor is to blame. The doctor is the hobo and not some stud getting their daughter into a van at night.

'My father will have nothing to do with me.'

'Is that so.'

'He threw me out,' she says. It is a way to stall, to allow her to run away.

'Does Mrs Crowe know that?'

'I didn't tell her.'

'I'll have to talk to her,' he says.

'Do you think I am?' she asks.

'A little girleen like you must be thinking, why was I born beautiful, why was I born at all.'

Betty is sitting on his desk while he writes a letter to the county hospital, all the while talking to her.

'She says her father doesn't want to know, threw her out.'

'Ah that's make-believe,' Betty says and they wonder then together who the father of the child might be.

'Didn't she give you any idea?'

'No, she clamped up. Johnny Belinda time ... Once it didn't go blue.' And handing her the bottle, labelled and slightly warm, he says, 'You'll need your cheque book for this, Bet.'

'There'll be hell at home ... Her father is a very heated man,' Betty says.

'Rosaries and ovaries, I don't know which does the most damage to this country. And to me.'

'Oh, Tommy, I am sorry.'

'Never mind ... You still hold yourself up with the walk of a queen.'

'I wish I did,' she says, a sadness in the voice and the long bone-drawn face.

'You'll probably have to wait around at the hospital for a while, so take her to see all the stone walls, round towers, mill streams and wishing wells that there are.'

In the museum they look at slides and photographs, read poems on exquisite yellow parchment, poems testifying to love and a woman's long-dimmed hair. Then they sit in a large room, just the two of them, Betty and herself, and watch a film, gull sound, waterfalls, the imposing sight of a poet arriving at his tower, his bride on his arm, a winding stairs, a four-poster bed, the voice of a commentator talking of Caoilte's tossing hair and the mystery of the rose. Suddenly, as if by some divination, she can see a person in a white coat, she believes that it is a woman, bent over a microscope, and in the damp daub of evidence, finding the two bodies, her own and his; body and antibody. In the dark she begins to plot, she will starve herself, she will starve them both, they will die separate, nourishless, listless deaths. Or so she thinks.

'It wasn't Galway, it wasn't Galway,' Mary is saying. They have pulled into the gateway of a demesne under a coppice of laurel trees.

'If it wasn't Galway, whose was it?' Betty asks.

'I don't know.'

'You must know, Mary.'

'There was a lot of us in a van, boys and girls.'

'When was that?'

'It was after the disco, there was drinking and people took off their clothes and things.'

'Is that true, Mary?'

'That's true.'

'How can I believe you,' Betty says, wearily.

'You can ... It was the night of the disco ... The doctor can compare the days and compare it. Tara will know. She was a witness, she was there.'

'Tara's mother is the last person I want to talk to,' Betty says, crisply.

'You said you wouldn't pull it out of me,' Mary says.

'Is it someone you love?'

'No.'

'Then you are shielding someone and for all you know he will do it to someone else, some other poor girl.'

'He won't, he won't.'

'What makes you so sure?'

'He's an older man.'

'This is disgusting,' Betty says, determining now that her father will have to be told at once.

'Not yet, not tonight,' Mary says.

'I'll tell him for you, I'll break it to him for you.'

'No ... That would be worse for his pride ... I'll tell him ... I'll go home and I'll tell him.'

She is running now, the top half of her body running and spinning but her lower part like a mummy, mummified. She is searching and hunting within herself for some other solution, some other person, some last avenue because Betty is in retreat now, she can tell from the spleen in the voice.

The wind blew dark and mutinous from under the laurels and rushed around the car as the country braced itself for a wet and hardy night.

✠

MONEY

She has not been home for several days on account of being sick, and having to be nursed in Tara's house. He looks with a glare when she comes in but within it relief at her homecoming. He has not shaven for days and the stubble gives him a convict's look.

'Where's Shep?'

'How do I know ... Everyone leaves me ...'

'I hope no one's stole him.'

'Who'd want him,' he says and then in a lower voice says, 'That other matter,' unable to say the word. She nods to mean yes, says she needs money for medicines.

'What medicines?'

'Medicines,' she says boldly.

'You weren't in Tara's house last night, I called over.'

'I was in Betty's house, she invited me.'

'Oh, the Countess ... Wouldn't even come in to say hello.'

So he had been looking through the window and had then stationed himself so that he could growl as she entered and call out to shut the door and not to let a draught in. He was still in his pyjamas, the tea slopping onto his saucer.

'She couldn't come in. She was in a hurry.'

'Too damn stuck up she is.'

'You should dress yourself.' She could hear her mother's refrain in her own. Her mother's mild rebuking on those few occasions when he was contrite and her mother had the upper hand.

She busied herself, tidying, stacking the used dishes onto a tray, boiling the kettle and saucepans of water because of the immersion heater not working, lifting the trampled torn shreds of newspaper from the floor which, in his anger, he had flung there and stamped on, telling him nicely to dress himself and that she would cook him a bit of breakfast. He comes back humming.

'Is Betty's house nice?'

'Oh, a palace.'

'Did she have a fire?'

'In the kitchen.'

'Not as good a fire as ours, I'd say.'

'No, but it's a stove that stays on all night ... It has tiles around it, with skiffs and sails.'

'Did she ask after me?'

'Oh, she did ... She said that you brought me there years ago and her husband picked me up in his arms ...'

'Will I ever forget it,' he says, warming now to the memory, the moment, oh so long ago, poor Mick, Betty's husband, being told he had two crooked eyes. He laughs and chews on the scones she has buttered for him, scones Betty gave her as a little farewell. His anger is lifted and so she broaches it lightly.

'I'll need a bit of money to get the things.'

'So that's why you came back ... You need money ... Not how are you, Father.'

'We need tea and bread and butter and you probably need cigarettes.'

He takes the coins out one at a time and lays them on the stove in a little cylindrical pile, some clean, some tarnished. There is not enough. She needs the bus fare to get to Dublin. Dublin is her destination now, not the city she visited with her mother, with throngs and shops and Pizza Huts, but a place where she will find refuge. She read of it in Tara's magazine, this very secret house where distraught women could shelter and even the name of it is like a beacon to her.

'I'll need more money than that,' she says, scooping it into a little cloth purse.

'There isn't more until Ryan pays me for the grazing.'

'I'll ask him,' she says.

'You will not ask him, Missy, I'm boss here. I'm book-keeper.'

She lingers outside the shop window, wondering whether she will say she has forgotten the money or that her father is coming over later on. One or other she must say. The woman inside is pregnant and moves about like she is proud of it, her stomach pushed forward, a fleshed-out trophy.

'Are you lost, Mary?' the woman says as she comes out to pick up some parsnips that are fallen from a box. Her voice is soft. She has six children already. A mother. The parsnips are clean shaven and Mary has a longing to cook them and eat them. It is like that, not able to eat at all and then these longings.

'I forgot my money,' she says quickly.

'Never mind, you can come in and get what you want.'

At the cash desk as she puts the few things down the woman says, 'What is it, Mary, what's wrong with you?' and for an instant she thinks that she can and will tell this woman, this mother, with her soft voice and her lovely soft pink neck on which pearls could rest, but she doesn't, her tongue refuses to.

'Here,' the woman says, picking up a chocolate box with a wide red ribbon round it. 'I never sent flowers when your poor mother died.'

'I'd rather the money,' Mary says and the woman opens the till and takes out a note but somehow there is a chilliness in it.

She cannot look up at the woman for shame, no more than she could look at herself, because she has turned beggar now.

✠

BROKEN LEG

Coming through a gap it happened. James slipped, then lost his footing on the churned up ground, the avalanche of muck and slurry heaped around the gateway, where the knacker to whom he had let the grass chose to fodder his stock.

He falls, tries to get up, slips again, then slithers across a gully, wheezing as he reaches in vain for the gate which has swung to the opposite side. Around are the stupid and menacing animals, trying to pin him in, and as he fends them with his forearm he falls a second time, hears a light snapping sound and knows that he has broken something.

Rising, he struggles to balance himself on the good side, the unbroken side, when his ankle gets wedged into a hole, and making one last teetering effort to reach the branch of a tree, he misses, falls face downward and knows that he has broken the leg as well. The pain is excruciating, yet the limb feels weightless, separate from him. He lies there, calling, shouting through shrouds of rain and dark, the animals encircling him, a bull, with a ring on its nose, in the vanguard.

At home she is waiting for him to come back, guessing that he will be drunk, wondering which of the neighbours will be his escort to carry him up to bed. When he has gone to sleep she will take the money from his wallet, and will get herself to the city, and beyond that her calculations do not go.

When Shep lets out his warning bark, she runs to have the hall door open so as to prevent her father from kicking it and what meets her instead of the usual drunk and plaintive excuse is a man with mud on his face being carried in on a stretcher by two strangers, one of whom she knows slightly.

'What happened?'

'What happened! I could have been left for dead ... Why didn't you send out a search...'

'He's all right ... He hasn't broken anything,' one of the men says.

'All right ... I've never known such pain in my life...'

'It's the fibula ... He's displaced it.'

'Displaced it ... I'm to carry four stone of cement for the next six weeks ... Can't lift my hand ... Can't blow my nose.'

The dark-haired boy is telling her how he heard the roaring from the far side of the river, ran across, but couldn't move him, had to retrace, to find someone with wheels, and found Dave who was on his way to bingo.

'Faith, we got him to casualty fast,' Dave says with a certain pride.

An argument ensues then, her father telling the two men to carry him to the sitting room where he will bed down on the sofa and her saying that it is better he be brought upstairs, to his own big bed.

'Put me where I tell ye,' he says to the two men who stand bemused, their hands slack on the poles. He is citing his reasons for wanting to be downstairs; one thing is to be near the kitchen where Mary can fetch his meals and the other is to have access to a telephone, so that he can call a doctor if things get worse.

'They won't get worse ... All you have to do is lie still and take the painkillers,' Dave tells him.

'You see that room there ... That's where I'm going to settle.'

'It's too dangerous,' Mary says, 'the sofa isn't wide enough ... He'd only fall out in his sleep.'

'We can put a ring of chairs around it ... a creel,' he says.

'Upstairs,' she says with a startling assurance which surprises even her and causes the men to smile, possibly recognising in it the small victories scored with their own parents from time to time. He does not answer for a moment, his hissing breath conveying the rage, flummox and disbelief which he feels. They have already lifted the canvas over the banister, Dave scaling the stairs slowly, his friend shouting at him not to bump into the holy statue half-way up. Unable to lash out at her he curses their clumsiness, saying they have broken it again, he can hear it unmesh, saying they are not fit to move a hog let alone a man.

It is as if a storm wind had come, hard and clean, and split the house in two, her father upstairs, herself downstairs, fourteen sloping steps, a long hallway brown and dust-swirled, the china knob of a door, hers to turn, to fasten him in the night.

DAWN LIGHT

In the dawn light the long windows looked like Christmas, sheer films of frost with little nodules here and there like the blobs of cotton wool in the draper's window. She stands in the drive until she sees the tassel being grasped and the blinds shooting up. She knows it is Betty's room because Betty took her up there to give her a splash of perfume to cheer her up.

When Betty opens the hall door, she is in her nightgown and her hair is unkempt. There is no smile, no semblance of a welcome, because she knows why the girl has come and she wants no part in it. Also to be found undressed makes everything more irking.

'I'm sorry,' Mary says.

'Don't you have any other words, only thanks and sorry.'

'There was no one I could go to.'

'Have you told your father?'

'I can't tell him. He'll kill me,' and then illogically she adds, 'He has a broken leg and a broken arm.'

'What has that got to do with it?' Betty says.

'When I said my mother was better dead I meant it,' Mary says in reply.

'What are you telling me, Mary?'

'That I can't tell him.' And staring into the woman's face and beyond it to the inner person she adds, 'It wouldn't be a right baby anyway ... It would be a freak.'

'Why do you say that, Mary?'

'Will you bring me to England?'

'I'm not your parent ... We're not even related.'

'I didn't go to the disco that night ... Tara is a witness ... I was sick, I had bruises ... She saw them.'

'If we are to do anything about this, Tara or her mother must not know.'

'Then you will bring me?'

'It's going against God, it's going against everything I believe in.'

'God can't be this cruel.'

'Look, Mary, I have to think and I have to take advice.'

'I'll pay you back ... I will.'

'I'll have to talk to one or two friends.'

'I know what they'll say ... You know what they'll say ... Give me the money and I'll go myself.'

'You're under-age ... You can't go.'

'My father would not do anything to stop it.'

'Why do you say that, Mary?'

'He wouldn't,' and although nothing is said or promised, the very act of allowing her in and down the long hall with a muttered apology about the storage heater being gone off a sort of compact is made between them.

Beside the kitchen stove Betty's clothes are laid out on a chair, arranged as for a performance, but also with a solemnity, the way a habit for the dead might be laid out. There is her skirt, her jumper, her underclothes and her stockings which have retained the shape of her legs and the dip of her instep. She takes them to the pantry to dress. When she re-emerges Mary sees that she has been crying and runs to her, now clutching her, employing every last scrap of hope and terror, sobbing, sobbing, 'Don't let me down. Don't let me down.'

'I don't know where or how to begin, but if we must do it ... we will do it,' Betty says, very quietly.

'I would have it if ... if ...'

'I know ... I think I know what you're saying,' and crossing to the wall mirror Betty takes a hairbrush from behind it and begins to brush her hair roughly as if to chastise herself. Then she puts on her stockings.

'Don't look down at my chicken legs,' she says.

'My mother always admired your legs and your style at mass, she used to talk about it when we were walking home.'

'The irony is that I, we tried very hard to have a child … My husband and I, we longed for a child … It broke his heart I think.' And reaching she puts her hand out to ask for her boots to be passed across. They are black patent boots and she licks the tip of the lace before threading it through.

✠

ANOTHER COUNTRY

It felt strange to them, to Betty and to Mary, and they were strange with each other, walking around, moping until the time. Houses squeezed in together and so many television aerials and so many different races. It was not how she thought England would be. Because they were early they sat in a little green enclave in front of a statue which had six heads, the colour of anthracite, supported on the one body, the faces all different, different manifestations of courage. Under the statue she read – 'This figure is erected to replace another figure destroyed by vandals to whom the truth was intolerable.'

So it was here in this big strange city it would happen, far from home. Its passing would be here, far from home.

In the place itself they were offered a choice of tea or coffee by a Spanish woman with large sleepy eyes. She was examined and then shown into the room of the head person who was sitting with Betty and who offered her tea or orange, whichever she preferred. She said to Mary that there was nothing to be afraid of and showed her a drawing of the ovaries and the tubes going into it and it looked like an armchair with wings. She shut her eyes. She didn't want to see. She simply kept saying 'Yes' and 'Yes'. It could be done on the following morning. It would take ten or twelve minutes at the most. Did she want a local anaesthetic or a general. A general.

'She wants to be asleep, sound asleep,' Betty said. The woman consulted the chart then and told them the exact time and told Mary not to eat anything before.

'How could I put your mind at rest?' she said as they stood up.

'It's all right ... She's just dazed,' Betty said.

'Maybe she would like to talk to one of the other girls ... Let me see who might be willing.'

'Yes ... That's a good idea ... That's a very good idea,' Betty said.

Mary was let go down alone.

The girl she saw was Mona, older than herself, blond and chatty. She got her to sit close on the bed and made fun of the paper nightie that she was wearing.

'Break my mother's heart it would,' she said. 'I had to pretend that I'd come shopping ... I'm going to buy a load of mugs ... With "Greetings from London" ... I'm not that blasé. Not really ... But you have to act brave ... You have to put on a good show ... Do you know what the doctor said to me, Asian fellow, he said, beautiful girl like you, how did you get caught out. And I said to him, I'm a terrible woman, that's how I got caught out.'

On the table beside the bed was a paperback book and a photograph of her boyfriend – Gabriel.

'That's Gabriel ... Handsome devil,' she said and kissed it and confessed that no matter what, she loved him to bits. Said that he nearly died when she told him, went mental, went green, they sat in the car and smoked sixty cigarettes in an hour. What to do. What to do. Not an easy thing no matter what you do. Gabriel working flat out, working a hundred hours a week to get the money.

'Are you scared?' Mary asked her.

'Not yet but I suppose I will be ... nearer the time ... I was awake all night and then I gave myself a talking-to, I said, think of eight months from now and out to here ... It's not that I don't like kids, because I do ... How many weeks are you?'

'I don't know.'

'You'd better know.'

'Not many.'

'No beautiful guy?'

'No beautiful guy.'

'What ... Some shit come up to you at a disco, say I love your earrings and where have you been all my life ... You're so special ... Love to know what they feel ... Still we'd be lost without them ... We'd be shrews ... Gabriel can do anything he likes with me ... He knows every bit of my body ... Why are you crying?'

'I'm terrified.'

'Look. Listen. It's only ten minutes ... You'll be brought in through the flip-flop doors ... You'll have had the anaesthetic ... And when you come out you'll probably be crying ... They told me I'd cry ... Everyone does ... It's only natural ... Would you like to meet up when we go home?'

And without waiting she writes down two numbers, her work number and her home number, remarking however that the home line is troppo busy because her little sister is dating.

A nurse came then and said, 'Doctor says you're coming down earlier ... Someone has ... has ...' and the voice trails away.

It was like she had just been quashed or the light that was inside her switched off; she went ashen then flustery, then asked if she had time for a cigarette, even a puff.

'I better go,' Mary said.

'Do you want to come up after?'

'Better not,' the young nurse said. 'She'll be groggy ... She'll be out ... Better not.'

They felt very close then, Mary and her, on account of feeling so alone and so afraid.

'Look me up ... We'll go on the razzle-dazzle,' Mona said, managing a smile.

'What's your name?'

'Mona ... It's on the bit of paper ... And you?'

'Mary.'

'Jesus wept ... We'll be a right pair ... Me a Dub and you a Mucker ... We'll paint the town ... The Dancing Queens.'

CASSANDRA

Noni's finest hour has come. She already pictures herself on some sort of illuminated dais, the people coming to give thanks to her for what she has done. She pictures how she will relay it, in what detail will she not describe the random action of her moving from the range in Betty's kitchen across to the window where the phone lay, debating as to whether or not it was improper to use Betty's hairbrush and then chancing on it, the fluke of fate which made her look down into the wastepaper basket and see. She will give pause before she enlarges on the shock which she endured at the thing which stared back up at her; a geisha, all tresses and come-hithers, the black print, the vile black print which read, 'Unwanted pregnancy – confidential advice.' She will describe how she bent down to pick it up but at first was too frightened to go on reading it, knowing that she was on the brink of a most terrible discovery and then the clues falling in together as if by a piece of wizardry, the fact of Mrs Crowe saying they were off to Dublin, yet getting English money in the bank, buying Mary a nightie and a toilet bag, hiring a taxi from the city twenty miles away, in case a local driver informed. She will tell them too how in that instant she re-saw the pictures of the conked and bleeding infant Roisin had showed her and how she felt Our Lady's sad tears dropping down on their little village.

When Lizzie re-enters with the mountainous load of logs, Noni is in the rocking chair, bleating her anguish, her neck and cheeks giving way to rampant patches of colour, gasping before she speaks, before saying, 'Like a good woman will you pass me my handbag and get me a drink of water ... I need to take my tablets.'

'What's come over you, missus, is it the change?'

'No, Lizzie, I've had that . . . A long time ago.'

'I never had it . . . Because I never had a monthly . . . I escaped it all,' Lizzie says, laughing.

'Lizzie, could you go upstairs for a few minutes because I have to make the most important call of my life.'

'Is it your husband?'

'You'll know soon enough, Lizzie, and when you do you'll need tablets.'

✠

REVELATION

'It's me. It's me.' Noni shouts up from the lower hall, a galling glee in the voice.

'Make me a cup of tea,' he shouts back to marshal his thoughts.

'It's more than tea you'll want,' she says, barging through the doorway, a sheet of paper across her heart, saying that she is not sure but she may faint, what with the shocking news she brings. Walking towards the bed she thrusts the piece of paper at him and he barks back that he has not got his glasses.

'I'll read it for you,' she says and in a voice both stiff and halting she calls out the name of the clinic in London, the unwanted pregnancy and the guarantee of confidential advice.

'What the hell has that to do with me?' he says.

'Everything ... Everything ... Mrs Crowe and your daughter are gone to England to that very place ... and it can't be Mrs Crowe's, can it ... So it must be Mary's.' She is waving the newspaper which she has glued together with ridiculous Santa Claus Sellotape as she launches into the miracle of her discovery.

'I said to Lizzie that I would go with her ... She dreaded going to that house alone ... She's terrified of their dog ... So I said, I'll come with you ... And she's out getting wood for the stove ... And didn't God lead me to it ... James MacNamara. Didn't God make me walk across to that wastepaper basket and bade me look down and guide my hand to pull it up.'

'Show it to me,' he says and grabs it. If he were on his feet now there would be some way of countering this, but he is not on his feet and this woman's eyes are hopping mad, rejoicing at the importance which is now hers. She is telling him how having found it she had to hold on to a chair, what with the shock, her heart condition, and then she remembered being in the bank and hearing Mrs Crowe asking for English money, and next by a spectacular piece of good fortune she finds out from her ex-daughter-in-law, who works in the airport, that they have travelled to London that morning.

'Deceived me,' he says.

'But why did you allow it?'

'Allow it ... I wasn't told it ... Mrs Crowe came here and told me that she was going to Dublin to see a sick relative and that she was bringing Mary for company.'

'And you didn't smell a rat?'

'Why would I smell a rat?'

'She came and got clothing.'

'She packed a few things, she said she would be asking you to bring me my grub ... We agreed where she would put the key ... That's as far as I know.'

'The guards will have to get onto it at once.'

'Keep the guards out of it.'

'What sort of father are you?'

'I'm in agony and you come in here raving.'

'Raving ... This is evidence ... Proof ... Murder on our hands.'

'I think you're getting carried away.'

'If you don't tell the guards I will.'

'You will not ... I'm her father ... Ask a guard to come and see me ... This is my business.'

'This is not your business ... It's the whole country's business ... Oh my God, Sodom and Gomorrah,' she says and remembers aloud Roisin telling them of the chain factories in England where death was on offer at cut price.

✠

MEN

'James.'
　　'Francie.'
　　'You nearly did for yourself, I hear,' the guard says, standing in the bedroom door and having to stoop a little.

'My God but you're tall ... I thought I was tall ... But you're a few inches above me. How tall are you?'

'I'm six six ... I was in the Vatican last year and the woman behind me prodded me, she said there is no standing in the Vatican, and me kneeling!'

'I'm sorry to put you to this bother ... If I was mobile I would have come to you,' James says.

'How's the pain?'

'Pain ... Don't talk to me about pain ... And do you know what's worse than the pain, the itch. In here,' and he hits at the plaster, 'is scalding me.'

'You were lucky they found you.'

'I was ... It could have been Secula ... Seculorum ... Damned slurry nearly did for me.'

'A man is better off on a tractor ... With the rainfall we get walking in fields is a hazard ... I was reading somewhere that inch for inch we get more rainfall in this part of the country than elsewhere ... That's why people don't thatch their roofs any more, it rots.'

'Oh I'm not walking fields again and risking my life.'

'Have you many cattle now, James?' Looking at the poor man's unshaven face and the goggling eyes he feels embarrassed at having to ask him anything.

'Not many . . . I'll sell the whole lot of them and sell up and move out.'

'You'd be heartbroken anywhere else.'

'Francie, I'll tell you something . . . I am heartbroken . . . Since my wife died there is not a night that I have not cried. And cried.'

'Mrs Burke came over to the barracks full of wind and bluster . . . It's about your daughter.'

'Oh, she was here, blathering.'

'She said that Mary is gone to England.'

'She jumped to a conclusion . . . Mrs Burke did.'

'Is your daughter not gone to England then?'

'I'm not sure . . . I was told that they were going to Dublin . . . On a shopping expedition.'

'And you a sick man,' Francie says, inwardly relieved, thinking now that Mrs Burke, notorious for her tongue has made the whole thing up.

'Children nowadays love gallivanting.'

'Don't I know it . . . We had a daughter . . . I say had, we have a daughter, hides in her room, won't speak . . . Won't eat . . . If I were to tell you what she did last Sunday . . . My wife thought that she would do a bit of continental cooking . . . Anything to get Lydia to eat . . . So she gets mince and tinned tomatoes to make a spaghetti Bolognese . . . Now I grant you it is not an easy thing to eat, to navigate onto a fork, and of course you can't cut it up because that is *de trop*, but I declare to God my Lydia decides to eat it with her hands, painted fingernails the colour of beetroot, her hands picking the dinner up like it was muck or stirabout . . . Show some respect for your mother, I said . . . And all she does is laugh . . . Laughter . . . Next thing she's sticking her tongue out and I pull her up by her hair and my wife is shouting at me, don't touch her, she didn't mean it . . . Treating her like a china doll . . .'

'Television has them ruined.'

'It has . . . How old is Mary?'

'She'll be fourteen . . .'

'She wouldn't have the right to travel to England . . . Mrs Crowe is breaking the law.'

'Wait a minute . . . I think I'm wrong . . . I think she's a bit more,'

James says, eyes and forehead breaking into tight creases, admitting somewhat ashamedly that with all his woes he doesn't know his own age, let alone his daughter's.

'Is there any chance that you could light me a cigarette,' he asks plaintively.

'Certainly.'

'Have one yourself.'

'Didn't I stop,' Francie says, patting the folds around his stomach, saying it was the most barmy thing he ever did, to endure not only the agony of giving them up, the nail-biting et cetera, but then to end up with a belly.

'You should do exercise for that.'

'What exercise ... I'm in that barracks six days a week,' he says and admits ruefully how much he loves chocolate. He takes pleasure tapping the new packet upside-down, then easing one cigarette out, lighting first one match, then a second because of their being damp, and in the puttering flame he sees the man's aghast eyes.

'Hurry on, can't you,' James says.

'You have the craving.'

'I don't know what I have.' And then in a sort of supplication he raises the arm in its yellowing cast and says, 'I wonder if I could get you to find me somewhere ... I want to get out of here ... It's dreadful ... Depending on Mrs Burke to come and bring me a cup of tea.'

'Oh she's a harpy,' Francie says, his eyes taking in all the features of the cold and comfortless room, a stained quilt, ashtrays, a chamber pot under the bed, desolation.

'I'll tell you what ... My missus goes over to the grave, her mother's grave every evening ... I'll get her to bring you a flask.'

'If I could just get away,' James says, a fraction too urgent.

'What get away ... You're a cripple.'

'Everything is getting to me ... Memories, too many memories,' and hands back the cigarette which he has actually bitten on, tobacco threads spewing out of the wet paper, asking like a child if he can have another, apologising.

Francie starts to pace, it is only when he paces that he can put his thinking cap on. He is thinking that there is something amiss, a man wanting to get away, not wanting to discuss the gravity of what has happened and biting biting on a cigarette like a maniac.

'Why don't you sit down,' James says.

'Oh, I'm all right ...' Francie says, leaning on the windowsill, thinking, this man is in a flummox and also thinking that it would be quite reasonable for a man to be in a flummox under the circumstances.

'Look,' he says. 'I hate to have to question you but the thing is I have to, it's my job ... Mrs Burke is of the opinion that your daughter is gone to this clinic ... Jesus ... I can hardly bring myself to say it ... Your daughter is gone to have an abortion ... Now we can't allow that ... We have to put a stop to that...'

'My daughter wouldn't.'

'Well, the name and address of the place was in the wastepaper basket ... And it's hardly Mrs Crowe that would be needing it ... So let me ask you ... Did Mary seem strange ... Did you notice anything odd ... Did you see her being sick ... Did she stay out late?'

'Out late ... She was off with Tara day and night ... Ran away for nearly a week.'

'Hello hello ... I wasn't appraised of this.'

'Didn't a guard bring her back ... Two guards ... A man and a woman ... Roaming the streets of Galway.'

'Have ye cousins there?'

'No cousins ... She was staying with some fellow, some hippie ... He plays on the street.'

'So she was away in Galway and you have reason to believe that she co-habited with this stranger and now she is missing ... You were deceived ... They did not go to Dublin ... Two tickets to England were purchased in the East of Eden travel office.'

'I'll kill her.'

'Well, before you kill her we better get her back and in tandem with that we have to bring in this suspect in Galway ... Where's the phone?'

'It's downstairs.'

'Jesus, we have been wasting precious time.'

'What are you going to do?'

'The law of the land, James ... The Law of God.'

'Get that scoundrel first.'

'We fire on two cylinders at once,' and as he hurries out he grabs the cigarettes and matches and apologises to his absent wife and says, 'I'm sorry ducky ... Stress ... Mega stress.'

✠

GUEST HOUSE

Reginald who owned the boarding-house fussed and chattered over them as he poured their tea through a strainer and said to please, ladies, try the crumpets with the homemade marrow jam. He knew why they had come. Some girls stayed with him and some in the rival guest house across the way. His favourite cat Moo was wrapped around his throat nibbling him. She was the colour of mica and had knowing eyes.

'Nice ladies. Nice ladies. Would the nice ladies like a little show just for a laugh?'

He worked in a place, you know, a place, naughty ladies, teasers, who spent the night taking their clothes off, girls with foam on their bubs, the men all eyes, all eyes, drunk blokes trying to get up on the stage for a feel, but not allowed, no sex involved, none whatsoever, all fantasy, girls just taking their clothes off and flinging them to the blokes.

Betty didn't know whether to say yes or no as they didn't want to offend him. He ran off then and brought back his little lizard attaché case and opened it to show his several costumes, his spangly things and his leather. The girls in the club spent fortunes on their costumes. Some going all science fiction and the others getting little black numbers from Montmartre. His was just old-fashioned stuff got at flea markets, bazaars.

He left the room and returned in a beaded dress that was sleeveless and skimpy, tucking his pony-tail under the net of a marmalade-coloured wig. His legs and knees looked buckled and underfed but he gained confidence as soon as he stepped on the pouffe which was his little dais. Up there he pouted and curled his finger at one or the other and said 'I think I'll have you,' then would switch his attentions to the other and back again. All of a sudden in a light voice he sang a song which Billie Holiday, his heroine, used to sing. 'Nice lady. Should not have died like that in the gutter.'

There were naughty stories from the club and naughty scenes, risqué, which he would like to tell but he daren't, he dare not because of being with nice ladies. He would pass the jug though. They need only put a copper in. It was for fun. In the club that's when things hotted up, the girls cracking the whips, the men outdoing each other, putting wads in, thinking they might get a feel, or more.

'One mustn't. Naughty. Naughty. No sex involved . . . None whatsoever . . . Only fantasy . . . Only dreaming . . .'

When the telephone rang they all jumped. Naughty. The moment he called her Betty seemed to sense it.

'Mrs Crowe . . . Mrs Crowe.'

They stare starkly at one another. Betty put her cigarette down, picked it up at once, drew on it mannishly, as if to say, 'Don't let anything go wrong now that we've come this far.'

BETRAYAL

'In Jesus' name get home here.' It is Dr Tom, his voice so loud and so close he might just be in the other room.

'What's happened?' Betty asks.

'The whole country is looking for her and looking for you ... You left a fucking clipping behind.'

'I tore it up ...'

'Well, you didn't tear it up enough ... Two women visited your house ... One of them found it and went to the guards ... The guards went to her father and next thing they come to me ... What had I done, what had I said ... Had I referred her ... Finito.'

'She's having it first thing in the morning.'

'She is not having it first thing in the morning.'

'It's all fixed ... The time ... The theatre ... The fee.'

'I'll go to gaol.'

'Don't be so melodramatic.'

'Betty, you don't know the medical fraternity ... They're under the thumbs of the bishops ... If you don't come home I'm finished ... My practice is finished ... I have nine kids and another on the way.'

'I always thought you were a friend,' she says, suddenly stung by being told of another on the way.

'I was a friend and you bloody well know it ... You needed a friend, a lover, and a doctor and I was all three to you, all three in one. That'll come out too ... Every fecking thing will come out ... All the dirty and half-dirty linen.'

'I'll never look myself in the eye again and I'll never look you in the eye again if I give in to this, if I fail her.'

'It's her or me … And I'm not loaded … I can't flash a cheque book.'

'Bastard,' she said and put the phone down.

In the hallway she waits, looks in the mirror and then marches in, announcing it, as if it is the most reasonable thing in the world.

'Pack your stuff … We have to go on back home,' her voice very quick, to avoid contradiction.

'Home?'

'The guards are waiting for us … I've committed a criminal offence and so has Dr Tom … How's that for a mess.'

'Naughty … naughty,' Reginald says, tucking the pink boa back into a long box with the slyness of a ventriloquist. 'Mustn't have naughty men, policemen, knocking on my door and looking at my treasures, my frou-frou.'

'You go … I'm not going … I'm staying,' Mary says.

'On what … You haven't sixpence.'

'Reginald will,' Mary says, her hands going up in some sort of idiotic flounce.

'Reginald won't … Reginald can't … You are a ward of court and I have to hand you over to the guards,' and saying it she begins to hurl things pell-mell from the side of the wash basin into the two bags, careless as to which is which. She is angry now. Angry at her own stupidity. Being roped in. Tears. Suicide … Every trick in the pack.

'Let me hide … Please let me hide … Say I ran off…'

'It's nothing to you if I go to gaol or if Dr Tom goes to gaol?'

'Such nice ladies,' Reginald says, holding up a long string of jade, waving it as he might a wand, to mediate.

'Sorry, Reginald … Sorry … Just get us the bill.'

'The room is as I quoted … I won't include the extras, the tea,' he says, hurrying out to frank her banking card.

'What's a ward of court?' Mary asks.

'They'll tell you that … They'll tell you that.'

*

In the plane they do not speak. Betty has the window seat, is drinking brandies, staring out at the dark, her forehead against the cold opaque glass, wishing only one thing, one thing, that they could stay up here in the heavens forever, drifting through forests of harmless cloud and being set down in some lost unmapped region. Stray wisps float into view, like doilies or little wandering skeins of fleece which soon get swallowed up in islands of blue. Neither of them has touched the tea or unwrapped the chocolate biscuit. Their elbows retract each time they touch, the small space between them a chasm. A fillet of red cuts across the sky then, like a bulletin, raw and brutal, the colour of things to be.

She knew that it was not long before they would be down, she could tell by the noise of the engine, a stalling noise, and she envisaged the people waiting for them, the locals and the strangers, their being met and then led away for questioning. It would never be forgotten or forgiven. She would become more of a recluse than ever, avoiding the neighbours in the houses all around, people like herself, filled with curious and escalating suspicions, and this despite the Cruiskeen Lán, the Lass of Aughrim, St Bridget's Wells, the Vale of Avoca, the High Road, the Low Road, the Sky Road, Moore's Melodies, Kitty O'Shea and the Uncrowned King of Ireland. She had not been drunk in a long time.

'Watch her,' she says, jumping up as Mary, with the sick bag to her lips, runs down the aisle.

'Is she your daughter?' the hostess says in a whisper, leaning in, not wanting to embarrass her.

'Watch her.'

'She'll be all right ... Young people get very excited.'

'If she's not out in two minutes we will have to break down the door.'

'Why?'

'She's not my daughter ... But she's threatening to kill herself.'

'Holy smoke ... This isn't for me ... This is for someone higher up,' the young hostess says, all composure gone now as she gallops towards the cockpit, the soles of her very new shoes raised high, the price ticket still on them.

When the plane came to a standstill Betty reached for their coats and their eyes met, and they flinched, the flinch of traitors.

'I wish I could have done more for you,' Betty said quietly. The look she got back she would always remember, not because there was accusation in it, not that, there was only bewilderment, and underneath it, this veil of softness, so soft, so trusting, soon to be slashed.

WOMEN

A rumour has started up as if by prophecy. Women are whispering, asking, waiting, waiting as they might for the apocalypse.

'Oh, sacred heart of Jesus.' It is Tara's mother, flinging herself onto a chair, in her own steam-filled kitchen, stunned from what she has just read. Noni has brought her the clipping of the place, has glued it together with absurd Santa Claus Sellotape, and together they ponder.

'Who else knows?' Tara's mother eventually asks.

'Her father and the guards . . . That's all.'

They vie with each other as to who will expire first, whose heart is weaker or stouter, which of them as mothers has not always dreaded an eventuality such as this. They compare stories about Mary, remarking on a brooch she wore at her mother's funeral, the long hair which she refused to have cut, would only have tapered, the smirk as if butter would not melt in her mouth. Presently they rebuke each other for wasting valuable time.

'We should start with Tara . . . Tara will know,' Noni says, her eyes opening and shutting on several other pursuits, such as searching up at the house, searching for a diary or maybe even love letters.

'Yes, Tara must know something,' her mother says and exclaims at the thought of that harlot sleeping in Tara's room, sharing Tara's bed, infecting her with sin and vileness.

'I have to go back to her father . . . You should see him . . . Above in the bed . . . Bucking.'

'I'll go to the school,' Tara's mother says, dragging the saucepan to one side, putting a prong in the bacon, then deciding it is pointless anyhow, since no one will be eating a dinner that night.

'Mummy ... Mummy, what is it?' They are in a corridor by a wall, the window to the classroom in full view and Tara's mother shouting, palpitating as she holds up the manual, reading out loud – 'The hymen which partly blocks the vagina is the gift wrapping proving that the product is untouched.' She reads it three times, then, striking Tara across the cheeks with it, calls out the next thing which she has memorised, 'O for orgasm ... The big O.'

'It was only fun.'

'Fun ... Am I climaxing ... Find his G Spot ... Let him find yours...'

'It came with the magazine...'

'Filth.'

'I've done nothing ... I really haven't.'

'Your friend Mary MacNamara has.'

'Is she dead, Mummy?'

'She would be better dead ... She's having a baby.'

'Oh, Jesus ... Oh, Mary,' Tara says and repeatedly blesses herself.

'When did she have her period?'

'I don't know.'

'What is I don't know?'

'She bought Tampax ... We both did, and mascara.'

'Have you a period?'

'Of course, Mummy.'

'Stop your mummy. Are you sure?'

'Where's Daddy, let him ask me.'

'This time, Tara Minogue, he will not save you ... Imagine your father reading – "the average female orgasm lasts five seconds ... beat the record ... make it ten ..." – He'll whip you.'

'Oh please, please, Mummy, don't show him that, it's just girls' talk ... It's just trying to be grown-up.'

'Did she confide in you, answer me.'

'No. No.'

'Did you know she was pregnant?'

'She was sick but...'

'But...'

'I thought it was the stew, it's often gone off.'

'What did she eat?'

'She ate rusks.'

'Was she sick all the time?'

'Mornings, morning sickness.'

'And you, you told no one.'

'She said it was an ulcer because her mother died.'

'An ulcer is not morning sickness ... Your father has an ulcer, it's a pain in the gut.'

'You know Mary, Mummy ... You can't get two words out of her.'

'What boys was she with ... Locals or blow-ins...'

'I don't know ... I never saw her with a boy.'

'Whose child is it, Tara?'

'Is she really having a child, Mummy?'

'Worse, she went to England with Mrs Crowe to get rid of it.'

At this Tara begins to tremble and asks her mother if they can please move away from the view of the window because she would rather her friends did not see her having a breakdown. She is crying. In her mind she is retracing the night of the disco, going into that room, the atmosphere of terror, Mary's bruises, her clothes on the floor beside her father's shoes, things so awful that she blanked them out. Now there is another awful thing.

'You are keeping something from me, Tara Minogue.'

'I'm not, Mummy ... Honest, I'm not.'

All she can think of now is the night before last with Danny, his saying he pulled out in time, but suppose he didn't, suppose one speck was left, suppose one of those little wiggly things was left inside her the way it happened with Mary, what then, ruin, ruination; herself and her best friend the two Mary Magdalenes of the parish.

'Mummy, take me home. I have awful pains ... Awful pains in my tummy.' And she grasps her mother's hand to massage it, to take her troubles away.

HEAD TEACHER

It is Tara's mother who breaks it to the head teacher. He is in his armchair, slouched, having tea and cake, his clothes smeared with icing. At first he refuses to believe it.

'Ask the guards,' she says gloatingly.

'This is tragic ... This is a tragedy.' A sultana that has adhered to his front tooth gives him a joker's look. He puts the cup down. He has always thought of himself as a man who could pick things up, he has thought of himself as a communicator, the shepherd on the mountain sort of thing for the boys and girls in his school. He has cared for them. He is angry with himself now that he did not pick that something up. He begins to piece things together. Mary hanging around his door, lingering after school, reluctant to go home, a little smile of apology on her face. Saying no, no, when asked if there was anything she needed, books or a heart-to-heart. Next day again hanging around, his joking her about being the robin redbreast on the windowsill. He recalls that he asked what was the problem. None, she said. None. He asked if she would prefer to talk to a female. No. She did not need to talk to anyone. But her eyes spoke. There was a desperation in them. He asked if it was of a sexual nature maybe, and at that she ran off. He did not pursue it because he was embarrassed. He had failed. He seemed to sink lower and lower into the crumpled cretonne of the armchair, defeated.

'Well, it is of a sexual nature,' Tara's mother says.

'My hunch is ...'

'Is what?'

'I am not sure I can put it into words ... It's not a boyfriend ... It's something more devastating. More shameful.'

'If it was that she would have gone to someone, the guards or me, or you or someone,' Tara's mother says as she starts to march about the room.

The woman in the dun cardigan seemed to be transformed then, seemed to levitate before his eyes, frothing, sermonising, depicting a night paradise of foul pleasures which the girl enjoyed; woods, bogs, callows; undressing herself for any man, any man, married, cracked, single, and what's more, proof of it, the proof of the pudding of it, soiled undergarments on their land, seen by her very own eyes and her very own dog when out for a Sunday stroll, a whore's remains it was.

'She'll need all the friends she can find,' he says gravely.

'She'll need watching,' she says, fiercely. What he saw beneath the outrage was the jealousy of a thwarted woman seething over her own lost, never-ever-tasted delight of being thirteen and fourteen and fifteen.

'I still think it's a case of a cousin ... Or an uncle,' he says half vaguely.

'She has no uncle,' she says savagely and cites the fact that less than a week before Mary's father came to their door to fetch her, believing she was there which she wasn't, and where was she after midnight, in whose embraces was she.

He rose then and went to his desk trying in some way to be rid of her. She saw that, and she hated that and she hated him for the cravenness, the soft spot which he and every man under the sun had for young, malleable flesh.

'We will have to nurture her,' he says.

'Nurture her,' she says, her fist mashing the stuff of her tweed pocket.

EVENING LIGHT

A group had gathered to meet her. There was Mrs Burke, Tara's mother, her friend Dympna and two women whom she did not know. Her father was not there, probably because of his fall. She waved as if for a homecoming, and seeing their expressions, shocked, appalled, her hand just hung in the air.

The young girl with the short slashed hair and steel grey eyes spoke to her sharply – 'We're glad to have got you home ... Your father is glad and every right-minded person in the country is glad.'

'Your father put us in charge of things,' Noni said, deferring to Roisin, and said, 'This is the woman who saved you ... The two of you ... Without her I could not have coped.'

'A little thing that hasn't harmed you ... Would never harm you ... Totally dependent on you for its life,' Roisin said, inflamed. 'Already a person ... Its sex, hair, eyes, fingers, fingernails already there ... And what is it doing, it is listening to the music inside your womb and thinking that you are its friend.'

'It was not the child's doing ... It was that Betty one with her blood money, her Judas money,' Noni said.

A strange woman came then with a mild voice and a mild smile and took her hand and said, 'Fear not, child.' They were all turning into a blur, their hats and their jewellery and their crooked smiles, all vying with each other as to who was in charge, who owned her. It seemed like another world, London did, the anthracite faces, Mona in the paper nightgown and Reginald with his feather boa and his naughty naughty. Beyond the glass partition she saw Betty being led away and there was in it something so cold and so matter-

[151]

of-fact, that she saw at once that there was no future for her, no
ransom.

'The hand that rocks the cradle,' Eilie, the mild woman, was
saying and she went on about women not being the Cinderellas of
society any more and women were defined by motherhood and
singled out by motherhood and the room was swimming now as
she asked if she could sit down.

'She's just acting ... acting,' Roisin was saying.

'We love you to death,' Eilie was saying.

'By this time tomorrow you would be asking yourself why you
did it ... You would be completely destroyed by what you had done,'
Roisin said and held up her wristwatch to affirm it, vexed at getting
that dazed dopey look.

'Are you too sick to talk, Mary?' Noni asked.

'We all love you to death,' Eilie was saying.

'I need to know why you made that decision ... When you
made that decision ... Was it in my house ... When you were eating my food and enjoying my friendship?' Tara's mother asked
her.

'Oh, Mrs Minogue ... Don't be hard on her ... She's back now
... She's safe,' Eilie says, and drawing Mary aside she spoke very
quietly as if it was in the confessional, asking did she realise the
miracle that had happened, that it was that thing, the little life
growing in the depths of her body, which brought the truth to light,
the whole sordid business of the rape, that the little life was the
saviour and that it would also save the rapist, because all rapists
long for the day when somebody would find them out and put a
stop to what they know to be shameful but which they cannot
control. If any of her daughters was in the same predicament she
would see it for what it was, part of God's design, and Mary must
see that too, see the pregnancy as a solution and not a problem, as
a gift from God.

The doctor had been standing above them for a few moments, a
young man, tall and completely attired in oatmeal tweed, coat,
scarf, shirt and trousers, all of slightly different but complementing
shades of oatmeal, and his doctor's bag was beautifully polished.

'Mary,' he said, quite friendly. She knew him slightly because he did locum sometimes at home and she had gone once to collect a prescription for her father.

'Shall we repair,' he said and led her to a still smaller room in which there were just two chairs and a rectangular glass table with pointed edges. Noni felt furious at not being allowed in with them, because after all she had been the instigator, she was the one to have found out and gone to the guards and got Mary's father to sign a letter for the solicitor, saying that on no account must she be allowed to leave the country again.

'You're very quiet ... Are you somatising your pain, Mary?' the doctor said.

'I have no pain,' she said.

'Well, you're not well, you've been sick and you're dehydrated,' he said.

'Where am I going to go?'

'I'm going to recommend that you spend a few days in a hospital, you need to be strengthened; they'll need to confirm the pregnancy and then await orders.'

'From who?'

'Well the guards from home, the Attorney General, the Department of Public Prosecution.'

'Does everyone know?' she asked, blinking with shame.

'You should have told someone, you should have told your daddy or your friends, people are there to help.'

'They're not,' she said, but she did not dare look at him.

'I'd like you not to think of me as one of the bad guys ... I don't have a jaundiced view of the world or my patients ... I had a patient who would not eat or drink, she thought Satan was in the food, but after a lot of visits, I got her to take something ... I'd like to do the same with you,' he said and all the time he was frowning, as if he was puzzling something out. He said that there was something he felt he must tell her, that although he was a Christian he had difficulty at times reciting the creed and that was a test of his faith, just as her faith was now being tested by God.

'I'd like to be dead,' she said, vacantly.

'How would you die, Mary?'

'Poison.'

'Who'd give you poison – no one, not a chemist, not a doctor.'

'I could jump.'

'Suppose you only broke bones ... Or let's say for a minute that you succeeded ... How do you know that you wouldn't have to carry that baby around with you in the next life, for all eternity ... Think of that ... Moreover is to die the last act of a living person ... I don't know ... You don't know ... There was a queen in Bohemia beheaded, yet she went on talking, she was clinically dead but she spoke ... We don't understand these mysteries and we are not meant to.'

As he rambled on she thought, he is not talking to me, he is talking to himself, and for a minute she was tempted to tell him the colliding inside her head, how all these objects were flying around, toothbrushes, bottlebrushes, clothesbrushes; wondering if it meant that she had gone mad.

'Do you like anecdotes, Mary?'

'I don't mind them.'

It became insufferable for Roisin to leave them alone, and as she hurried in, her eyes sweeping the room, she scoffed when she heard his soft bland words about hard choices and the usefulness of talking about suicide thoughts and even transposing them into pictures.

'Rubbish,' she said.

'It's a very real option to a person who sees no way out,' he says, irked at her intrusion and her superiority.

'It's not your child,' she said suddenly to Mary. 'The way your tonsils are yours or your mane of hair.'

'It's not yours either,' Mary said, the words a beautiful explosion that seemed to float out of her mouth and blacken the face that was only inches away.

In the flat landscape outside, the sky was a dome of navy, the clouds to either side heaped, capacious, an aeroplane soaring through them like a flickering bird of fable.

POWER

'Feel that,' he says. PJ has come into the room ebullient, beaming. A week away from her and he's bursting. She won't feel it. She remains yoked to the leather armchair, china blue eyes pale, sizzling like a pale blue fuse burning into him. She is wearing the necklace he gave her, the rubies.

'So you're back,' her voice curt.

'You know I'm back and you know I'm glad to be back,' he says, winded from the stairs. He opens his shirt so that she can touch his chest and compliment him on his tan. What she remarks on instead is that he has put weight on, he has been slipping on that diet.

'In the bosom of your family,' she says, tartly. 'In the bosom of your yacht.'

'At sea people don't speak.'

'At night they do.'

'We were always off with crowds in bars ... Sing songs and all that.'

'Oh, his eminence, our leader, singing a rebel song or a humble ballad.'

'I'm a plain fellow, Geraldine, and you know it.'

'A plain fellow who has made it to the top of the ladder, PJ.'

'Look ... I was dreaming of this ... Coming into the room ... You here ... The blinds drawn ... Not able to keep my hands off you.'

'You said you would ring.'

'I did ring.'

'When?'

'I rang Sunday ... I got your mother.'

'She never told me.'

'Well I can't be blamed for that.'

'What did you say to her?'

'I asked her if she'd any tip for the race.'

'So you didn't ring me, you rang my mother to ask for a tip.'

'Jesus. I'm like a hunted beast.'

'Who's hunting you – not me.'

'My wife ... My family ... My devoted staff.' He kicks papers and portfolios with a lusty spleen.

'I'm not hunting you ... I'm not really ... But six days is six days, Jock.' Now she is soothing.

'Did you see the new shower ... did Vinnie show it to you ... All the gadgets?'

'It's super.'

'Will we have one?'

'Maybe.'

'God, you're in a foul mood.'

'My dear mother knit you this,' she says, taking a sleeveless pullover from her basket where she has also brought her nightbag in the hope that they might go away. Out on the mountains he is a different man, they are both different, swaddled together.

'Now she's a good woman ... She's on my side,' as he holds the pullover, then smells it, smells the new wool.

'Jock, is it ever going to change?'

'Of course it is. We will walk hand in hand into the sunset.'

'Say it, Jock.'

'We will have our little Grey Home in the west.'

'How can I believe you?'

'Didn't that woman with the cards tell you?'

'She did.'

'So.'

'I'm getting on, I'd like a family.'

'We're enough of a family ... We're soul-mates.'

'You love your children.'

'Of course I love my children – what do you think I am, a robot?'

'And you say it's them that's keeping you there.'

'I will not see them turn into hooligans and drug addicts.'

'But you will see me withering away.'

'Withering . . . You're a slip of a girl in your pillar-box red . . . Did I buy you that?'

'No, you didn't.'

As she crosses to shut out the last sliver of light he pinches her, and the stuff of her skirt does not have sufficient yield to allow a man to feel the flesh, and in the violet dusk now they kiss and whisper, admitting to all that was waiting to be said the moment they met. They begin to undress, expert at it, garments flying, laughter, the words of a song, her asking if he wants a peek-a-boo when they are interrupted by a knock on the door.

'Holy Jesus.'

'Don't answer it.'

'I told you I'm a hunted beast,' he says and puts his bare arm through a crack in the opened door to receive an envelope which he thrusts across the room and which misses the desk.

'I don't want to get my hair wet, Jock . . . I had it done and we are going to dinner . . . We are going to dinner?'

He pushes her to the inner passage, whistling.

'Peek-a-boo. Peek-a-boo.'

'I might even hide behind the curtain and watch you.'

'Wasn't that in a horror movie?'

'It was . . . *Psycho* . . . Well I'll psych with my little eye that Geraldine won't be worried about the hair on her head when she comes out.'

'We are going to dinner . . . aren't we, Jock?'

'I want to hear a lot of little yells, a lot of little yodelling.'

'Not in here . . . We need to be up the mountain.'

'Yes, in here . . . I want to christen that shower.'

'Why do you like them – the little yells?'

'Yo Jock . . . Yo matador . . . Zmell de bloodz o' de torros.'

'Matador,' she says. 'What does Matador think of yo stockings which require neither garter nor suspender, kept up by suction?'

What he thinks is no other man should see that alabaster arc of thigh, edible, smackable, his. His.

'Why didn't you show me when I came in?'

'I wanted you to guess . . . To spy with your little eye.'

'You're some woman.'

Amidst the jubilance and skirmishing, trying to duck each other under the powerful jets, he hears knocking again, repeated knocks which he knows to be a summons, even the pauses being Conor's way of transmitting the urgency of things.

'Oh shite.'

He comes out, face blazing, the towel robe back to front, and shouts to Conor through the locked and padded door – 'What is it ... What is it?'

'It's concerning the envelope I brought up from the Attorney's office.'

'Can't it wait till morning?'

'It can't ... He has to speak to you right away.'

'Feck's sake.'

'A young girl went over to England ...'

'Oh, the love that lingers.'

'She didn't have the operation and she's home now, but the guards are afraid she'll go again.'

'Like hell she will.'

Suddenly he is not Jock, or rather he is the other Jock, the one Geraldine recoils from, the one who will not suffer contradiction or tampering with his great office. The smiling blushing gallant put to one side now like one photograph overlaid with another; cold, pugnacious, asking without words why in feck's name she has come out of the bathroom, why she is standing there in her slip, shoeless and stockingless.

'Conor knows me,' she says and by that also saying Conor has seen many a thing, has had to effect deafness in the car during torrid rows, then has had to leave his driver's seat and walk up and down a freezing road for the steaming reconciliation.

'I have work to do,' he says roughly.

'I suppose you will go down now and be the statesman and do the right thing ... Yourself and that feelingless fish of an attorney.'

'I did not appoint him ... I inherited him.'

'But you'll give the green light.'

'Look, if it was up to me I'd give her the government jet to get straight back across the salt sea.'

'But you won't because you might be out of power.'

'I've been out of power before ... You know that ... So don't call me chicken.'

'Hundreds of girls go, Jock ... Including me ... Why one law for us and one for some poor girl?'

'Because she came home, stupid.'

'Defy him ... Tell your attorney to sit on it for forty-eight hours ...'

'He has the power to restrain her ... He's only consulting me, out of, out of decency.'

'Decency! Men who can turn off the heart valve the way you turned off that fucking water jet.'

'What business is State business of yours?'

'None, Jock, none. I'm just crumpet. And oh, much as I have loved you for the last ten years, I've hated you ... I've seen you in action ... Power ... Power ... The mighty ambrosia ... Anything and everything and everyone would be sacrificed for that power.'

'Vinnie will take you home.'

'I'm staying.' She sits on his desk and begins to remove the various pieces of jewellery, and with a sneer as he sees them being thrown to the floor, he says, 'Oh here we go, oh here we go, divorce papers again.'

'Fucking paste jewellery,' she screams, but he is already gone.

Vinnie will come up and she will go home and obey. A week will pass, bickering with her mother, then will come one of his boyish letters about love, about friendship, the enduringness of love, a poem, Yeats, who else, and it will all start up again because she is crooked too, lonely and crooked, two lamentable things to be.

The gauds of beading along the floor are like tears, inflated and violet from the shadow of the drawn blind.

✠

SUPPER

The panelled room ready for its little coterie of distinguished guests imparts an atmosphere both gentle and hallowed, a room which has housed great minds, heard great debates; its age reflected in tiny things such as the frayed and faded colours of the pale green wall-silks, and in cornices here and there a cupid with an arm or a big toe missing and the unseemly sight of a bit of rusted wire poking through. The two men stand by the fire discussing the bane of a squeaking shoe. One is the host, Judge Martin Cooney, and the other is his guest Hugo, who has arrived to take up a diplomatic post.

Hugo, the foreign gentleman, has raised the topic because no matter how he furls and unfurls his foot his shoes will not stop squeaking and this, in such a rarefied atmosphere and his first visit at that, and the Judge the highest, the most venerable in the land. Coming up the stone stairway he noticed it, and now in the vast room it squeals at everything his host is telling him. They stand, as is the custom, before one fire and for the latter half of the evening, when they partake of port, they and the other guests will repair to the opposite end to be greeted by an identical fire of dull, listless, unvarying flame.

'Not a patch on the real thing ... But no one wants to carry up coal nowadays,' Martin says, and touches the marbled breasted front of the chimney-piece which carries the proud brown patina from years and years of roaring fires and licking flames.

'When I was a young man and took a girl home, a squeaking show on the staircase meant no tendresse, no cat's pyjamas.'

'Quite.' Martin smiles. His is an automatic circumspect smile, his long face having the yellow of vellum, his dentures that bit too bulky so that they seem like masonry, filling his small mouth and framing his thin womanish lips. Any talk of tendresse, cat's pyjamas, wenches, or trysts on stairways, angers him, topics which some of his learned colleagues revel in, ever panting to lower the tone and allow things to degenerate into smut. It is cigars one minute, the efficacy of the humidor in that shop in Nassau Street, and the next minute it's a woman's breeches. He has had the same salutary wife, Agnes, for forty-odd years and though she is unpopular and thought to be bossy by some of his colleagues and nicknamed 'the bantam' he has found his connubial life quite satisfactory. His wife has carved a name for herself in the nation's echelons by donating an Italianate figure of the Virgin to her native parish over in the West.

'They are not even new shoes ... That is the curious thing,' Hugo is saying as he looks down and clouts one foot with the other.

'It may be the temperature in here,' Martin says, eager to get off the subject and move on to salutary things, his love and pride in a real fire, the times in his grandmother's house long ago when they gathered mushrooms and roasted them on hot coals with a pinch of salt.

'No ... I washed the bathroom floor and was somewhat liberal with the detergent.'

'You washed the bathroom floor?'

'Yes ... My wife, you see, has not arrived yet ... Otherwise hers would be the squeaking shoes.' His appointment being recent he has come on ahead, is living in a service flat and spending his spare time searching for a house in the nearby mountains, a house such as his wife had dreamed of and done a water-colour of. A dovecote abutting a river or purling stream.

'I find if I don't wear a shoe, the leather goes a bit dry and that can lead to a squeak ... But it's a different squeak,' Martin says, hoping to bury the topic.

'The shoe misses the body's essences and perspirations,' Hugo says and is the recipient of another frigid and toothsome smile. Martin is asking himself if this man can be imagining that he is avant-garde, sounding off about perspiration, or does he think that he has come among cavemen.

'So you're settling in nicely,' he says.

'We love this country ... My wife is a Joycean scholar ... When we were engaged she insisted that I read aloud to her, Molly Bloom's ... How do you call it?'

'Soliloquy.'

'Soliloquy ... Not the same as colloquy?'

'The converse.'

'Is it true that your great Mr Joyce carried a pair of miniature knickers in his overcoat pocket, to amuse himself?'

'No idea,' Martin says, relieved at the sounds of jocularity, two colleagues entering in a garrulous froth, colleagues who had bitterly opposed each other at the bench all day. Donal, the senior barrister, is telling Tim, a junior, about a very dire case of delirium tremens in which he was assailed by biting dogs, dogs under his bed, up on the bed, at his throat, every breed and denomination of dog.

'It got me off the booze,' he says and taps the place where a belly once protruded, then undoes his belt to show where a new hole had to be punched by his shoemaker. Introductions are done, and in an impulse of exuberance Hugo repeats his own and his wife's admiration for Molly Bloom, then asks mischievously if it was so that Mr Joyce showed a special interest in micturition.

'Could be ... Could be,' Donal says, rummaging through his Latin data for a clue, then suddenly hitting on it and decrying with an angry thrust of his fist – 'A peeping Tom ... Nothing but a literary peeping Tom ... Or should I say a peeping Jim.' Drove him mad it did, this worship of highfalutin pornography, no appreciation whatsoever of the earlier stuff, the courtly verses, the psalms, the epiphanies of monks and the grand laments written for the wild geese, cream of the country's aristocracy forced into exile to serve in foreign regiments. 'Our Wild Geese shed their blood on the continent and have had great wines named after them,' he says staunchly.

'Very great wines ... Very great bouquet,' Hugo says while Danno, entering in ruddy disquiet, overhears and opines that the bouquet of wines and women differ from man to man and from equinox to equinox.

'Also differ whether she be standing or couchant,' Hugo says.

'Quite so ... We have a mountain here called Leabasheeda, Bed of Silk. How is that for an ongoing couchant,' Danno says and asks his host if their foreign friend has been shown the listed lavatory with its listed lavatory chain.

'Shall we nigh forth,' Martin says, ignoring the question and welcoming the wobbling sight of the butler in the doorway bracing himself to announce dinner.

Gowns are donned, Martin having to suffer further smut from Danno about the good men, the many good men who have undressed in a ditch, and as they prepare to go down, Ronan, a young solicitor, arrives flushed and stammering. It is established that Hugo will head the procession with Martin, and so out into the cold passage and down the stairs to more squeaks, they enter the dining room where an assembly, mostly youths, noisome but somewhat abashed, rise to bow and scrape. So many bowed heads and of such different inclinings it begins to seem as if the oak beams themselves and the solemn cankered faces depicted in the paintings have vivified, to participate in the time-honoured obsequious ritual.

At the high table as they wait for the first course Hugo studies the motto, a green cresting on a porcelain plate, '*Non mutare* – we shall not change.' Differences of opinion arise as to the sagacity of such a creed, and Ronan, the young solicitor, his gown falling from his sloping figure, tells them that a guru whom his wife consults is of the opinion that change is the only stimulus for spiritual growth.

'They're all chancers ... those gurus,' Donal says.

'Now now,' Martin chides him and says they must not give the impression of being insular, East and West having much to teach one another.

'Didn't a monk rape two women in a temple ... Brought them along miles of serpentine dark corridor and pounced.'

'Ah, the old reliable, the tricolour of fish,' Danno says with gusto to a butler on whom old age and craven dutifulness has taken its toll. He shakes uncontrollably as he puts down the plates, each one an identical serving of watery prawns, white trout, and rolls of smoked salmon filled with sour cream.

'Never look a gift horse,' TP, an older barrister, sometimes garrulous, sometimes sullen, says, then raises his plate ceremoniously and begs them to consider how the seas are being fished bare and the sea floor destined for famine because of man's incipient greed.

'Only maggots,' Danno says.

'Sshhh ... Grace. Grace,' Martin calls and they each rise.

Benedictus nobis is intoned and repeated throughout the room, and once again with his gravid smile Martin turns to Hugo and asks if he is surprised by the brevity of their grace.

Through the vast hall conversation is resumed, a mickle and merry noise regardless of what is being discussed, glasses are clinked, tongues let loose and at the top table little rivalries and sparrings begin, each determining to interrupt the other and enlighten their visitor on the quirks of the country.

'What of Master L'Estrange,' Martin says, pointing to an empty place, a desertion he does not tolerate. Master L'Estrange has called off. Reasons unknown. Real reason because he despises them all, is above them all and does not wish to break bread. The men differ in what they think of L'Estrange and parry insults as to whether he is the real thing or a very clever imitation of the real thing.

'He has his little confraternity of admirers,' Martin says to Hugo.

'There's no one to touch him ... Brilliant man,' Danno says.

'I wouldn't call it brilliance ... It's more a flair,' Martin says, but to no one in particular.

'Come on, Martin, you know he's got *it*,' TP challenges him.

'He's an actor, the way we are all actors at the bench ... He throws his hands up ... He demurs ... He plays little games with his witnesses ... I've seen him reduce them to tears.'

'Don't gripe, my Lord,' TP says and moves his chair so that he is no longer facing his host.

'I am not griping ... I simply wish that he had had the courtesy to tell us he was not coming.'

'It's probably slipped his memory, he works day and night, a workaholic,' Ronan says, his cheeks blazing from one glass of wine and their bantering, beads of sweat along his forehead.

'Oh come on, Ronan ... That's infantile ... We are all workaholics ... But we are not all prima donnas.'

'He's taken cases no one else would touch ... That's why he's hated ... That's why he's slandered ... That's why he's had arson attacks on his house,' Ronan says, half rising, as if he might wallop someone.

'May I propose a toast to our honoured guest,' Martin says over-courteously, his glance down the length of the table augmented with pique. Nothing about the evening is to his liking and he is thinking of fish pie at home in the TV room and early bed.

'Why don't you just say that you hate L'Estrange's guts,' TP says, refusing to let it die.

'On the contrary, I like the man and I enjoy a *causerie* with him.'

Winks are exchanged, toasts are drunk to all present and to other great men who jousted and imbibed at the same table; wine is swilled, the water jug passed clumsily from wrist to wrist, its brackenish hue alluded to and explained away because of the iron and iodine in the virginal regions from whence it springs.

'Folklore ... Folklore,' Danno says, and praises the wine not for its bouquet but because there are buckets of it.

The dinner does not look appetising; the hacked and bleeding strips of beef on a silver salver somehow impart the frenzy of the slaughterhouse and the vegetables are a mush.

'You have served abroad,' Martin says to his visitor. 'Now tell us some strange occurrences.'

'Many, many ...' Hugo says, meditatively.

'For instance?'

'For instance among certain primitive tribes; even to this day, they believe in head-hunting.'

'Isn't that a banking expression?' Donal says.

'Its origin is more primitive ... A baby is born and an elder in the tribe is put to death.'

'Savages.'

'Well it's one way of keeping the population down,' TP says, guffawing, suggesting that the idea be passed on to the bishops.

'Which bishops – the brimstone or the fleshpots?'

'What fleshpots are you talking about?' Martin asks, livid.

'The ones that go to Thailand for their fun,' Danno says.

'I think our friend is getting a very wrong impression of our country,' Martin says.

'Not at all,' Hugo says, and returning to the topic of head-hunting he explains how the soul of one is believed to enter the soul of the other.

'Sure they have no souls,' Donal says, smarting because of the insult to bishops.

'On the contrary, they revere the soul ... They put hooks and cages around a body to keep the soul from flying away.'

'Well I'll tell you something, you'll have your soul well vetted here ... So get your hooks and cages, sir,' TP says.

'Must I watch my p's and q's?' Hugo asks.

'Put it like this ... If you decide to commit a crime, pick your locality,' Danno says.

'Meaning what?'

'There are some jurors who will just not convict ... Murder, manslaughter, bestiality, rape ... All the biggies,' Danno says, beaming.

'Rap his knuckles,' Martin shouts down.

'You know it's true, Martin ... We were on cases together ... We saw it happen.'

'That's sour grapes ... That's because you lost.'

'That's a known fact,' Danno says and cites the case of a commercial traveller who again and again took up with foreign ladies, took them for drives, gave them chocolates and candlelit dinners, then on the last night on some lonely by-way had his way and yet, and yet, always got off because of living among these passionate tribes who had no time for the law.

'So you must tell me where I indulge my amours ... My little peccadilloes,' Hugo says, pleased to find them so animated.

The butler is standing by his Lordship, whispering, then putting down a note, his hands trembling exceedingly.

'You mean now?' Martin says, scanning it.

'Yes, my Lord.' And so with an irritable wave of his napkin, and muttering some terse apology, his Lordship rises and again a conglomeration of bowing while at the top table wonder is voiced as to what the urgency must be.

'I think you've given him a nausea attack, Danno,' TP says and instantly Danno prides himself on how he can always ruffle respectability.

'Methinks me knows,' Donal says and whispers to Tim, the pair of them having ignored most of the jawing and guffawing, while they discussed certain political rumblings, some phone bugging about to be discovered.

'What is it, Donal?'

'I'm not sure ... But I had a call from PJ ... He was mental, chucked a wobbler ... The Attorney General had to act over some brat ... Some little slut about to pour piss on the nation's breast.'

When men of honour, men of *gravitas*, meet at this inappropriate hour and in this bibulous atmosphere, they know at once and they act. First principles. First principles. When Judge Cooney sees his friend and colleague, Aubrey, eyebrows in a nervous twitch, a petrified clerk standing beside him, he knows that it is something significant. It takes only minutes for the clerk to read the submission sent by a country solicitor from the West, outlining how a girl under-age had gone to England to terminate a pregnancy, had got cold feet and had come home, but the fear was that she would go again and that there were some all too willing to assist her. A court is convened there and then, and though he is devoid of gown or wig because of the lateness of the hour, all protocol and formality is maintained, and having heard the submission read for a second time the Judge agrees that she must be stopped because the unborn shall not be removed from the jurisdiction of the court. He grants the injunction there and then with the assurance that it will be ratified in an actual court the following morning.

'Notify the guards, the solicitor and her parents,' Judge Cooney says.

'Mother dead, my Lord.'

'Where is the girl?'

'She is in hospital, here in the city ... Her mental state is unsound.'

'Notify her ... The right to travel *simpliciter* cannot take precedence over the right to life.'

'A doctor who examined her said she was in despair.'

'*Despair of salvation*

Presumption of God's mercy
Contradicting known truths
Envy at another's spiritual growth
Obstinacy and sin – the five sins against the Holy Ghost. Notify her Aubrey.'

'We will, my Lord.'

'You did well, Aubrey ... You acted with speed ... What we need now is a bit of legal magic to copper-fasten it and by the way we want no leaks ... We want this under wraps ... This is something our friends in the media would salivate over.'

'It will be under wraps, my Lord ... It's in everyone's interests including the girl's that nothing gets out ... It would destroy her privacy, her peace of mind if it were to become public.'

✠

SAVIOUR

In the tiny ward where she lay alone, Mary could hear babies crying, harsh cries, registering different kinds of discontent. They sounded like bleating lambs and she wanted to get up and drive them out into the fields. She stuck a pencil first in one ear, then in the other. Beside the bed there was a pencil, a notepad and a phone. There was also a bunch of flowers but no name on them. She imagined it was the young nurse Ruby, who had confiscated them from some other patient, pretending perhaps to bring them to the chapel, to put them on the altar. Various people had spoken to her and the matron had told her that the legalities were being sorted out. She had had no tests yet because of being weak from travelling, because of the vomiting, but she would have them the next day.

'Your teeth will rot if you only eat custard,' the young nurse said as she brushed her hair. She said it was a crowning glory and that Mary must never cut it, never.

'I'd shave it if I could.'

'Ah now, don't be saying that ... The worst is over ...'

It is dusk when the other woman comes, tall and bulky, her eyes concealed behind thick spectacles, bandaging on her legs. She closes the door then heaves her shoulder to it, heave-ho, then crosses to the bed and from a linen cloth she produces Bibles which she has filled with markers. The markers are shreds of flowered wallpaper samples, with acorns and rosebuds on them. She leans in over the narrow bed, a furious strength to her voice, a phantom's conviction –

'But to those who did receive Him He granted authority to become God's children, that is, to those who believe in His name, who owe their birth neither to human blood nor to physical urge nor to human design but to God, God ... Are you listening?'

'I don't know you,' Mary says, too frightened to pull the emergency bell because of what might happen in the intervening moments before help came.

'I was seeking evidence of God for days, I have pondered the bounteous love of God and it revealed itself to me tonight when you came here. I was bidden, bidden.'

'You were not bidden,' Mary says.

'Do you realise that that child inside you, that soul could be the next prophet. It is written that a second prophet is coming to save mankind. Why has the sun become black as ashcloth and why has the moon turned red as blood ... Answer me, answer me. Why? Because of you and people like you, that is why. Why is there no peace on earth, why is there no peace in East Timor or Russia or Bosnia or Somalia or here at home ... Why are there wars, why, why ... Because the wrath of God is unleashed because of the millions of unborn children ... The blood of three million unborn children is weeping down and the sun which is the Lord has turned black with sadness and His Holiness the Pope is black with sadness and the moon is red as blood.'

'Go away,' Mary says, her voice muffled because she has gone under the covers, only her eyes showing.

'Oh, yes, I can see that you are afraid ... You fear the words of the Lord as Jezebel did ... The dogs shall devour Jezebel and none shall bury her so sayeth the word ... When Jezebel heard Jehu entering Jazreel, she painted her eyes, adorned her head and when Jehu arrived and lifted his face to the window, two or three eunuchs looked out at him and he said, "Push her out, it is me," and they pushed her out. Some of her blood bespattered the wall and they trampled her down and when they came to bury her they found nothing of her except her skull, her feet and the palms of her hands, so that none could say this is Jezebel. The same is true of you.'

Then stooping down, in a wild whisper, she says, 'Uncover yourself.' Her eyes and her voice verging on lunacy, spittle flowing from her as she runs a relic over the naked body, stooping lower and lower as if to see through the wall of the flesh itself, and into the womb, talking riddles to it and shaking Mary, shaking her so violently that the bed rungs judder.

She backs away then, staggering, pausing for breath, and after a moment seems to levitate upward into the dusk-filled room, her glasses half off, her little nurse's cap askew, turning another page of her book and spouting it without having to look down, her voice strengthening as if there is a bellows in her.

'The serpent vilest of all the field animals tempted you, O serpent which tempted the first woman to eat of the fruit of the garden, we have found you. Wail, O Cyprus, and wail, O Sebasha, for an infant whose mother would slay it. Woe to her who treats with scorn the rock of salvation. Thou shalt be of unsound mind.'

From beyond the room they can hear voices, and walking backwards now she hisses, 'I have set before you life and death ... Therefore choose life that you may live ... I will know ... I will know.'

Opening the door she hovers, the outflung arm a token of her returning.

✠

LUKE

Long matted hair that hadn't seen a brush or comb in weeks. If there was one thing Guard Fahy could not abide, it was these louts, the lice upon the locks of the nation, balladeers with their ethnic this and their ethnic that, never did an honest day's work, bastards begot on their travels, at Fleadhs and Siamsa, bastards rolling in the mire, never washed from one rendezvous to the next.

'Why have you that clock,' he asks staring at the two aluminium wings flopping out of a torn pocket.

'I just bought it at the pound shop … I have to go up north tomorrow,' Luke says.

'Is that so.'

'Yes. Have to catch the first bus.'

'You've never had an alarm clock before?'

'Never needed one.'

'Holy Christ … You know something, I don't think you'll be catching that first bus.'

'I have to … I'm teaming up with a mate … We're collaborating.'

'Is she tasty?'

'He's a bloke.'

'You realise that everything you say will be taken as evidence.'

'I'm innocent. I told the guard when he picked me up.'

'Ever been in a police cell before?'

'Never.'

'Are you sure … Are you positive of that?'

'One in Glasgow.'

'And was it the same little perversity … Deflowering a minor?'

'I hadn't a ticket for the Underground.'

'You've put a porker in her.'

'You have the wrong bloke,' Luke says, his voice pipey and the words in his mind far stronger and more assertive than what comes out. He cannot stop shaking. His clothes flap on him as they would on a scarecrow. Who can bail him out, who give him a character reference – only his mates from the Fleadhs, but these civic guards would shred that. Two minutes more and he might have escaped. Nora, the girl in the bookshop, had given him the tip-off, said that they were looking for him all morning, had been asking where he lived, when at that instant one of them came through from the art gallery at the back and put the cuffs on.

Nora took the bohráin, said she'd mind it for him and nursed it like a chalice as he was being herded into the back of the van.

'This girl and I ... did not know each other.'

'Oh you mean you weren't on first names.'

'In the biblical sense.'

'This is druidic ... She stayed in your quarters ... Your quartier ... Remind me, are you en suite or have you to go half-way up the landing?'

'I slept in a sleeping bag, it's in my room. I've never been in this kind of trouble ever.'

'Well you're in it now, Mutt.'

'I only let her stay because she was homeless.'

'There are hostels.'

'She had no money.'

'You let her stay to get your nuts off.'

'I've never touched a woman ... Ever.'

'Oh ... Blessed Oliver Plunkett ... Or do I mean Matt Talbot,' Fahy says, calling upon the harp on the wall, the nation's blazonry, with its tight, bronzed strings, to commend such an example of purity.

'By all accounts she was a good looker,' the guard says as he runs through the questions on his notepad.

'Look,' Luke says, cupping and uncupping his hands as if he is holding a frightened bird in them. 'I see beautiful girls every day ... One more beautiful than the other and I don't ... I don't.' He is looking down at his hands raised in this humble suspension of trust and he laughs, an almost bitter laugh, and thinks, 'They want a bloke ... The place she came from they won't penetrate ... They won't be able ... So it will just have to be me. Only a moron would think otherwise.' His sight starts to go. It is always like that when he gets stunned, always. It happened the day the train pulled out and Angie was not on it, her luggage on the floor, she having rushed onto the platform to get a coffee, but not returned; opening the luggage hours later and finding books in it, books she had stolen from a pub shelf, to give a bit of weight to the suitcase, to pretend. A soft-seeming girl with woodland. Only a moron would trust.

Through the window on a curved branch he saw something move but could not tell whether it was a bird or an old curled-up leaf; yes, he was blind, his sight was gone.

'Why don't you answer?' the guard was shouting at him.

'There's no point.'

'Why don't you answer?'

'Because ... I am already damned ... I've already done it ... Even though I didn't.'

'Oh, the usual left-wing tripe ... Let me tell you something ... We are a civilised force ... As advanced as any country in the world ... We have forensic testing, fingerprinting ... DNA ... We'll take blood from you and blood will be taken from the foetus and in a laboratory it will be decided if they match.'

'I'll give all the blood you want ... I'll give it now.'

'You'll give it when the doctor gets here,' Fahy said, scanning his questions and then looking up with a sneer – 'You had her ... How many nights ... Not to mention mornings?'

'She stayed three nights.'

'I suppose you perform better in the morning when the dope wears off.'

'The landlord knows me ... He'll vouch for me.'

'We might as well get to the nitty gritty ... When did you lay her ...'

'I wouldn't. I couldn't.'

'She says you did.'

'She's lying.'

'That's only for starters . . . She's above in Dublin awaiting criminal charges, she's a ward of the courts . . . This is no hole-in-the-corner job.'

'Let me talk to her.'

'You bought her a jumper.'

'In the pound shop.'

'You had intercourse with her.'

'I did not . . . I'll swear on the Bible I did not . . . I want a lawyer . . . I'm entitled to Legal Aid.'

'You can get your Legal Aid when we get a written statement from you.'

'I'm innocent.'

'Ten minutes of fun and ten years in clink . . . Disproportionate.'

When Luke sees his Fair Isle jersey and the tin box – a corset box as it happens – with his letters and songs and photographs, he reels in shame, it is as if they have just undressed him.

'So what have you got for us, Colm?' Guard Fahy asks of the young guard who is whistling lightly as he holds out the trophies.

'Take a sniff of that,' Colm says and they engage in a discussion as to whether it is Afghan or Moroccan.

'And what else?'

'His social security book . . . His mother's letters and his will.'

'He's made a will, good. Did he leave me the silver,' and reaching for the social security book he brandishes it in front of Luke aglow with righteousness. 'Nice, cushy . . . When you think that we have a living on the street . . . That we put the cap down on the pavement, while we're fiddling the State . . .'

'I do it for love.'

'Could you repeat that.'

'I love the bohráin.'

'No no . . . You do it for . . . Please repeat that illustrious word,' and wresting it out of him, insisting that he say it, he snaps his fingers with the disdain of a man training fleas to go in and out of a matchbox.

'By the way,' Colm says, half snigger, half embarrassment, 'there was a lady in his room . . . Called me honey . . . She has a bone disease.'

'Christ, he's a pluralist.'

'She's not my girlfriend.'

Turning to Colm, Guard Fahy asks with exaggerated compassion if she too is in the family way.

'She was drinking milk and watching cartoons.'

'On our money . . . On our bloody money,' Fahy says, the lava of long-held hate and noxiousness bursting from him now as he paces. 'I work my butt off, seven days a week, I work overtime to buy shoes for my kids . . . I grow my own vegetables . . . I don't permit myself a drink, I don't go to the dogs, I don't go to the bookmakers while he and his ilk sponge off the nation, beget children . . . Holy Christ, I'd send the lot of them down the mine and dynamite it.'

Luke seems to be watching them and himself as though in a miasma. He watches them touch his things, contaminate them, sneer at his mother's disjointed letters while he breathes, deep and slow and cogitant.

'You didn't find anything else, Colm . . . Billets-doux?' Fahy asks.

'You'll find what you need to know in the inside drawer,' Luke says, blurting it out. They start to read her letter aloud, her fears about maybe being a mother, her asking him to come to her rescue, and spitefully they look towards him, knowing they have got the wrong man.

'So I can be on my way,' he says.

'Not yet, boyo . . . We're not finished yet.'

As the light failed in the cell Luke watched it eke out from the rectangle of milky glass which fronted the pavement, footsteps up above, people going home, the sighs of engines, cars revving, voices fluctuant, friendly under the stars, if there were stars; crouched and tightened, gathering his ribs into a knot of hardness, mineral hard, not allowing it to slacken whichever way he breathed, making a wigwam of himself. He counted numbers then, enlarging them and painting over them the happy golden colours of numbers glued onto birthday cards. They had not left him a bucket and he guessed why. They wanted him to wet himself and witness the pool which would wander along the floor and be half absorbed into the concrete yet retain the particular haphazard and shameful traces of itself, that and the smell, so that they could call him pig when they came to let him out.

He quaffs the air loud with rain, behind him their cruel smutty barbs, their crooked jokes, runs past the river and the slop-green river bank, over a humped bridge, nearly coming a cropper on the pile of morning newspapers outside the corner shop, past the weedy allotment that leads up to his own digs where he does not even dream of halting, a zephyr; through a rustic lane now with over-hanging gardens, and on and on until he reaches the frontier of the sea, endless, horizonless, the turbulent waves far out with a rav-ishing turquoise glint to their underbellies and the near ones lapping and gentle, for him to immerse himself in. This, his des-tination. He will erase all traces of the civic guard, of the stinking, leaking cell, of this or that girl who stopped to hear him play and made eyes at him, and above all of the girl he had taken for a wee waif and who had done him wrong.

No one will get near him again, no one will drag from him that troth which he has been keeping for the right woman and which even in his cretiny he had once believed Angie to be, had settled on the ring he would buy, the Claddagh ring, with two hands plaited on a golden mount, the symbol of two plaited natures. O lost enchantments.

He is crying and he cannot stop.

'Why are you crying?' he says, looking up at a famished star that has forgotten to pack in. He cannot answer. He cannot yet bring himself to say that he is crying not for what they had done to him, but for what he did by letting them read the girl's letter, and in the doing sullied himself.

✠

A LETTER

'Letter for you, Mary,' Ruby says. It was hand delivered and there was a signature on the back. It was from a cousin, a cousin of her father's, introducing herself because of going to be her guardian for the time being. Her daddy had approved it and the courts had approved it. It was a long letter and it was signed Veronica, with the name Linihan in brackets.

Dear Mary,

You will love my little house, I think, it is very comfortable and it is warm. Thank God for central heating. I will tell you a bit about it so's you can think about it while you are convalescing. You will have a space on the dressing table for your own things and you will be able to walk about in your bare feet in the morning if you like because I have a big white rug in the front room. Tell you what, your task would be to clean it, I mean not to wash it, but to keep it spruced. They sent a fork with it from the factory, a little fork to lift the tufts up. Would you like to do that. Of course you will have your studies to do and I understand that Sister Rosario is going to give you lessons free. She is a lovely person and has travelled to the US and abroad and you will like her. Did I tell you the house is called Shannon View after the river. We must not forget our roots, our woods and our rivers and our history above all. Now you may wonder why we are cousins. Well my father and your father were first cousins but your side were always thought to be the toffs. My husband passed away some years ago and I had really big death duties which I was not prepared for and so had to sell the big house and move to this small house but as I said, it is quiet and it is peaceful, a nice unstressful atmosphere, and because of the sea light – the sea is only a few hundred yards away – the changing

*light and shadow is peculiar. I challenge artists who try vainly to explain
the light and colour let alone capture it. One cannot catch mist in one's
hands. Neither can anyone who aspires to painting trap a light or colour.
As you will probably guess, I have let the cat out of the bag. I would have
loved to have been a painter but was not good enough at it and I have to
settle for patchwork. My garden is a real work of art, but it is not the best
season for it. I have trees and scented bushes. All fragrant things have a
soul. Did you know that. I am sitting here finishing this letter and trying
to think what you look like and what sort of voice you have and if we will
get along. I am sure we will. I have been told that you are a well-mannered
girl, though on the shy side. We will sit here in peace, the only sound the
hissing of a steam geyser for the coffee. Do you like coffee? I must confess I
have a weakness for it. I thought I would write you all this before fetching
you so that you would know me. I am thinking of you in my prayers and
will see you very soon.*

Your cousin Veronica

✠

DREARY DAYS

The two wooden table lamps had barley sugar stands and were covered with flowered shades in pink and blue. Pink for a boy and blue for a girl. That is what Veronica said. They would get knitting patterns and two sets of knitting needles and nice new balls of soft wool. Veronica herself would make a cot cover. She showed Mary the pictures. Basket of plenty.

This was her new home, this is where she would go to school from and get bigger and bigger. This is where she would be brought from when the pains came on. In the meantime she would have counselling. They were seeing to everything, her new family of bossy women.

Veronica laid the breakfast table before they went to bed – the cereal packet was got out, the two mugs with cherries on them and the napkins in green metal napkin holders. The shower was difficult to turn on but even harder to turn off. She never looked down at herself, her body was hateful, an alien. It didn't matter whether the water was boiling or freezing, she didn't care. The hot water came out in a trickle. There was talc and bath essence but she did not use them.

The fire in the front room was lit at lunchtime, and in the garden outside the plate-glass window, she could see a flame of the fire, free-floating, a banner in thin air, like it had no foundation, no grate to rest on, just a burning thing in the garden outside. In the room were three evergreen plants and a big bunch of Honesty, the silvery white discs like unconsecrated communion wafers. The birds converged at lunchtime too. After they took their helpings from the bird table they went and made a pattern on the top sprigs of a plum-coloured bush. To look at their dark shapes was to imagine that they had been appliquéd to it. They sang like billy-o, a song of gratitude. Sometimes one or other quivered, a tail quivered, or a breast quivered and a squitter happened during their impromptu concert.

After lunch was their walk. After the bowl of soup and the cheese scone, Veronica always said that they needed to work it off. Rarely did they meet anyone. They might see a dog in the distance and guess about its owner somewhere in the dunes. The sea wind bit into her, it went in through one ear and out the other and it was like being syringed by a shaft of cold. The side near the sea hurt more. She lost her head scarf there. It blew off and she ran to get it but the wind was carrying it down to the sea and she thought, 'This is bad luck … It's bound to be.' Her hands went funny colours like rhubarb. Her father's hands went that way and one day when he came in from counting cattle he asked her to warm them, to rub them up and down and she did but it was clean, it was a clean thing and there was nothing ugly in it.

Every day they went as far as the big yellow digger and watched while the driver picked up, or attempted to pick up, one of the big rocks and consign it down to the sea. It was because of erosion; the sea was eating into the sand and unless a reef was built, the sea would take over. The teeth of the shovel had difficulty getting a bite on the rocks, sometimes the driver had to try nine or ten times and they could see him getting furious. He never waved to them and they never waved. It was an unfriendly place.

The slow days with Veronica were chiefly composed of knitting and crocheting. Hundred of stitches went into doing those strips of matinée coats. Pink for a boy and blue for a girl. She would sit opposite Veronica because it was where she had been told to sit and watch the crochet needle loop forward then quickly backward then forward again so that a piece of straight thread was converted into a tight and unrippable little conundrum. Veronica kept her head down, her eyes on her task, her fingers scarcely seeming to move, a little frown, and all the time watching, watching from the side of her eyes. Even when she closed her eyes for her forty winks she was still watching.

A PET

Four women carried it in with a touch of ceremony. It was something in a shoebox. Mary had been looking through the window.

'Mary,' Veronica calls out and asks her first to close her eyes and then, when they have set it down, to lift the newspaper off. What she sees at first is a Pyrex bowl of water and something in it moving like billy-o and bubbles coming up.

'Do you like it?' the other woman, Peggy, says. Peggy is wearing a cap which reaches down to her ears. She has had cancer and has to wear a cap all the time, and each night at prayers Veronica has prayed for her.

'And look, there is a little rockery for it,' another woman says, holding in the palm of her hands a few stones. They make her put the stones into the bowl and then one of them tells her to touch it, touch her new friend, not to be afraid. It has two different colours, red when she stares into the water and gold when she looks at it through the side of the bowl. Through the side of the bowl it is longer and thicker.

'What will we call it, Jack or Jill?'

'Mary?'

'Mary ... do you want it to be called Jack or Jill?'

'Either,' she says.

They tell her to pick up the feed canister and read out the directions and the substances in the food.

'It contains protein, oil and fibreash,' she says, very loud, very nervous, and adds, 'Feed sparingly.' She must not irritate them.

'You wouldn't kill it, would you?'

'No.'

'You see, once you get to know something or someone ... Once you touch it ... Once you see a little soul struggling for life, you do not think of killing it ... Isn't that so?'

'Yes.'

'Now where would you like it to live, Mary?'

'There,' she says and points to the shelf next to the little black radio underneath a holy picture with the hanging rosaries; they are spare rosaries for when other women come to pray and have forgotten their own. They move to the fire and she stands looking in at it. It has three different movements, one when the mouth opens and closes a fraction, the other when it decides to make a dive and a foray through the water and the third, by far the most sinister, when it simply moves its little fins. Its eyes are the circumference of a small bead, a small black unfeeling bead, and the expression in its mouth is one of spite as if warding off others, enemy fish. Then, all of a sudden, it jumps out, it leaps out over the edge of the bowl and is on the side of the floor darting about.

'It'll die, it'll die,' one says.

'It's going blue,' a second says.

'The man said it would die in thirty seconds if it was out of water.'

'Catch it, Mary ... Catch it ... You're younger than we are.'

As she reaches to catch it, it slips from her fingers, and she grips it again, the slipperiness revolting her, and she chucks it with venom into the bowl.

'Good girl, good girl ... You saved its life ... You see ... That is your true nature, you would not kill, you would not kill,' and they look first at the fish which is utterly still from its peradventure and then at her, telling her that they trust her now that they know.

Outside the window a plump brown bird, the sole inhabitant of the bird table, lifts and lowers its tail again and again, mechanically, like a door latch, and in the wintery sky, the sun is a football of fire with muslins of cloud passing over it, wiping its face. If they were to ask her what she was thinking she would say, nothing, not thinking. But she is. She is thinking of the supreme moment when she will escape them.

'I can see you getting married one day ... You'll have a lovely quiet wedding over in the West,' one of the women says, and again they are saying how she would not or could not take a life. The words dinned and distilled into her, followed by the prayers, low and beseeching as they kneel around her; their smells, their twisted worried faces, their brooches, their stockings, their frizzed cottony hair, snaking her.

> *O most beautiful flower of Mount Carmel*
> *Fruitful vine*
> *Blessed mother of the Son of God*
> *Immaculate Virgin*
> *Star of the sea help me and show me you are my mother*
> *O Mary conceived without sin*
> *Queen of angels*
> *Queen of patriarchs*
> *Queen of all saints*
> *Tower of Ivory*
> *House of Gold*

And as they prayed and waved their beads and their scapulars over her, her stomach seemed like a porthole into which they were looking and prying.

Afterwards they had tea and the cake which Veronica had made and which they ate a lot of. They even put their fingers along their plates to lick up the chocolate filling.

'I can see you having a very quiet wedding in the country ... I saw it just now ... What you were wearing,' the woman said once again. A wedding. A word. Another word like death or truth or goldfish. She thought that words were the thing people used to suit their purpose, to stuff up the holes in themselves, to live lies, and that one day those words would be sucked out of them and they would have to be their empty speechless selves at last.

'Shouldn't we be thinking of names?' Veronica said.

'Diana is really popular now.'

'Ah, we want a name of our own – Siobhain or Maeve.'

'What do you say, Mary?'

'I don't know ... It's ages away.' Despite everything she did not believe that she was having it; it was a globule and she would believe it only when the feet pressed on the wall of her stomach and kicked and she would kick back, they would have a kicking match. It was as if Veronica knew, knew what she was thinking.

'Mary MacNamara, come here,' Veronica said and, as had become a habit with her, she pulled on her hair to chastise her, indignantly dropping the long, flecked strands into the fire.

Under her pillow there was a card. She was not sure which of them had gone up and left it. It said – 'Please do not break your promise ... Please do not kill an innocent baby.'

STRANGERS

'Cocks crow in the morn
To tell us to rise
And he who lies late
Will never be wise.'

The announcer's voice, syrupy, recitative, warning his listeners to fasten their seatbelts because the topic for discussion was one that was rocking the nation. The moment that she heard the word Magdalene she knew it was her and knew that she should not listen. Veronica set the radio clock each night for the same hour but never wakened, always saying that she had had trouble getting to sleep. They slept together now. Veronica said it was on account of the guest room being cold but it wasn't that. It was to stop her from running away. Often at night she felt a foot hooking around her own or an arm clutching her so that she moved further and further away, and twice she had fallen out of bed and had to crawl back in again.

The first person to speak was called Eileen and between her and the disc jockey there ensued a short skittish preamble about an Eileen character in a song who turned the spinning wheel but was really scheming to go off with her lover and leave her poor sick granny stranded. He asked Eileen, as he would ask the others, what she thought about this poor little girl made pregnant before she had even blossomed, this poor little waif in ankle socks, maybe listening in, maybe not.

'She's a slut ...' The voice was rapid and the breathing quick.

'Oh now that's a hard word ... That's a bitter word.'

'Look, Dave, a large proportion of our population are a hundred times worse off than her . . . There's people in wheelchairs . . . There's men out of work . . . There's battered wives . . . Senior citizens who don't see a soul from one Sunday to the next and we're supposed to cry for this little schemer – well don't cry for her, Argentina.'

'Eileen, I'll have to leave you there because Seamus is on the line – Seamus.'

'Dave, I think the poor kid is a human football. Men in grey suits deciding what should happen to her.'

'Well who should decide?'

'Not them, Dave . . . They never gave a woman a good time of it.'

'What would you be calling a good time of it?'

'Oh you know . . . You know . . . Take her up to Monty . . . Think what someone might slip into her stocking.'

'Seamus, you're a bard. I can see that. But we can't have you corrupting our maidens. And now to our listeners who have just tuned in, this morning's theme is the little girl, the wee Magdalene, whom many say should be free to leave the country for whatever purpose . . . Are we wrong to keep her or are we right . . . Magdalene versus the nation.'

In the interim there are advertisements for coffee, insurance and foreign holidays, then once again he returns to welcome his callers – 'Good morning, Ashley, and thank you for giving us the benefit of your time and your cogent reasoning.'

'Dave, thank you . . . I nearly came to blows in the pub last night . . . Everyone on about it . . . Everyone spouting . . . Leave her alone, I says . . . Let her go to England if she wants . . . We'll be judged in the history books as a nation of Neanderthals . . . Let the girl go.'

'The law is the law, Ashley, and we have to abide by it.'

'Shag the law.'

'Oh now now. We can't have that sort of language . . . Kate, I'll come to you . . . Give us your wisdom on this.'

'I'm disgusted . . . All you people with liberal tendencies is what's destroying the country . . . It gives me the gick.'

'You're not a fan of hers, I see.'

'I'd send her to the laundry that she's named after . . . I'd make her scrub.'

'Thank you, Kate, thank you for your words ... Of course you're all one hundred and ten per cent right, and now we go over to the West to hear what Josephine has to say ... Are you there, Josephine?'

'I'm here, Dave, and I'm crying, I'm crying for the little mite, this little girl, and I'm crying for the little soul inside her and I'm smiling as well because you see the little life is what has saved the rapist, is what has saved the child herself.'

'Could you clarify that, Josephine?'

'As you probably know, Dave, rapists long to be found out; they long for someone or something to put a stop to their shameful deeds and that's what happened ... God made the little girl conceive a child and this unborn child is the hand of the Saviour leading them to the bed of the crime.'

'I'm not sure about that, Josephine ... As far as I know, nobody knows who the father of the child is.'

'They will.'

'If you say so ... You're all one hundred and ten per cent right, and now it's time for a little song, a little early morning tendresse, the haunting voice of Garth Brooks – "She's Every Woman".'

It was just as it resumed and a woman's voice was becoming heated that Veronica wakened, sat up, pulled at her and said, 'Why are you listening ... Why are you listening to this?'

'I don't know how to turn it off ... You told me not to touch the machines.'

'Why didn't you waken me?'

'I want to go home,' she said, the hot tears filling her eyes.

'What are you talking about?'

'I want to see my father.' She did not know why she said that, but as soon as she had blurted it out she knew that she meant it. She was lonelier with these people than she had ever been and afraid in a different way. She thought that if she threw herself at her father's mercy he must now find it within himself to help her, to show some of the pity that he had shown with the mare, the night the foal bustled inside her.

'I know you ... And your tricks,' Veronica said and began to pull her hair, but this time vehemently, as a child might pull the glue from a doll's head to take not only the hair but the scalp beneath it.

'You're staying right here ... We have your father's authority ...
I am your mother now ... I am your surrogate mother,' Veronica
said, and from a drawer hauled out the letter which had given her
that licence, that owning.

She was afraid then of everything about Veronica, the high-
pitched voice, the eyes that could mind-read, even afraid of the big
black pleated skirt that took up one whole side of the armchair,
armour, waiting for the powerful body to step into. Afraid.

THE TRUTH

James cannot even raise the blinds in his bedroom. Permanent dusk, clutter – his dinner plate, cups, empty cigarette packets and the shadows of the branches outside swaying back and forth, breaking in on his cruel predicament. Strange voices hollering up, a motor car come and gone.

Noni, his only contact with the outside world, giving him bull, relating each and every variation of the drama, what neighbours are saying, men are vowing to go out with shotguns and track down whoever wronged her, others calling her every dirty name under the sun.

'I'd be lost without you,' he says each time as she arrives with his dinner or his tea, a woman whom he cannot abide, a woman who would go down into anyone's stomach for news.

When she is alone she calls out her own name but when escorted she shouts, 'Visitors ... Vissies.'

'Who is it now?' he says, sitting up, disgruntled, going through the twice daily pantomime of cursing and asking her to pass him the calendar so that he can count how many more days he will be such a burden.

'Don't say I'm not doing my best for you,' she says, scolding.

'Who is it now?'

'Two very nice gentlemen, who have come to listen to your story.'

'What are you talking about?'

'Journalists. They want to defend Mary and help find the rapist.'

'Rapists.'

'Now that's not a nice thing to say,' Noni says and then the Angelus bell strikes, giving him a moment's respite, a desperate and fitful stab at thinking, his life caught and circumscribed by this woman, and now worse: the story has leaked and by whom and to whom and how much.

'How did they get to know of it ... I thought it was all *in camera*?' he says aloud, making an elaborate, though not devout, sign of the cross on his lips and down his front.

'Someone leaked it ... A clerk in the court leaked it, after the private hearing.'

'Oh, I'm not surprised ... A nation of informers ... Always were, Robert Emmett met his doom that way,' he says, his mind now shuttling as to what he should do.

'Where are they?' he asks abruptly.

'They're in the sitting room.'

'Jesus ... Poking around.'

'They're very nice men ... Very well dressed ... I couldn't leave them outside.'

'What can I tell them ... I can't add or subtract anything to the sorry tale that is.'

'You can defend your good name.'

'Against whom ... Against what?'

'You are a pillar of the community ... You want that known. Printed.'

'These fellows are not after pillars of the community ... They're after dirt.'

'They're sorry for you ... They think how you must have suffered.'

She's leaning over him now and he has the distinct and unnerving feeling of being smothered.

'My hands are tied,' he says, a filigree of ash about to drop on the quilt, except that she nabs it with a scrap of newspaper, which she holds like a scoop.

'You have a big opportunity to help yourself and help Mary,' she says, adding the name as an afterthought because she would like to see the girl flogged.

'No one can help the creature now.'

'Since it leaked, all sorts of busybodies are muscling in on her case ... The Fors and Againsts ... Smart Alecs who want to challenge the courts, overturn the ruling and get her out again ... Can you imagine ... Their minds are sewers.'

'They have no right over her ... She's my daughter ... Let her come home here and I'll mind her ...' and in the emptying husk of his being he thinks that if he can be cunning, that if he plays it right, he can send an open appeal through them, saying he wants his daughter back, he wants her to come home, all the while restive and fidgety, twisting and turning, passing through every mutation of a cornered man.

'I can feel your pain ... Tell it to them ... Touch their hearts.'

'I'll tell them that there's no need for her to be in Dublin ... With strangers ... I don't know why I gave my permission ... You all pulled it out of me. You came here like troops, you and Father Gerard, and that hysterical one with her leaflets.'

'Mary had to be in Dublin for the doctors and the psychiatrists ... She had to be within the jurisdiction of the court,' Noni says, getting stroppy now.

'I'm not going to be bullied ... I have to put my thinking cap on ... I want to prepare my thoughts.'

'Oh, they have to see you today ... It has to be now.'

'Why does it have to be now?'

'They've been around for two days and they've been talking to people ... They have a story.'

'What story?'

'They've been to the guards ... They've talked to Father Gerard ... They saw Betty ... They photographed her house.'

'That bitch.'

'You're right ... She told them something awful ... I don't even know if I can repeat it.'

'Repeat it. You ignoramus.' Each word, each inflection bringing him closer to the abyss.

'The reason why she took her to England was because Mary said it would be a freak ... It wouldn't be a right baby at all.'

'What freak?' he said, foaming now, gesticulating, pointing to have his jacket and his hairbrush handed to him, protesting before God that there would be no freaks in his family, in his bloodline, and those who spoke such calumnies would swing for it.

✠

ALLELUIA

Alleluia, alleluia, I will not make you orphans
  Says the Lord...
  I will come back to you and your hearts will be full of joy...
Alleluia.

Mary merely mouthed the words, answering the given responses, kneeling and standing when others knelt and stood, all the time her eyes darting towards the doors at the opposite end and the aisles which led to them, trying to determine which would be the fastest route. Although mass was being celebrated the atmosphere was casual, almost irreverent, people wandering about, lighting candles, an obstreperous beggar leaning into pews demanding money. It was a sung mass and Veronica elbowed her to join in, pointing to the page number in the cloth-bound hymn book.

The church was radiantly lit, floating spheres of gold and white gold around the altar, rays of it seeping into and emphasising the gold leaf in the stout polished pillars of marble. The tabernacle door was crusted with ornamented eaves comprised of gold needles, like pine needles, but effulgent, trajectories of colour leaping like sunbeams to darken the wine in the cruet and give a blush to the adjoining cruet of water. By comparison the side aisle was gloomy, a rose window spilling out purple and indigo onto hats, caps and bald bowed heads of ageing penitents.

Women carrying hessian bags with wooden handles took the first collection. Mary had no money to give. Veronica did not allow her money in case she ran away. Since the phone-in programme on the radio, they took turns watching her, so that she was not alone, not for a second. The collection money was dropped quietly and covertly into the bags which the two women then carried to the altar steps, bowing down as they handed them to a second priest.

It was an unusual sermon. A young man told of the works he and others did for the poor. He stretched his arms in all directions to demonstrate how palpably close the poor were, in their dingy houses and their dingy rooms to which he repaired every evening to talk to old people, lonely people, mothers with young children and battered wives. He was asking the faithful to give generously and for this collection Veronica did give her a coin. It was cold from Veronica's pocket. The man went on to tell them of a holiday place which his organisation had bought, a little villa by the sea where some of these poor wretched people might be able to go for a day or two if everyone gave generously.

The Scripture was then read by the priest in a very impassioned voice − 'I am the alpha and the omega, the first and the last, the beginning and the end, happy are those who will have washed their robes clean so that they will have the right to feed on the tree of life and come through the gates into my city.'

She was both hearing and not hearing, and as the time approached she began to tremble, believing that at the very moment she would falter, her legs would simply refuse to bring her out.

Luck was on her side. Had Veronica been one of the first to go to the rails for communion, Mary would have had to follow, whereas what happened was that a great surge of people rose, jostled, storming to get there first, pushing each other, elbowing each other, like people at a mart. So many overcoats, so many hats, some with plumes, some with daft woodland feathers, brushing together. She rose when Veronica did and followed and then allowed a few people to come between them, pausing, turning, as if she had forgotten something, or grown faint, and then gripping the side of the pew and moving backwards, backwards, passing through the open doorway flanked by men who seemed not to be there as worshippers at all but as onlookers.

Outside, she almost tripped over a beggar woman who was on the steps holding a plastic container, her eyes, her jaw, her lips and all of her moving in a strange and twisting distortedness, her only way of asking for money, because she was without speech.

'I'll come back another time and see you,' Mary said, tearing through the gateway and down the passage with sheet after sheet of plate glass, clocks, watches, more clocks and in the main street, songs and instruments clashing, and a man with goggles soldering an image onto a tin plate and her feet galloping, galloping. She ran — a running that seemed effortless, independent of legs, of lungs, something of an infallibility in it, since she was running for her life; buses and statues and people flying by, shouting to herself, out loud, 'I am free ... I am free.' At other times, she repeated the man's telephone number, forgetting that she had written it down, that she had hidden it on her person, the morning of the phone-in.

✠

INTRUDERS

They are having tea and biscuits, in Mr Hennessy's sitting room, biscuits which Mr Hennessy, donning his green cloak, dashed to the corner shop to purchase. The room is icy but beautifully furnished, lacquered walls, carnival-lustred, the fat crimson plaits of red weave like truncheons resting on the soft folds of curtain. One flap of the long table is covered with glasses and gold-rimmed goblets, and a tureen filled with china and porcelain bears the tag numbers from an auction.

'We've had a wonderful response ... People sending you letters and cards and money ... One wanting to send roses ... You are a popular lady.'

He talks very rapidly, not waiting for her to reply, and mostly she looks at things, stares, to hide her discomfort, at cups, paintings, a cartoon of Mr Hennessy being pelted with arrows and an exercise bicycle which looks inappropriate in the rarefied room.

They are waiting for Cathal, a solicitor, who as Mr Hennessy said would be the man to champion her cause, citing cases, notorious cases which Cathal and L'Estrange, the barrister, had taken on, wizards at their job and good men with it, good men.

At first the clamour seemed to be that of a crowd going by, revellers from a hurling match, their heckles rending the damp evening air and drifting up to the secluded room. Then the doorbell and knocker are summarily pounded and Mr Hennessy jumps and says, 'I think we've got guests, Mary.'

As he stands in the doorway with a shawl over his shoulders which he grabbed from a sofa, he is confronted with a mob telling him to hand her over, to cut out the fancy talk and to bring her out.

'You are a noisy lot,' he says, walking back and forth, rubbing his hands, studying the faces, some of which he has encountered before, craning to read the slogans on their banners, and all the while having to hitch up the shawl which keeps slipping off. The placards draped with rosaries carry pictures, mostly of the Virgin with 'Save the Baby', except for one with the simulation of running blood and which reads 'Thy Sister's Blood?'

'Deviant,' one shouts.

'We've had that little semantic tangle ... you and I, sir,' he says, talking directly to Manus, the heavyweight, who is standing astride his motorcycle, wearing only a waistcoat, a grey mobile phone on his shoulder, like a snake.

'We'll have your head on a dish, Hennessy,' another of them says.

'Oh, à la Herodias ... You do know your classics.'

'Cut out that ascendancy shit.'

'I'm afraid you people have no manners and I will have to ask you to disperse and put a note through my letterbox ... It is after all Sunday, the Sabbath day.'

'Henry the Eighth ...' a woman screams. 'Henry the Eighth seized St Patrick's cathedral and now they are begging Catholics to take it back, because it is rotten.'

'How you do deviate,' Mr Hennessy says tartly.

'Arse-licker.'

'Murderer of the innocents.'

'For the record, I am a pacifist.'

'Oh, like the little man in the loin cloth.'

'Are you referring to Gandhi?'

'Talk cuts no ice with us, Patsy.'

'I can see that ... I can see that some of you could do with a little higher education.'

His levity galls them, his high squeals of laughter at their ghastly insults – 'Toyboy' and 'Arse-licking bandit'. He imitates their accents, their wording – 'Fy is dat', he says, to madden them.

There are about twenty in all, men and women, mostly young except for one daft little woman in a grey beret who capers about, talking, chirping like a clockwork bird. Suddenly she effects a paroxysm – 'Thrice was I beaten with rods, once was I stoned,' then sticks her tongue out at him.

'I am glad you know your Bible,' he says.

'We don't give a shite about the Bible,' Manus says, coming forward with the phone and telling him to speak to the media, to tell the media why he is holding a ward of court illegally, what he is having done to her in there.

'I have my own phone ... Thank you very much,' Mr Hennessy says while wishing that the poor beleaguered girl inside hearing the pandemonium will have the good sense to ring the police.

'I've got the newsroom on the phone here ... They'd like a word with you,' Manus says, thrusting a phone at him, insisting he speak.

'Do not come near me with that filthy thing ... Disinfect it,' Mr Hennessy says, taking a few steps back into the hallway to forestall Roisin who is pressing forward.

'You better give her over ... Because you are breaking the law,' she says.

'So are you, my dear ... Trespassing on my property.'

'We can have the police here ... They'll bring her out.'

'As far as I know you are not very fond of the police ... You and the police have your little run-ins ... I've seen you down in O'Connell Street, with your brochures and pictures, haranguing people.'

'Do you mean this?' she says, and brandishes before him the postcard of the battered foetus.

'Oh, charming ... It must be yours ...' he says and wonders if he would like her to fetch a 'bottie' while to their amazement and consternation, he side-steps her and retreats into his own hall – slamming the door, putting the chain on it, as outside they start to batter it in furious outraged disbelief.

He passes without even glancing at Mary, opens a set of folding doors where there is a makeshift kitchen and in the small copper sink immerses his face again and again, repeating to himself some of their more outrageous slanders.

While they waited for the police to come, he busied himself, shifted some of the china, then began to prop up the lilies, some of which had drooped, in the big jug, and were likely to topple. Soon his white, pleated shirt was smeared with stains, senna-coloured, from the curled spidery stamens.

'Damn, damn,' he kept saying.

'It'll wash out,' Mary said, rising to get a towel.

'Oh, I'm not doing all this for just you,' he said sharply and she felt it like a blow of a cudgel, cowered, then retreated to the corner of the room.

He relented quite soon and fetching a towel to rub at the stains, speaking to her, but without looking at her – 'I'm glad it's to me you came ... Some of the others might not have been up to it, but I am ... I love a good fight.'

✠

CATHAL

'Am I in the black books?' Cathal said, standing in the doorway, tall, bearded, his hands very white, wearing a houndstooth cap which seemed a remnant from his more youthful days. He had been out on the mountains, he confessed, driving an old banger at a rally, and as luck would have it, it broke down and he had to walk miles to a youth hostel. Vale of Avoca.

Mr Hennessy escorted them both to a little parlour, all the while regaling Cathal with the story of the hecklers, their tattoos, their nose-rings, their freaking when he imitated one gurrier's 'Fy is dat'.

'So how are you, Mary?' Cathal said. They were alone, side by side, sitting on dainty chairs by a table with inlays of ivory and tortoiseshell. She liked him already, liked his quiet, and his reserve.

'Not so bad.'

'We'll do our best for you, L'Estrange and myself ... He's the genius and I am the plodder ... We'll do our best.'

'I haven't any money.' She blurted it out.

'Don't worry ... Money can always be found ... What I really need is for you to tell me everything, to help me make a case ... So we'll start with ... with ... How do you feel?'

'Afraid.'

'What are you most afraid of?'

'Everything ... The women I was with made me swear that I wouldn't harm it ... That I wouldn't kill it ... They prayed over me ...'

'You won't have to go back to them.'

'Could I go to you?' she said.

'I wish you could ... But you see, I will be acting for you ... So we have to keep things separate,' he said, and then added that it did not mean that he was not her friend, because he was, and would be.

'I know you are.'

'And will you be my friend, and tell me everything?'

'I'll tell you as much as I can.'

'We have to make a case ... We have to build it brick by brick ... L'Estrange can't go into a court wringing his handkerchief ... There'll be a man opposite him and he'll be shooting from the hip ... We have to do the same.'

'What'll happen if we lose?'

'We'll go to Europe.'

'It'll be too late.'

'I know ... That's why we have to move fast ... We need your daddy on board ... We need him.'

'No.'

'I can't even go into court without his permission.'

'You have my permission.'

'You're not old enough.'

'He won't give it.'

'Why not?'

'The disgrace.'

'Do you feel disgraced?'

'I do.'

'But think, you're not the only girl to have a baby out of wedlock, things are changed, parents stand by their children's child ... They even rear it...'

'This is not the same.'

'Why not, Mary?'

'My father would sooner that it was dead.'

'And you?'

'I'd sooner we were all dead.'

'I know it's a black hole ... I know you see no way out, but there is.'

'There isn't.'

'Look, we're a team, and together we'll talk to your daddy, we'll ring him up and tell him that we want to see him.'

'Will you talk to him?'

'I will ... But I think you would melt his heart more.'

In the hall she dials the number, already cowering, not even sure if she has dialled correctly. As she hears the first ringing she imagines it reaching him and pulls the phone away from her ear to signal to Cathal to get ready to speak. She imagines the sound starting up in the breakfast room, then coming out into the hall and disturbing him where he is sitting, one arm on the stove, his saying to himself, 'It's that blasted telephone again.' After several rings she believes that she has dialled the wrong number and has to write it down and look at it to make sure.

'You see, I never rang it much,' she says, awkwardly, all of her trembling.

'You're OK ... You're OK.' He can sense the terror in her and has to stop himself from putting an arm around her as a protection.

'Take a deep breath and we'll try again.'

Round the house the wind is stalking, a keening lamenting sound to it, bending the weak stretches of rotted privet and dislodging the loose ornamental ball on the yellow pier. Shep is lurking by the back door, while his master, whom he has not seen in days, is above in bed, with the curtains drawn. Hearing the telephone, James bridles, and believing it to be that yokel of a journalist, he shouts to it, 'Leave me alone ... Leave me alone I said ...' As it goes on ringing, he thinks that it might be Noni, jubilant at having brought journalists to his bedside, or else that mope of a photographer returning to take another mug shot for his portfolio. Every other word his portfolio and the lad with a pencil and notebook writing down the names of the various saints in the holy pictures.

'Holy Jesus,' he says, pushing the stone hot-water bottle to one side, getting out of bed and with the two sticks making his way along the flat of the linoleum and then levering himself down each step of narrow stairs. He has to do it slowly, watching his steps, going to the next and the next, then losing his temper outright as the fecking thing rings off just at the moment when he has reached the cold and slithery tiles of the hallway.

The cream had gone cold on his coffee, had formed into little oily rivulets, but Cathal drank from it all the same, thinking; thinking how he would get her to open up to him. Three times he had asked if she wanted to tell him who the father was and three times she had said no, and that anyhow it would make no difference.

'Is it that you love the person?' he asks, and instantly and maybe because he had used the word love she begins to cry. They were quiet tears and in the dusk of the hall, he could not see, he could only hear, the sounds deep and mournful, not like a child's tears at all, not fretful, not babbling, and he knew then that she was telling him that which he had just got the scent of, the onrushing scent of, and that her tears were her way of telling him, her only way. Neither moved and he allowed her to cry and cry, her whole body yielding to it, overflowing, a full and awful consummation, and he thought to himself that there is really no such thing as youth, there is only luck, and the enormity of something which can happen, whence a person, any person, is brought deeper and more profoundly into sorrow, and once they have gone there, they can't come back, they have to live in it, live in that dark, and find some glimmer in it.

'Can I get you anything?' he said when she became quiet.

'I'm all right now ... I had a cold.'

'What do you think we should do, Mary?'

'I think we should go down and see my father and ask him to help us.'

'I'm glad you said that ... I'm very glad you said that ... I'll talk to him first, to pave the way.'

✠

JOHNNIE

It was to another house then, the same but not the same. Some things would be different, the steps up to it or the person who let her in, or the cold or the tiles in the hallway or the light switches or the smell. Every house had its own smell. There were happy and unhappy smells and she knew it as she crossed the threshold. The driver, who was over-friendly, kept turning around every other minute to express his dismay at her ignorance of the city.

'Never been to the Liberties ... Or the Botanical Gardens ... Or Glasnevin ... Or the zoo ... Now you're not going to tell me that you haven't been to Malahide.'

'Is that where we're going?'

'I wish it was ... Still, we're going to a nice area ... Very nice area ... Big trees and bushes, well-to-do people.'

They drove down the main street, past different monuments, past a hotel with various flags flying above it, past another monument black as coal, a man's iron overcoat held out and his hand raised in an imposing salute.

'People from all over the world go to Malahide Castle ... In the summer. I bring droves of people there ... It's beautiful inside ... It was in the same family for seven hundred years, except when Cromwell had it ... Ever hear of him?'

'Yes.'

'A malign man ... He destroyed Catholic churches ... turned them into stables ... The family got it back again ... Not any more ... Finished ... No heirs ... No sons.' He stopped all of a sudden to lean out to shout something to another driver, a friend.

'What sort of food do you like?' he asked her as they drove along, and not getting any answer, he rushed in with his own favourites, his specialities.

'I like sloppy foods ... Stews and things like that ... giblets, now they're the real Ally Dally ... Around Christmas you can get the goose and the turkey giblets, the both ... One's pale and the other's dark ... They mix marvellous, and you know another lovely flavour ... Hen cod's roe ... Melts in your mouth ... Mind you, the secret is the lard ... You have to get good tangy lard.'

'Can you stop the car,' Mary said, her hand splayed across her mouth.

Around the sapling where she had bent to be sick was a single card which she reached down for and turned over to look at. It was an ace of hearts. Supposed to be good luck. There was no grass or foliage to cover her sick with, only a small rectangle of sapless clay where a kerb had been dug up ... She put her handkerchief over it.

'What has you sick?' he said, linking her back and putting her next to him in the front.

'Did someone upset you?'

'No.'

'I mean there's chastising and chastising but a person can go too far ... I went to a public debate the other night, me and Jimmy, the fellow we just passed that shouted out, and there was this professor spouting, saying never slap children, insisted it was all wrong, even if the children were bold, and this woman got up and said that she had twelve children and she often slapped them and how many had he, none, none. And that's why he was talking through his hat.'

Going up the flight of steps to the new house, he took her arm and told her that she was to be careful, not just at night, but in daylight, in broad daylight, on account of there being people with knives and with syringes, pushing drugs, grabbing purses, bringing the country into disrepute.

'Mind yourself,' he said, then pushed the beautifully polished bell, and from his pocket took a crumpled card, his last one.

'Maybe some Sunday the missus and I will take you to Malahide ... That's if she hasn't divorced me.'

She looked down at it and then looked up at him, gratefully.
'You're called Johnnie.'
'That's me ... I'm your man...'

MRS B

The woman who let her in was friendly, a big woman, still with her hat on, saying she had not time to take it off since morning, what with three teenage boys and a husband all in constant need of food. Food, food, food. She was Mrs Winnifred Fitzsimmons, but always known as Fitz.

As they went down the hallway and into the kitchen, a young boy who was drinking a mug of coffee got up and went out, muttering and blushing. The blackheads on his chin looked sore, as if he had been scratching them.

'Don't blast us out with too much music, Brendan,' his mother called and shoved the boiling kettle back on the hot plate. 'Tea or coffee?'

'Either,' Mary said.

'We're all very angry at what's happened to you ... Very angry and very sad,' she says and turns then, to introduce Mary to Mrs B, who has come in with a basket of clothing to be ironed.

'This is Mrs B ... and she is our guardian angel.'

'Hello,' Mary says.

'Will we tell her what we sometimes see in the garden?'

'You can tell her,' Mrs B says.

'We have a flasher ... Quite harmless ... All he wants is attention ... A bit of attention.'

While she is talking and getting down the cups she has twice to answer the phone, once from someone outside to come for an appointment and the second time from a member of her own family announcing that he has a fever and demanding food.

'You feed a cold and you starve a fever,' Mrs B said. 'Tell that to my big hungry son,' their mother said. Mary wondered if these sons knew and what she would say to them and if they would all eat together or if she would have a tray in her room.

'Yes, we are all very sad and very angry,' she said again, putting particular blame on the media, the news hounds who had no respect for privacy.

'How long will I be here?' Mary asks.

'Well I've offered to keep you for the whole time ... But it's not up to me, it's up to the State ... It's up to the psychologists ... No one's life is their own any more.' Hearing it, her eyes go blurry again, and so as not to waver, she stares at a picture on the wall with the paint spread on very thick, the crude tracing of a spatula, a seascape, the sand rough as if animals are scraping a way through it.

'What sort of food do you like, Mary?' Mrs Fitz is asking.

'I ... I don't mind.'

'I'll tell you what, I'll get my husband to do one of his world-renowned curries and after it, we'll show you slides of our holidays ... Would you like that?'

'That would be lovely.'

'Wait till you see us ... Two old fogies like us ... On sleighs ... Riding down the mountains at night, holding lighted torches in our hands ... Singing and telling each other that we love each other ... And we do ... We do.' And crossing once again to the ringing phone she whispers to Mrs B to ask their visitor if she has any little bit of washing, for she must have, from all that toing and froing.

'You'll have a cup of tea ... You will ... That's grand ... Ah, you're very good ... I used to do the five days and now I do two ... Nicest woman in the world ...' Mrs B says, sitting now that they are alone, Mr and Mrs having gone to play badminton. 'When I had the lump removed Mrs Fitz came every day to the hospital ... Four in our family died ... I thought I'd go before my sister ... I didn't ... No good of a doctor prescribed tablets on the phone for her, didn't even see her ... If he'd examined her we could have raised the alarm ... She's gone now, and my lump is gone. I'll never forget the nurse saying, "You may come back without a breast, Mrs B ..." I didn't, I'm very lucky ... They had to cut the lymph glands though. Do

you see that floor ... It'll be shining in an hour ... You can skate on
it ... Don't look sad ... Don't you let people upset you ... You want
butter, you don't ... That's grand. All the years I'm here and I've
never had a cross word ... They are like my own family ... Yes,
cancer is in the genes they say ... My poor mother knew she had it
... Used to talk about the unknown ... Her fear of the unknown ...
Prayer is the only thing ... Do you pray, you do ... Grand. If you
say a Hail Mary from the bottom of your heart you'll get what you
want ... It has to be from your heart not just your lips ... You're
very quiet altogether ... When you stand beside somebody dying
it does something to you, you can tell, the eyes ... the rattle ... then
the beautiful thing is, the smile, once they are gone ... Seraphic or
whatever it's called ... The Good Shepherd bringing them straight
to heaven ... No more fear of the unknown ... You're a very nice
girl ... Your mother and father raised you well ... You're a credit
to them ... I'll be in here two mornings a week and you can come
out to my house if you like some Sunday ... It's in a grove but I'm
on a height ... You can see the mountains ... When I come on
Friday I'm going to bring a leaflet ... It's a woman who's taken on
the sufferings of Christ ... Her hands and her feet bleed ... I think
it's the stigma it's called ... She'll help you ... I'll pray to her for
you ... From the heart ... Almighty God we need to pray for the
world we live in ... Sin city ... I saw a programme with a man in a
g-string hoovering and a woman, not a young woman, sitting on
an armchair looking at him ... It showed the back of him ... It
affects children seeing that sort of thing ... I turned it off ... You'll
have another cup of tea ... You will ... You won't ... That's grand
... I'll tell you what I'll do, I'll bring you with me to the Halloween
party ... You can cut up the barm-brack ... I won third prize last
year ... I went as a flower girl ... Imagine it ... I had this big hat
with heather and what do you call it and I had to walk up and down
with my basket like I was selling flowers to people in motor cars
going by ... I came third ... I got this beautiful little beauty kit ...
Lovely creams and things ... You can dress up too ... What is it,
what's wrong, love ... Oh, my poor love, I think I know, I'm not
supposed to know, but I think I do.'

✠

LONESOME FATHER

I t was Mr Fitz who read it while they were having breakfast. They had breakfast every morning in their four-poster bed and Mrs Fitz always teased him about the rag of a newspaper he ordered.

'We're in trouble,' he said.

'Who's in trouble?'

'Our little friend ... They'll be on to her next.'

'You mean Mary?'

'I'll read it to you ...

The lonesome father of a young girl whom the world has christened Magdalene cried out last night for help to find the callous father of her child.

'Someone took total advantage of her,' her father said. 'Anyone who would do that is a hard case and will have to be punished.'

The grief-stricken man spoke for the first time since his daughter's midnight dash to England and spoke not only of his disgust at the brutal advantage taken of her but of other people, so-called Samaritans who were prepared to help her to commit a heinous crime, adding tragedy and criminality to what is already a tragic situation.

'They have no decency, these people,' he said. 'If they had any decency they would have brought the poor distraught child back to me, not whisked her to a death camp in England.' The Gardai are doing a house-to-house search, interviewing friends and school-friends to see if any light can be shed on who is the father since Magdalene herself is unwilling to speak, a matter which according to social workers and psychologists is quite common in a traumatised person and attests to the sweetness and fidelity of her nature. The help and co-operation of the public is vital.

'There must be someone who knows,' the angry father said from his bed where he has been invalided with a broken leg and a broken arm for the best part of a week.

'Just give me a Black and Decker . . . And I'll saw this bloody plaster off myself and go and find him,' the tearful man said. Neighbours are rallying at all hours, women arriving with flasks of tea, evident anxiety in their expressions and understandable fear for their own daughters, shock is palpable as this dark and terrible story unfolds and has put the hurt into the land itself, the hurt of a young girl who was too ashamed and too bewildered to ask for help and who took, as one neighbour put it, 'the blindest way out,' but as she went on to say, 'Jesus loved her enough to bring her back to us.'

More than one family in this tightly-knit community which boasts farm land and dense forestation have had the similar tragedy of an unwanted pregnancy but always with support and solidarity behind them so that a child born out of wedlock was not considered a foundling as it might have been in the dark days of even a decade ago. Mass and rosaries are being offered daily, both giving thanks to God for the rescue of the young girl from the fate of the scalpel and the hope, the very zealous hope, that the culprit will be found and any further catastrophes averted. A man has already been questioned but was allowed to go free and the search is now concentrated on a huge area of forestry, where it is hoped clues might be found, especially a blue gemstone diary in which the young girl confided her secrets, according to her best friend, Tara.

Her father, now on tranquillisers, says there is only one small ray of light in all of this which is that she is with friends, she is in a warm and friendly environment, people comforting her. The poor girl, unable to think straight, uttered worrying threats on the air journey home from England and had to be comforted by a stewardess and helped off the plane to a waiting police car, whence she was brought to hospital suffering from shock and acute nausea. Not knowing who or where to turn, she expressed the wish that she would rather be dead. Cards and well-wishers have been flowing into the family home, the girl's whereabouts being a secret, and what better way to conclude them than with this letter from a priest, which her father invited me to look at.

Dear little Magdalene, I call you that because I think it is a name that you would not shy away from. Of her Jesus had said, 'He who is without sin among you, let him be the first to cast a stone.' It's a strange thing to tell you but I know you even though I know nothing whatsoever about you. I don't know if you have grey eyes or brown eyes, maybe you have dimples, maybe you have long hair, maybe, maybe. I can just imagine what you are going through, the deep ache, the awful sense of failure, being used as a football by all and sundry and thinking that men in gowns with wigs are deciding your fate. You have reason to be angry and you have reason to be cross with God and man. Believe me, I know what you're going through. You need love. You need a platform to express your anger. You need someone to listen to you. You need to be able to sit down and tell the world what the abuse was like. You need to go back over those sleepless nights and get it all out. I can just picture you by a fire, talking and talking, a little girl with dimples, the down of youth on your arms and on your legs, aged before you had even blossomed, and now everyone is bossing you and you are not being allowed to decide for yourself. Let me tell you something. I feel that you are a great person, I feel that what you have suffered has made you a great person. Give birth. Do not run away now. Do not be governed by the court of law or all the people telling you this that and the other. Go through with it and see how strong you will be and how proud. I pray for you and your little friend. Make no mistake, it is your little friend. Once you believe that you will be all right. I love you with all my heart.

'I am not looking for pity for either my daughter or myself . . . I am looking for justice,' her father said, the week-old stubble on his chin as grey and as stark as the tears which, despite his efforts, well up in his sad grey eyes. The Gardai are confident that they will find the man but as one senior Gardai put it, 'That lovely home is broken forever and so is our beautiful, wholesome happy parish.'

Their wholesome parish will never be the same again.

'Something fishy,' Mrs Fitz says.
'I'll say.'

'We better ring Cathal.'

'So that's why she won't talk … That's why. She's like a mute,' Fitz says as he reaches across for the telephone.

DIRTY OLD TOWN

'Your daddy will come round,' Cathal is saying. Hearing it, it is as if it has already happened. They're driving through sun and rain, hidden elongations of sun in the slants of rain and bronzed highlights on his soft black beard. Your daddy will come round. It is as if it has already happened. He plays a song to keep them company, the same song over and over again.

> *'I found my love by the gasworks crying*
> *Dreamed a dream by the old canal,*
> *Kissed my girl by the factory wall*
> *Dirty old town – dirty old town.'*

The mountains in the distance are soft and hazy, inverted moulds of varying purple, and the little towns they pass through all have their different emblems of pride – tubs of flowers, bunting, the winning flag from a hurling match played months before. Out of the town the fields with silage bags, crows satiny black, congregating and dispersing old, squat trees with waistcoats and jerkins of ivy around them. The big wide rivers a greeny brown and frothed in parts as if treacle has been stirred into them. Your daddy will come round.

They do not know it but her daddy is already up. Soon as Noni showed him the rag of a newspaper and the insinuations in it, he told her to order a car and get him to hospital because that plaster was coming off, he was not going to be Joe cripple any more.

'It might not be set,' Noni told him.

'I don't care if it's a banana,' he told her and hit out with a crutch, later having to pacify her with garments which belonged to his dead wife.

'Heard a siren from the dock
Saw a train set the night on fire
Smelled the spring in the smoky wood
Dirty old town – dirty old town.'

'Do you sing, Mary?' Cathal asks.

'Not really.'

'What are your hobbies?'

'Oh ... Cooking,' she said it just for something to say.

'When you get back to school, you should learn languages,' he says. The 'when you get back to school' was the same as 'your daddy will come round'. He was telling her the pickle he got into on his honeymoon, in Moscow, years before: how his wife lost her wedding ring during dinner and his having to bribe head waiters and doormen to go down with him to the heaps of rubbish, their searching for half the night and his having to fork out dollars each time one of them flagged and lay down to sleep.

'Did you find it?'

'Oh yuh.' A strange cadence in his voice.

As soon as she saw the chapel spire, the blue-grey shaft solitary in the sky, she floundered, became agitated, thought she was going to be sick, asked him to slow down and later caused him to pass their own gateway without warning. The gates were open and had stones to them.

'I can't go in ... I can't go in.'

'We've come all this way, Mary.' It was the first show of irritation in him and all she could do was reach out as if to touch his coat sleeve, yet not touch it and say flatly, 'He won't let me go ... If I go in there ... He won't let me go.'

Shep sniffed her out at once, came bounding and leaping up outside the car window, his tongue a maelstrom of speech as if to make up for not having been there to greet her. 'Get down ... Get down,' she said, making cross faces, but his excitement was too much, his delight that she had come home. She should not have come. Everything was made worse by her coming back, everything seemed to be watching her, the trees and the dipping strands of ripped paling wire, that and a strange cat, a queer cat, with a queer look to it. Even the house looked shook and all along the field, like some wandering spirit a white mist travelled in shallows. Only the shrubs which her mother had put in were thriving. Devoid of flower or leaf they were nevertheless filled with colour, a purple colour like blood flowing through them. Nearly everything reminded her of blood. Her father's, her mother's, her ancestors', her own, and thinking how none were separate and yet none were kin. Cathal would come out with some good news. She would be able to tell it by his bashful smile. He would not say it at first on account of being shy, he would say something ordinary like 'We have to get our act together.' They were probably in the room where it had happened. The good room. Good. Bad. Just words. Shibboleths.

'Get down ... Go away.' She was not looking at Shep any more, she was looking away, pretending not to know he was there. She was looking at the two trees, the selfsame trees that she had often seen from the bedroom window, the chestnut to one side and the ash tree to the other. When she was young, one was her father and one was her mother and she used to have a little daydream that she would put her arms around each one and walk them together and loop a garland around them. Ten, twenty times a night she leapt out of bed to pray, in that long ago time, yet could not silence the sobbing, a sobbing within and without, human cries, animal cries, unearthly cries as if spirits clustered in every clod of earth, feeling and needing those cries, that expiation, as though from it all would be resolved into a bright, afflictionless paradise. Except that that did not happen.

Shep kept looking away, a bit crushed, the raggy limber ears no longer cocked; looked back, then looked away again, sighting something in the far corner of the field, maybe a bit of the moving mist that mimicked the leaps of a hare or a rabbit.

They sit in the cold room and Cathal bides his time, allowing the man to ramble on, the happy family they were, his beautiful wife, his clever daughter, shining at school, winning things at school, winning all before her.

'As you know, I want to try and help her,' Cathal is saying.

'I'm glad of that ... I only wish someone would help me.'

'I thought that article in the paper was pro you.'

'Pro me ... I should never have let the hooligans in.'

'Still, he treated you sympathetically.'

'And why shouldn't he?'

'Some of these reporters are sharks.'

'He had no right describing my bedchamber.'

'They always do that, for ambience.'

What Cathal is watching are the movements, the shifty movements, the rising to get an ashtray, then mislaying it, sinking into a chair, then sitting forward, alert, a man *in extremis*. 'How is my daughter?'

'She's as well as can be expected.'

'Where is she?'

'She's around,' Cathal says, watching the man's back now as he looks through the window fearful of invasion.

'Does she talk about me?'

'Well to be honest, she doesn't talk much ... She's quiet.'

'Always was ... Quiet ... Deep water ... Like her mother.'

'She did say one thing though,' Cathal says. 'No one could beat you singing "Danny Boy".'

'Is that why you drove all this way?' Again the mad swivelling in the eyes, the not wanting to be caught out.

'No, Mr MacNamara. I drove all this way because I want you, I need you, we need you; we will have to take her case to the Supreme Court and I simply don't have the right.'

The man has got up again and this time with his slippered foot is kicking an empty cigarette box which he has dispatched onto a mound of ashes.

'What the feck do you need me for ... You're the lawyer ... *Homo sapiens*.'

'You're her father.'

'I am.'

'Then you have to OK it.'

'Do you want every guard, every superintendent, every vigilante, every bishop and every priest on my doorstep.'

'If you love her you'll do it.'

'Of course I love her ... She means everything in the world to me ... Or did.'

'All I am asking is your signature on this piece of paper.'

'How do I know that she sent you?'

'I think you do know that she sent me,' Cathal says over-calmly. They sit in a listening silence, the still air like chain-mail around each one. Cathal thinks that it is a matter of minutes before it comes pouring out, the botched, infantile admission, except that he is wrong.

'What does she say she wants?' James asks huffily.

'She doesn't know ... She has even said that she wanted to be dead.'

'Who wouldn't want to be dead?'

'Not a lovely girl like Mary with her life before her.'

'She should have come home herself.'

'It was my idea that I come to you.'

'She should have faced me.'

'We don't have much time to waste.'

'Springing this on me, without warning; it is more than I can take ... it's more than ...' James says. He lights a match as if to search for the word, allows it to burn down and from it lights another, staring down into the sulphurous glare as if he might discover something in it, then he looks up, his fingers blackened, the expression on his face pitiful almost, almost asking to be challenged.

'Why don't I get out of your way and maybe ring you this evening,' Cathal says.

'Give her that,' James says, taking from the sideboard a wedding photograph of himself and his wife, uneasy in their good clothing. 'And that,' he adds, picking up a little jug.

'Anything you'd like me to say to her?'

'I'm a luckless man, always was ... Before I married ... After I married ... Never stood a chance ... After my wife died I asked them to send me somewhere ... An infirmary ... Anywhere ... But they wouldn't.'

'You wouldn't want me to tell her that.'

'Why wouldn't I?'

From the bay window James watches, watches the man shut the gate, then sights a second figure in the car, her, sees her look in his direction and look away, then crouch down, then the vehicle speeding recklessly in spite of Shep running in front of it to try and impede it. From him a last expiration of hope. She was out there and did not come in. Did. Not. Come. In. Of all the wrenchings of his life it is the worst. He closes his eyes to try and see her, to try and catch her, but she is running in that plaid coat, towards the sky, the skyline, and beyond it into infinity.

✠

MARY'S DIARY

Cathal is in Betty's sitting room by a french window, holding the diary which she has just given him. Before he turns the pages he already knows what he is going to find, he can tell by the chill in his spine. The cover is purple and blue and has on it the name of a gemstone. The entries are scattered and between some pages a flower on its withered stalk and on the centre page her mother's mortuary card, glued on.

The first entry is entitled – 'Man'. It was about an Ice Man which had been found, the Ice Man's clothing and the Ice Man's tools.

'The Ice Man was well prepared for the alpine chill. His basic garment was an unlined fur robe, made of patches of deer, chamois and ibex skins. His well-worn shoes were of leather and stuffed with grass for warmth.'

> *'I lost a World – the other day!*
> *Has Anybody found?*
> *You'll know it by the Row of Stars*
> *Around its forehead bound.'*

'I play with the bits of thread of my jumper. It isn't to change anything, nothing can be changed. I try to make it into o's and a's, to tell me my future. Except that I have none. It's seven o'clock on a bright summer's evening, the sun, the glorious sun showing up the dirt on all the window panes and my father gone to bed early, drugged himself with tablets because of his loneliness and trying, I think, trying I think, not to harm me but the harm is done.'

'He brought me to a hotel to make up for things. I wasn't hungry. The owner was snappy – "I have trifle, I have pavlovas, I have creamed rice pudding; what the hell do you want?" My father and he drank. There was a wild turkey splayed along a stained-glass window pane, the pink, pimply dead neck jutting from it and each bit of its speckled wing separated from the next bit. A doctor had shot it in Buffalo. The smell of the drink made me sick. I sat out in the hall on a carved chair. There were cups and saucers in a glass case, the saucers resting against a maroon velvet backing, the cups had magical flowers and magical forests on them. I could hear my father singing inside.'

'I was sent home from school because of being sick. My throat was all thorns. He nearly ate me. He came downstairs in his under-clothes. Why are you home. I'm sick. You're not sick. You're a mollycoddle. He said to go out and play. I half-played, skipped, but I wasn't up to it. I kept falling. There was a seat in the hedge that a workman made, a little armchair and I sat into it. I thought I'll cry because I have no mother, I'll have a big bout of crying and maybe after that something will happen. He called me in. He was in the kitchen drinking tea and he told me to go up to bed.'

'With the money for my birthday I got a plaid coat. The blood stains won't show. They will soak into the cocoa and henna and gold yellow patching. I have this feeling that it will happen when I am outdoors, on a road, going off somewhere. But it won't show. I will welcome that blood. I will drink it.'

'Jesus Christ ... When did you find this?' Cathal is asking Betty.

'After I came home ... 'Twas in her school bag ... I left a note for the priest ... I left it in the sacristy ... I more or less hinted ... You see after everything that happened I was too afraid.' Her voice apologetic at having to admit it.

'This country ... This fucking country is full of people who are too afraid – what are we afraid of ... The truth ... The stinking truth. Of ourselves.' And bending then to pick up a sprig that has slipped out, he says determinedly to it, 'I love this child and I am going to save her.'

'I prayed that someone would come and knock on my door.'

'You knew all along.'

'We all knew, all along ... But we were dumbfounded,' she said.

Looking at her unslept eyes, the tensed hands, in stark contrast with the portrait on the wall of a winsome and assured woman, he relents and says, 'I will have that cup of soup, after all.'

THE RACK

Did. Not. Come. In. Why had he not gone out there and dragged her in.

He could not have envisaged the next hour even if he had tried, him shouting from room to room, yet all alone, alone but hounded, hunted, driven into a corner, the very entrails of the matter about to spill out, voices, handcuffs, interrogation, disgrace. The rack. His one chance to escape and he had thrown it away. She would not have refused him, that much he knew, because of her nature. In the hands of others now. Being quizzed and requizzed. Betrayal. Sweet Jesus.

Brightness, appalling brightness imposing itself upon a room and upon him, alone and desperate. It is only a matter of time. He knows that. He sits forward on the chair, his fingers tapping things. Rat-tat-tat. Talking to himself.

'They will not break me.' He says it again and again. He does not know what he is saying. They are words. Just words. Triumphalist when said to himself. Empty, hollow, when practised on another. They ... will ... not ... break me. On the floor are the three cut-glass ashtrays heaped with butts and toads of damp ash. On and off he has cried. All his ruinous life coming to a head in him as he looks about a room that bore all the trademarks of a once breathless bride. Artificial tea-roses, points sharp as spears, plunged into a sudden efflorescence of sunlight. Dolls in hooped crinoline. Grinning ghosts.

He can hear the dog announcing a car coming up the drive. He does not even attempt to hide. They will not break me.

The guard shouts his name from the vestibule – 'Mr MacNamara
... Mr MacNamara.'

'Sir,' he calls back and rises with a bonhomie of a man going to
the races.

It is Murphy, Murph, a guard well known for his obstreper-
ousness, pleasantries in his voice, his jowls something else.

'We want to bring you over to the station for a while.'

'What is it now?'

'Oh, just routine ... There's been a bit of a development ... Your
daughter was around today ... We have to get our books up to date.'

✠

MURPH

'**S**omething rotten,' Murph said as he came out, smelling under his armpits, smelling his rage. What the feck was the world coming to.

'Do you think he did it?' Donal asks, his back to a wall, an expression of fear and shame on his young features.

'If he did it I'll have to be put in a corral,' Murph says and reaches for the carton of milk and slugs it. The pain in his gut is something awful, it's ripping him.

'Is your indigestion at you?'

'I thought we got that fecking thing fixed,' Murph says, pointing to a clump of newspaper which is stuffed into a hole in the window, where some raver had taken a shot at it.

'Billy came and he fixed it ... It fell out soon as he left ... The putty must have been rotten.'

'Why didn't you sweep the glass up?'

'We've no dustpan.'

'This is sure one swell day.'

'What did he say?' Donal asks. They can hear James calling, shouting, saying he wants to go home, that there are cows to be milked.

'Bull.'

'What kind of bull?'

'Hypnosis ... We can hypnotise him and the truth will come out.'

'He has a point there.'

'Shut up ... You don't know what you're talking about.'

'Sorry.'

'I'm sorry, Doe ... I'm just ... Well, any man would be ... Any father, any brother...'

'Oughtn't we ring the super, this is getting heavy.'

'We'll ring no super ... I'll get a statement out of him, like a dentist, tooth by tooth, Donal.'

They sit in their shirtsleeves, the newspaper rustling, their elbows on the table, a bag of toffees between them. Donal is fidgeting with rubber bands, slipping them on and off like rings. They are waiting for the moment, the moment when he will break, wanting it and at the same time repulsed by the spectacle of it, that moment when a human being grovels, cringing, asking for mercy, the abasement, not a pore of pride left.

'You were in there a good while.'

'I let him shoot his bolt ... Often when they talk, they contradict themselves ... They spill.'

'What did he say?'

'Folklore ... Fucking folklore ... As a kid he was sent off to college, educated by priests, and used to slip out to the races where he always backed winners ... Was so renowned for backing winners that even priests asked him to place bets for them ... Net result he got expelled ... Back to the old homestead ... Empty except for himself and a potboy ... Parents dead ... Gongs starting up in the night ... Shades of his ancestors.'

'Did you ask him straight out or did you couch it?'

'I had to first suffer the long rigmarole of romance ... How destiny struck ... A young prelate by the name of Tuohey ... A mountain man comes to him and says that he wants to learn to ride ... Unfortunately could not stay up on a horse ... Consequences, thrown several hundred yards ... Broken collar bone ... Ambulance ... A week later James, our good Samaritan, in an errand of sympathy braves the bog roads and the wild night and scales the mountain to enquire after your man ... An older woman lets him in ... A younger woman with earrings takes his coat ... Lovely fire ... Lamplight ... Mulled wine ... You wonder why I fumigate, Donal ... You wonder why I perspire ... Rage ... Rage at how these vermin try every trick in the pack.'

'He looked shook when he got here.'

'He'll look shooker when I'm finished with him ...'

'Did you get in close.'

'Oh further folklore came ... The young woman admitting to a longing for her own place ... Her own animals and her own fowl ... Independence ... In other words, marriage, and so in a very abbreviated space of time they are betrothed ... Wedding bells ... Then a veil is drawn.'

'What do you mean ... He clamped up?'

'I mean that no one has a fucking idea of anyone else's setup ... Even if they sleep in the same bed ... Were you happy I asked him ... Were you content ... Answer me that ... And I see the lip going and a rag of a handkerchief coming out so I think that we now have to ride roughshod ... No more Valentine cards.'

'So you hopped the ball.'

'Exactly ... I said to him you lived alone with your daughter. More verbal diarrhoea. How lonesome he is ... How lonesome life is ... How a man alone can go off his head ... How man's nature is to talk to someone ... A woman ... A kind and caring woman and by Jesus if he doesn't produce a bit of worn paper with a quotation ... "As matter desires form, so woman desires man." Aristotle.'

'I wonder where he got that.'

'I lean across to him ... eyeball to eyeball and I say "You lived with your daughter ... Right ... Right, he says ... Were you black-guarding her ... I might have shouted the odd time ... Did you ever hurt your daughter ..." Sudden change of tactics ... Flouting his rights ... He does not have to say anything ... He can walk out that door ... He can be referred ...'

'He knows his law.'

'Law my arse ... If he did it, I tell you, you'll have to put me in a coral.'

'But why wouldn't the girl talk ... Why wouldn't she tell her solicitor?'

'Shame. I've seen it before ... Often ... They feel dirtier if they tell it ... They feel they're to blame in some way.'

'Are they?'

'Look, Donal, I am not a clinical psychiatrist and I do not want to be ... More moonshine ... Motivation and transference and a lot of university bull ... If he did it I want to see him behind bars, bound up to his oxter ... I'd sooner a man that shot his child or cut a throat.'

'We've no proof,' Donal says, trying to calm him.

'We know the following – she's up the spout ... She ran away from home ... She did not have intercourse with the yodeller in Galway and she wrote this ... This: "I do oH's and aH's with the thread of my jumper ... The sun showing up the dirt on the windows and my father gone to bed early so as not to harm me ... But the harm is done."'

'Ssh ... He's trying to break the door ...'

'OK, Doe ... I'll teach you ... Let's go in there ... Let's target,' and he is filled now with wild rampaging energy, the pain in his gut forgotten, a beam on his face, enquiring if the little intermission has helped James, enabled him to refresh his brain cells.

'You can't keep me here against my will.'

'We can keep you up to twelve hours, buster ... If I were you I'd co-operate ... You see, the finger is pointing at you.'

'By who?'

'We have evidence – heaps of evidence. Fellatio, penetration, the works.'

'Is this a joke?'

'No, this is an interrogation.'

'You can't keep me here.'

'Your daughter went missing and you didn't report it, why not?'

'A neighbour did.'

'But not you – isn't that bizarre?'

'To tell you the truth I was hurt ... I thought she did it to punish me ... We had a bit of a row.'

'What was the row about?'

'Some family squabble.'

'It was about you feeling her up, wanting to have sex with her.'

'I want a solicitor.'

'What do you want a solicitor for ... You haven't been charged with anything ... That's unless you're ready to confess.'

'Confess ... Feck ... Who do you take me for ... Oscar Wilde?'

'Did you touch your daughter?'

'Touch my daughter!'

'Did you get her to touch you?'

'You're mental.'

'So are you.'

'There was a hooligan in Galway.'

'He's out of the picture ... He's clear ...'

'And I'm in the picture?'

'Correct.'

'I'm a widower ... I'm a father ... I'm a broken man.'

'Why are you changing your story?'

'I don't have to take this shite.'

'Co-operate and you'll be helping yourself ...'

'I didn't do it ... I know I didn't do it.'

'Why would you say "I know I didn't do it", are you hearing voices — You had sex with her, admit it?'

'You have sex on the brain.'

'Why did you hide from the social worker ... Why did you run away ...'

'I had business with a farmer ... We buy and sell horses.'

'After you had got her in the family way?'

'I'd want to be a maniac to do a thing like that.'

'You know what's sad ... You don't see reality ... Your number is up and you can't see it.'

'I might have kissed her ... The odd time ... A father does.' The eyes wide open now, the bluish whites aghast and empty of every dreg of hope, wishing that someone, most likely himself, would take a razor to them, leaving only the blind untelling sockets.

'Continue,' Murph says.

'I wish I hadn't,' James says, the voice faltery.

As Donal rises, the down on his face seems to sprout, a foolish yellow pollen against the sudden burning pink of his cheeks, and for a moment it seems as if he has suffered a seizure and is asking to excuse himself. But it is not that. The rubber bands on his knuckles which are now bunched seem like some boxer's device as he makes a dive at the man.

'You did it ... I know you did it ... I felt it just now.'

'Relax, Donal ... Relax.'

'I know he did it ... You're an animal,' and the socking of the fist in the confined space of the room comes like something theatrical, the jangling of the filing cabinet, the tall figure of the man drooping, then falling phantom-like, his face down, and Murph with a terrible and pre-emptive knowledge of what this means – shambles, cold, stark, retributive, fucking shambles.

'Go out,' he said to the young guard, his voice hoarse. 'Go outside and leave this job to me.'

MONA

'**O**h flying it ... Flying it,' Mona says. They are upstairs in Mary's bedroom, Mona chain-smoking and drinking hot whiskey, spitting the cloves onto a saucer. She glows with excitement, describing their all-night vigil outside the Dáil, their crowd and the other crowd swapping insults. Insults!

'We were waiting to see yer man ... PJ. Looking up at the lighted window ... We read next day that he was in Rome ... The gas it was ... One old harridan pokes her placard at me – she's a street-walker, I've seen her at the corner of Leeson Street – don't be daft I said but she wouldn't let up, kept asking a guard to arrest me. Ever have your clitty kissed, it's gorgeous I says to her and blew a load of smoke in her face. I thought she was going to have a stroke. How are you?'

'I'm ... I'm ...'

'Ah, you'll be fine ... You'll be flying it.'

'These women terrified me ... They said it has a soul.'

'Look ... It's the size of a ten pence piece – it hasn't a soul or if it has, it's not their sort of dried-up turd.'

'And that I'll be suicidal forever.'

'Am I suicidal?'

'Are you, Mona?'

'I think about it, always will ... What would it have been ... Maybe it's mad but I say little prayers to it ... I think of it as up there somewhere.' Her voice softer now and the dark creeping into the corners of the room.

'How's your boyfriend, Mona?'

'Gabriel ... the beautiful Gabriel. Gone ... I broke it off. It was all tense when I got home ... Me bleeding a lot and him sulking a lot. He wasn't ready for a kid. Down the road maybe but not now. He's no money ... I've no money ... I love him to bits though,' and for a second her voice ceases, then she rallies and launches into the hospital saga, having to go back to hospital and the cow of a nurse asking her what religion and her saying non-practising Catholic; the doctor quite rough too, the looks he gave her, left the yoke inside her while he took a phone call, being kept waiting, waiting, awful chairs, pink and blue, pink for a girl and blue for a boy, pictures of babies everywhere, galling.

'I don't know what I want to do ... Whether I want to go back to England even if I could ... Even if I can,' Mary says, slightly ashamed.

'You've got to be a babe ... You've got to fight ... Fight for the freedom to say yes or no, to do yes or no ... Fight for others ... That's what it's about ... That's what life is about,' Mona says, and she seems old then, old and dredged.

She rises and crosses to the window to grasp the tassel of the blind which has been tapping incessantly. The pigeons, quiet and smoke-coloured, are coming in for the night, settling themselves with a whoosh of wings under the slates, and from the honeycomb grid of the gas fire there came the intermittent spit of hot white sputters. The story Mona was telling and that she had not ever told before was from way back, a kid, going to the mountains as kids with her mother and father and aunts and uncles and how the kids did not want the grown-ups following so they threw rocks at them and went on up to play and fool around. Then on the way down spotting an ambulance and the word being passed up, how her Aunt Anna had been killed, hit by a rock, stumbled and fell all the way down and no one saying anything, no one saying whose rock it was but everyone thinking it was theirs.

'I would have called it Anna,' she says, her voice husky with the admission of it.

'I don't know what to do, Mona,' Mary says.

'No one can tell you what to do ... Only yourself ... That's what's so hard ... That's what so terrible about living,' and she puts her hand out, a smooth plump hand with a little array of rings, and they stood clasped, silent, listening quietly for the frightened things flailing their hearts.

✠

VIGIL

Through the blinds she can see the shadows, shadows of people, and the fitful thrust of candle-flame forking and waning. She can hear them. Since dawn they have stood out there, praying ceaselessly, a quiet well-behaved group, ringing the doorbell at a reasonable hour and requesting to see her, to give her gifts and show their solidarity.

'How did they find out?'

'That's what Fitz and I were wondering; spies, spies.'

'I can't.'

'You won't see them ... But we have to move you ... There will be journalists here before long, it'll be a circus.'

'Can't I hide?'

'I know it's home ... And we all love you ... The boys wanted to go out with kettles of boiling water and saucepans of porridge to pour on them ... Like they used to do in the tenements when the bailiffs came.'

'Where will I go?'

'Cathal is sorting that out ... There are places.'

'Places!'

'Look, trust me, it'll be a nice place ... You won't be sent back to Veronica ... It won't be for long ... Because guess what?'

'What?'

'The good news is, your father has given his permission for us to fight your case ... We're going to court ... It's a matter of days ... So come on ... We have to dress you up ... We have to dress me up ... And we have to go out there and bluff our way past them.'

'They'll stop us.'

'You don't know my Fitz ... He has a plan of campaign ... Got the good car out of the garage ... We don't want to risk my jalopy ... We'll fly past ... You'll be in my long coat and my Lady Godiva hat ... We'll have umbrellas ... I'll thank them for coming and say that unfortunately we have to see our attorney ... We'll get into the back seat like royalty and be driven off.'

'Did Cathal say why my father gave his permission?'

'I think ... The guards have been at him.'

'He must feel bad.'

'Do you hate him, Mary?'

'He was the wrong father ... That's all.'

'And yet, you're you because of him ... That's one of life's strange mysteries.'

Maybe then, sitting on the bed as she drew on her stockings and looked down at her goose pimples and thought how ugly she was and how much uglier she would become, maybe then the little current of hope died in her.

'You should be over the moon ... We've got what we prayed for,' Mrs Fitz said, and gave her a little pinch.

'I don't want to have it and I don't want to kill it,' she said.

She started to run then, a run so fluid and prodigal it was as if she had been practising forever and was in the last throes of some terrible determination, as if the walls themselves cushioned, flung her from one to the other with an alacrity, and her body answered, careless of what fell or what was toppled, and in each chase finding a newer, wilder bate of energy, running now as if she was only speed, only vertebrae.

'Mary ... Mary ... What are you doing?' Mrs Fitz said, trying to hold her back, but she did not stop to listen nor to answer, her body was the answer, running it out of herself, running from that room to the hallway, the stairs, the passages, rooms she had never been in and a box room full of fancy dress clothes and Christmas decorations, down a back stairs to a lower hall, the stifling drone of automatic prayer filtering in, and when at last she fell onto a heap of old bicycles, the entire family were standing around but no one spoke, because of the violence that had been let loose, and in some ways they were afraid of her now.

WELL-WISHERS

S he sits on the bottom bunk in her new room, dusk descending in the convent garden outside and the Michaelmas daisies scrunching up their eyes for the night. The clip-clopping of a dray horse on a street beyond. A man buying and selling junk. They had passed him in the car on their way. She is with an order of nuns. She is still shaking from having to pass that crowd of people, a coat over her head, her shoulders hunched as if they had arrows, overhearing a man telling Mrs Fitz that they had only to name their price.

She looks at the medals, the leaflets, the letters and then begins to read at random.

The baby is always taken out alive. He will breathe, move and cry. The child is then butchered, head torn off, abdomen punctured with a sharp knife and left to die in a bucket. Read this nine times every hour and you will be saved.

You need love, you need privacy, you need encouragement. You are not to blame. Be angry with God and he will listen. In his eyes you are holy. Tell him what the abuse was like. Do not do the wrong thing. I am not your psychiatrist, I am not one of those smart alec judges, I am not even your poor father but I hold your hand, believe me I do. So many bigshots using your misfortune, loud-mouthing about you and your feelings. Don't listen to them. Be brave, Mary. May I call you Mary? Let the country be proud of you. Let us all stand up and cheer and say she won, she gave birth, she was good, she was great, she came through. I pray for you and the little mite inside you – Your New Friend.

The third was in capital letters on the cardboard of a shoe box.

Ignore the gobshittery ... It's your show ... Fill your cunt ... There are guys out there would love to shag you senseless but I am not one of them, I am a class act, I am a good solid reliable ten-fucks-a-night plumber. See you at the GPO.

People were awful, people were dangerous, people would crucify one, the people one knew and the people one did not know. That last admission was the most terrible of all and the most frightful. Maybe that's what people meant about getting old: it wasn't the years, it was the knowledge. She had that now.

She tears them up but it is too late, they have stitched themselves into her mind and are talking back to her, to the room and to the world, and always would.

Her own letter is a scribble and is addressed to no one –

I don't hate you, you know I don't. If only you were my sister or my brother but not my child. If you could be spirited out of me that would be all right, more than all right. It is just that I cannot bear you. I am asking your soul to fly off now and wait for the right mother. But I know that cannot be.

The garden had become dark and the clopping horse back in its stable. A pastoral silence.

She did not even tiptoe as she went out.

✠

MEN OF DESTINY

She is back with Mrs Fitz and together they are looking at the evening paper and studying the five faces, the five judges who will hear her case and decide.

'He's not such a bad fellow ... He could be all right.' This is Mrs Fitz telling or rather assuring herself of something she thinks she knows.

When people do not know, when everything is suspended and the future a thicket enveloped in darkness, equivocation, chance, people huddle together and tell little stories, exhume little skeins of hope, cite a good dream they have had, or remember when they last saw a rainbow.

They study the faces, the wigs, the spectacles for hints of anger or disgust that might lurk behind the semi-smiles, as Mrs Fitz gives her opinion of each one – 'Now he's tougher, it says here that he's not regarded as a liberal on moral issues ... And this fellow, he's a youngster, never handed down independent judgement before, when they're young you can't tell ... Often they have the hardest hearts ... I think I know him, Judge Fogarty, I know his sister ... She works in the museum ... They're a nice family ... They give a big party every Christmas Day.' Then looking at the fifth face, long, with a slightly smug smile and the lips somewhat accentuated as if there is lipstick on them, she decides that he's the one they should worry most about.

'I'd be afraid of him ... I'd be very afraid of him,' she says quietly.

They read the names and for some reason Mary begins to write them down, to memorise them.

'We'll put some more vitamin E on these scratches of yours and soon you won't see a thing,' Mrs Fitz said, picking up her wrist and looking at it, baffled, tender. 'Have you put the disinfectant on ... Are you sure. That nail was full of poisons ... any nail taken out of a wall is full of poison and rust and God knows what.'

'It's drying out.'

'I'm not cross, Mary ... I'm shaken ... We all were ... Mrs B nearly died ... You could have cut an artery. If that boy had not gone into the shed to pick up his jacket ... what would have happened. You would be dead ... Think of how let down we would have felt, realising that we had failed you ... You are not to go on thinking that you have no one ... No friends ... Because you have and you will have ... There is a life before you ... There's nature and friendship and love ... Why do you never talk, Mary?'

'I talk to myself.'

'What do you say to yourself?'

'Anything.'

'What are you saying now?'

'I'm saying that if I could be the judges and they could be me, that if we could swap and they'd know every bit of my life,' and she stops then and puts her hand to her mouth, ashamed of the habit of hoping.

'Look, we stand a good chance ... There are five of them this time ... Not one ... We stand a very good chance.'

They remain for a long time staring at the faces, trying to reach them, talking to them with the same kind of secret and prone hope as when talking to the statues of saints in the chapel, repeating the five names, Frank, Terence, Ambrose, Malachi, Diarmuid; juggling them so that it became Malachi, Diarmuid, Terence, Ambrose and Frank, metamorphosing them, sending messages to them in their fine houses.

OH MY DUCATS,
OH MY DAUGHTER

'The law is the law,' Frank says over-pompously, adding, 'Render unto Caesar that which is Caesar's and to God that which is God's.'

'I know the law is the law,' Molly says, thumping him, 'but bend it.'

'We shouldn't even be discussing this,' her father says.

'Everyone else is. Everyone is talking about it.'

Each morning he dropped Molly at school and up to now she mostly sulked with not a word exchanged between them because of being half-asleep or having had one of her scenes with her mother. Her mother and herself, aliens in a big house, the presence of one in a hall or a kitchen assuring an outburst of the other. Doors being banged, her mother accusing him of always taking Molly's side when all he wanted, when all any man wants is peace in his own castle, not rows, not barging, not women's screaming feuds as to whether a belt is missing or a dinner table not cleaned off.

'I wish I hadn't been put on this case,' he says.

'No you don't wish you hadn't been put on this case, you want to be on this case, you want to be one of the big shots in this country.'

'What I want and what I feel is my own business, Molly ... I never thought I'd be anything, only a moocher ... I never thought I'd get this far.'

'Daddy,' she says, her voice softer now. 'You can't let this poor girl down, you cannot let her down, she's a scapegoat.'

'Molly, if I heard that someone was going across to England to bomb Parliament, I would have to stop him, wouldn't I?'

'Yes. The him in this case is the rapist, that's who you should be pursuing, he's the one who has bombed Parliament, not her.'

'We shouldn't be talking about this,' he says flatly.

'Why not?'

'Not even your mother is allowed to talk to me about it.'

'My mother and you barely talk.' That much was true. His wife, who insisted on accompanying him everywhere and would sit in the courts with him if it were permitted, simply to keep an eye on him, his wife and he had not had a proper conversation in maybe ten years, simply mandates about whether the fire was going to be lit or not lit, when to turn on the central heating or if they should drive out to their mountain cottage where, on account of its being cramped, the tension rocketted. His thin droning wife, incapable of silence, yet never having a conversation with him. Oh yes, she made sure to criticise him before others, sure to flout his background, his ignorance, the classics he had not read but pretended to have read.

The one time he ever felt mastery was when he withdrew to his study to work on his cases, to sit most of the night turning the pages again and again, reading the same dry stuff, and suddenly his brain incandescent, agog, some chink, something which his legal mind could latch onto, a loophole, a moment of pure joy, as it might be to a painter discovering a new pigment. Sometimes during those nights he got up and went out into the garden and in the moonlight hit a few balls with a hurly stick and re-imagined himself in the fields, the stony fields of long ago, his mind like the leather ball itself, an acceleration to it, spinning out of mortal sight. Some little twist or turn within the labyrinth of the law which he could follow up and this feeling of supremacy and happiness, alone with the moon and the damp grass. That was his preserve, not this, not a daughter who was refusing to get out of the car until he promised to let the girl go to England.

'In Jesus' name, Molly.'

'Suppose it was me. Suppose I was pregnant?'

'It's not you and it better not be,' he says.

'But if it were me, Daddy.'

'Your mother and I would . . .'

'That bitch.'

'Molly, you are to go into that school or I will whip you.'

'Oh, I'm to go into that school, am I ... What do you think they're talking about ... You and your four eminent colleagues can send this girl to the stake ... It's a small country, Daddy.'

'Feck. I know it's a small country,' he says, catching a glance of himself in the mirror, his face like gruel, his eyebrows knotted together as if thinking, when all that is in his head is anxiety, and a mounting biliousness about the days to come, the bitter argument, the unasked for sagacity from every Tom, Dick and Harry.

'You would take me to England, wouldn't you?'

'Why the hell did the girl come home?'

'Say that to the cameras,' she said.

'I'm not the only one who is thinking that,' he says.

'But no one says it, not you and the four Judases with you.'

'We haven't even met yet, we haven't even heard the arguments, we haven't digested it, we haven't decided anything.'

'Digested it! I know what two of them will do anyhow.'

'You need the strap.'

'That *Opus Dei* fellow. Don't tell me he's going to have any mercy, oh no.'

'Who told you he's *Opus Dei*?'

'It's known, it was in the papers. It's a small country, Daddy, and as for Mr Thin-Lips with his family of nine, his first wife dead and his second wife ovulating, he got his two chances, didn't he.'

'Am I paying school fees for this impertinence?'

'Tell him that when you argue and digest.'

'We don't talk this female ovulation bull.'

'Oh no, you don't because you're not fourteen years of age and sick and vomiting and a thing inside you put there against your will, God knows how brutally, no, you're men, you're dignitaries, you hold the reins. Good men ... Wise men, pillars of society; and you go to mass and the sacraments every Sunday, Daddy, and you meet that actress in the lane at night.'

'What actress in the lane at night?' His colour is changing now, he does not have to look in the mirror, it's like a nettle-rash rising, scalding, scalding.

'I know for years, years.'

'We each walk a dog.'

'And your two dogs stand to have a chat ... I nearly wrote a composition about it,' she says, blithely.

'Thank Christ you didn't.'

'The two dogs have a pow-wow. Our Dolly and her little terrier, I bet you her terrier has a go ... I bet you Dolly is soppy ... Look, Daddy, I don't begrudge you. If you meet a woman with some bit of sparkle, why not, why not have a tangle with her in a lane at night and why not walk back home, looking at the stars and feeling that bit more romantic, but if you are that bit more romantic, Daddy, recall it, evoke it when you sit down to do your digestions.'

'We are not going to discuss this case ever again, Molly.'

'If you vote no, if you refuse to let her out, I'll get the biggest boo in there in that school. I'll be boycotted.'

'I'll vote as my conscience tells me, not a bunch of hysterical girls.'

'Boo,' she says and reaches across and kisses him, and watching her walk off in her uniform, not a girl and not yet a woman, he thinks life without her would be the catacombs.

✠

ON THE RUN

They let him out in the end. Play ball and the case against
him won't proceed. Plead insane. Insane. Insanity. He went
home and slurped back tea, made that one call, changed his
shoes and off, off. The blue-grey uncomprehending eyes not looking
down at his feet, not caring whether he is on trampling road or field
or hill or hollow. Play ball. Plead insane. He does not know how
why what. He has run out of cigarettes. When he touches his guns
with his tongue he discovers terror and beading like semolina from
long ago. Long ago. Nothing for it but the wilds. With the foxes
and their carrion. He has friends, he must have, people he has not
seen in years. Cousins or the descendants of cousins. Shelter. A
place to hide. A room in the rafters. Tea brought up and cold meat
with relish. But can he trust it. In twenty-four hours it will be
known. Or even less. Pissing rain.

He knocks on a door where there has not been a caller for ten
years or more. Weeds and briars in the jambs of the door.

'Anybody home, anybody home?'

The windows whitened with lime bleach. When the door yields
after a gargantuan shove he finds inside an old mattress ripped and
scrabbled, rain pools, and a rat, a she-rat with hungry whiskers,
suckling her litter. Instead of scurrying she sits, still, mothering,
vicious. 'So long ... So long.'

In the hotel five large whiskies in a heat. You want no more.
We'll serve you no more. I have to sleep, I have to lie down. No
vacancies here, sir.

The hackney driver all jitter, afraid of the countryside, afraid of
the barren countryside with only a television mast to distinguish it

from being a moonscape. Jacko will come up trumps. Jacko will do a Scarlet Pimpernel –

> *They seek him here*
> *They seek him there*
> *The French, they seek him everywhere*
> *Is he in heaven, is he in hell*
> *The damned elusive Pimpernel?*

Arriving in the backyard he finds Jacko feeding several calves from the one bucket, a flock of birds perched on his shoulder and above him three undergarments on a clothes line, frost-stiffened.

'Good morrow . . .' he calls out and crossing over he says in a less hearty voice, 'I'm on the run, Jacko.'

'You look it.'

'Can you hide me?'

'The guards are out looking for you . . . They're . . .' And he does not go on because they can hear the cars, the sound of the cars in the valley below, like screams rising up and into the isolation of the mucky yard, a fleet of cars it seems, although most likely it would be three, one from each of the neighbouring towns; converging then at the crossroads as if to reconsider, engines puttering, then soon starting up in a fast and final carousel towards their destination.

'I never knew you had such a good view of the lake up here,' James says, wiping his eyes on his sleeves.

'Let down by that fandango between your legs,' Jacko says, and then shouting it as if for the oncoming posse he says bitterly, 'And they call woman the weaker sex.'

WHITE FROST

Soft morning crisp. Starched low-lying lawns. The bristle of tyres along the untrodden suede of a quiet canal street and the gulls in ceaseless audacious peregrinations, moving fluently, dizzily as if obeying a ventriloquist's unseen hand.

Judge Mahoney opens his newspaper, impatiently scans. What have we here. Same things. Home news. World news. Writs. Crises. Nefarious deeds. A raunchy miss, skirt up to her coccyx, claiming her philosophy has changed people's lives. His choler from sleeplessness expressed in the rustle of the pages. Disquiet and bile until he suddenly espies something wholesome to read, a pleasant and heartening recollection of the old days and the old ways – fairy women with long dark hair, Cú Nimbe, the poison hound, penances and miracles in lonely places. Much regaled by this he speaks civilly for the first time to Jim, his driver, enquiring if the concert tickets are in apple-pie order; then he rings his friend and colleague, Diarmuid, and tells him to read the piece as it will do him a power of good. Neither allude to the business ahead, the weight on their breasts, dissenting voices, outcries no matter what they decide, blistering attacks on their persons, and their acumen, all of which could have been easily and expeditiously avoided if a certain Attorney General had sat on it for a pinch of time and put 'Gone fishing' on his office door. Oh, a very rood of piety and rectitude. The fact of its being the father all the more sticky. Rumour of the AG himself intending to come into court. L'Estrange no doubt up all night thinking his way into their five skulls, their five flummoxed skulls, and a girl somewhere in the city saying her prayers.

'What did we get for lunch today, Jim?' he asks.

'The low-diet melon and smoked turkey.'

'No one joining us?'

'You said not...'

'That's true, Jim ... I said not ... Today being a day of general judgement upon us all.'

✠

BLACK FROST

Alone with the road and the road's surface, counting his big mad strides he is. Winter at its most sere and pitiless. The frost like grains of coarse salt bristling in the ruts. Sun's rays. Sparkle. Sky a quilt of gold, rays everywhere.

'Good morning, James,' is what any passer-by might say, except there are none. It is a back road, a forgotten road, a nowhere. And no more truck with the Jackeens, with their dandruff and their wedding rings and their barrage of questions. No more. Where did you touch her. When did you touch her. How did it start. Did you fondle her breasts. Did you take her pants down. Did you take your pants down. In the fields which he crosses, fallen boughs, falling gateways, drinking troughs, the last he will see of his own environs.

He knows the tree that he will do it from. Walked there with a flashlamp the night before and Holy Christ wasn't there a bit of rope waiting, nylon blue, left by a passing Samaritan. Brought it home and studied it.

It is a big tree, in fact two trees, two huge grey trunks straddled to form a stout Roman arch under which any Barabbas might dangle and repine. A thousand-year-old tree, or more, the knobs, warts, boles and wounds attesting to a rigorous life. A few leaves left, tatters, tattered, a fidgety jingle. His stallion looked at him, glared, the livid eyes the colour of slate, pranced, lay down, rolled in the sour juiceless grass, got up again and then shat three thick steaming molasses-black balls of farewelling shit and galloped off to persecute the little teaser who was standing at the far end under a stone wall. Miserable in shape and colour as rotting dish cloth.

No more. Free of their words and their crass advice. Plead guilty.

Plead insane. When did it start. Why did it start. His blood about to be dispatched to Oxford to undergo a test. Why did it start. Why did it start. Who in the wide world could answer that for him which he himself did not know.

'I am paying now ... Aren't I.' He tells the branches of jewelled briars and the lone birds. It is as if he does not yet believe that which he is about to do. A fifteen-inch collar, always was, he says, blithely, as if it is a transaction in a shop. He pulls the rope down, slowly, with reverence, like a man about to be ordained. Being nylon, it won't itch.

'Can't have the itch,' he says. It is as if he does not believe it, or else believing that someone will come, he will see her, yes it would be her, the creature running up the fields to his rescue. The Jackeens who never got it out of him will be the ones to cut him down. It was as if it was still a game, feeling the stones along the top of the wall to make sure that they were loose, telling them that when he kicked they were to go, saying that he mustn't botch it, he must not be heard roaring like a ginnet to the surrounding countryside.

It was when the ground went that he began to holler. Ground gone, stones gone, and he up there in a worse nowhere, cradle and crater, beginning and end; out, back and around, crazed bumps-a-daisies. It was then he shouted, it was then he knew, it was then the words came, a great welter of words from the entrails, the help word, the hate word, the blast word and the love word, known to all men, compressed into the one word because it was only minutes, less; his breathing going and him still sashaying backwards and forwards, the blood leaving his face in waves, the expression furious and piteous; lips lifted over the teeth to say the first and last thing which man craves to say and ending in a terrified hosanna that was in the old tongue. He sought then to undo it and with a tugging that exceeded human might he pulled and pulled but the rope had already commenced the steady mathematical snapping of bone and the neck piping to be free was soon a crust of raw stigmata.

For witness, the frost-flecked house in a glittering dilapidation, fallen chimney pots and the winter pampases swaying in a soft and murmurous sibilance.

Quiet things to mark a violent passing.

HAND MIRROR

Mary is back among them. She is theirs for the day. Permission has been given. A local guard had wrangled it from her father. They are in a beautiful house which Roisin has been loaned. They are all assembled, old and new faces. They are of all ages, some very smart with shoulder bags and short skirts, the older women in their coats drinking tea, a nun reading her office.

'Why isn't it in the papers?' a woman who is wearing a skull cap asks. She had thought it would be in the papers.

'Oh it will be, it will be,' she is told and assured that the press and the cameras are outside the court waiting for the verdict.

'We haven't long to go, love,' Mrs B says to her; she is the only friend amongst them.

Mary has not seen the court, not even seen a picture of it. Veronica sits glaring at her with a look of reproach, the 'you betrayed me, you abused me' look in her eyes, and a girl with a club foot is busily picking out her favourite biscuits which are pink wafers with a pink puttyish filling.

Roisin has arranged for a press conference afterwards and mentions the names of the journalists who are coming. She is quite optimistic. Those poltroons and heretics down there would not dare overturn the constitution.

'One of them would,' the nun says tartly and they all know who she means.

Mary is told to leave that room and go to the bathroom to have her hair done. Someone called Breed is doing her hair. It is a vast bathroom, slop buckets filled with dried hydrangeas, their blue-green faces like the faces of mildewed clocks.

They will know in a matter of hours. An open and shut case. Maybe not. She can picture Cathal and Mr L'Estrange, very quiet now, biding.

'We will make a true Irish girl out of you,' Roisin says.

'Do I put her hair up,' Breed asks, lifting a long coil of it.

'Yes, better up ... Tidier,' Roisin says.

'I don't want it up,' Mary says. There is a moment's hesitation, a moment's bristle.

'All right, don't put it up,' and at that Roisin storms out.

'You listen to me ...' Breed says. 'If Roisin says double that hair pin, we double that hair pin ... Her word is law ... Understand?'

Mrs B comes and kneels by her and whispers to her — 'I found that book I told you about ... It was in a trunk ... Do you remember I told you, about a little girl on the moon ... She's gone there to live with her aunt ... Her mother and father died ... Can you hear me, Mary ... I have a very soft voice ... Don't look so sad ... Smile.'

'Will you stay near me ...'

'You're OK ... They mean well ...'

Lipsticks are then discussed, the choice being between strawberry, fuchsia and raisin. She is told to spread her lips wide. She is told to smile. Smile. She is told to pout. The lipsticks belong to Madeleine, the owner, who is in Ukraine on business and, imagine it, has had to buy a second fur coat because of the freezing temperature.

'Two fur coats,' Breed says. 'Wouldn't they be bulky?'

'I'd like one,' Mrs B says and holds a hand mirror for Mary to see herself.

✠

BROTHER AMBROSE

Judge Mahoney and Judge Hanna have come out separately for a breath of air. From the several churches all along the quays bells are ringing, summoning the faithful to morning mass, cordant, discordant, liquidy matins, boomerangs lauding, gold gonged, holy.

'Do you mind if we talk?' Ambrose asks, a red muffler up to his lips, his face blotched.

'Not a bit,' Frank says, still smarting from a last minute harangue on the phone from Molly.

'I didn't sleep a wink.'

'Oh now ... The ravelled sleeve of care.'

'What do you think will happen?'

'An avalanche ... That's what will happen ...'

'I think right will prevail ... It'll go against her. It should.'

'The law, Ambrose ... The law is a labyrinth and clever men learn how to use it.'

'You mean you are going to say yes.'

'I will listen to the evidence and maybe yes I will say yes.'

'I thought you were a family man.'

'Boy, when you're my age, you'll have a few liberal welts beaten onto your arse.'

'We can't disgrace our country.'

'Our country will not recover from this ... Our Attorney General opened a right can of worms.'

'He did the right thing ... The honourable thing.'

'By his own lights, yes ...'

'That's slander.'

'I'm sure he's a decent man ... I'm sure he's led a decent sheltered life ... Never had to rough it ... Never stood around bars and got his nose bloodied, and neither have you, Ambrose.'

'If we let her out we know where she's going ... We know why she's going ... To an Auschwitz in England.'

'And if we don't let her out she might kill herself ... Weigh the deaths ... Two as opposed to one.'

'That's horse-trading ...'

'Roman senators cut their teeth on horse-trading.'

'That suicide could have been a stunt.'

'It is not a stunt, Ambrose, if you pull a nail out of a wall and try to slit your wrist.'

'But she did it sideways ...'

'Do you think a child of her age would be familiar with the correct way of slitting a wrist?'

'You want to canonise her.'

'Believe me, I don't ... I wish she had gone and done what she had to do and left our lovely constitution with a ribbon round it.'

'We're a Christian country ... We're a model for the whole world.'

'We're pagans, Ambrose ... Pagan urges run in our blood ... Pagan love ... Pagan lust ... Pagan hate ... It's why we need God so badly.'

'The unborn shall not be moved from the jurisdiction of the court ... It's written ... Sacrosanct.'

'Don't give me catechism, Ambrose ... I have it coming out my ears ... When I was a youngster I read the great trials, *Bodkin -v- Adams*, I acted them in my aunt's shop, I was weaned on them. The great advocates, my heroes.'

'So you don't know how it will go either.'

'I don't know what L'Estrange's submission will be, but it will be good ... It will be more than good ... He uses the law ... He takes it like a lump of lead and he does alchemy with it. Wizard.'

'I hope that I won't be the one to tip the balance ...'

'Maybe you will ...'

'You'll hate me for it.'

'I won't ... We're not politicians ... We're gentlemen of the bar ... If I were to take off all my clothes when we go in there, not one of you would bat an eyelid ... In my club they gossip if I have a second lump of ice in my whiskey.'

'I'm going to go in now and go down on my knees and ask God for guidance.'

'Ask yourself the big question ... The worst act of a desperate man, woman or child.'

'That's making sentiment of the law.'

'Suicide can strike anywhere ... Anyone ... Any time ... Even thou, Brother Ambrose.'

'You're trying to frighten me.'

'I had a brother ... Did it just like that,' and he grinds his teeth as if he might have been the one, the wretched one who provoked it.

'I love this country and what it stands for,' Ambrose says.

'We all love this country in our own crooked way ... And by the way, I didn't queue up for this case either,' Frank says and brings his very delicate white hands up to his face to cover it, to convey weariness or perhaps antagonism.

They walk in silence then, the wind pouching in under their gowns and lifting their hems up so that they look like caricatures of men, arms athwart, groping and gasping for respiration.

WAITING

'She wants to be alone,' Breed says.

'What else does she want?' Roisin asks tartly.

'Oh, leave her alone,' Mrs B says. 'She says she'd rather hear the verdict from one of us.'

'Put her in the dining room and lock that door ... I don't want to hear that she has bolted.'

'She won't ... She's not well ... She's sick.'

'Sick?'

'I had to give her a hot-water bottle ... For the pain.'

The women repair to the front room, one group clustered around a giant television, a smaller group by a glass table, several hands trying to work the radio, one telling another to put it back where it was, rings and knuckles jousting, each professing that she knows exactly what to do.

As Manus comes hurrying in they sense that there is something amiss.

'Where's Roisin?' he calls.

'She's over there.'

'Tell her I want to speak to her alone.'

'What is it, Manus ... We're all family here.'

'What is it, Ma ...' Roisin says.

'They're going to let her out.'

'Who says?'

'I got a tip ... One of the clerks tipped me off.'

'When ... Where?'

'There ... I was down there ... They're all down there howling, the "let her out" crowd.'

'She's not going out ... She's not,' Roisin says.

'We'll know in the next half an hour ... The Judges are conferring ... But it seems it won't be long,' and looking he asks where she is, says with a sort of sneer that he's never seen her.

'She's resting,' Veronica said.

'Listen, all,' Roisin says and stands on the kerb to be that little bit taller. 'If they let her out we go in there as a group and we do everything under the sun to persuade her not to go ... We each do our own thing ... She can't go ... She doesn't want to go ... She'll regret it until her dying day if she does go ... We have not lost ... Whatever they say ... Rubbish, we are not going to lose ... The country is behind us ... So never mind the legal scum ... We'll overturn it ... We'll win.'

'Well, fasten your seat-belts, guys,' Manus says and sits cross-legged on the floor, his splashed helmet like a scalp between his knees.

✠

MARY

Chairs. More chairs than she has ever seen in the one room. Cream-coloured slip covers. Brasses. Big bulky ornaments. A stuffed eagle with a blood-red beak. Chinese bowls with nothing in them, a silver cake tray. Bottles of wine in a rack. Their footfalls outside, their voices. Table mats in a big pile. A thin lady carved in brown wood, the same shape the whole way down, her hands in a dainty fold over the pouch of her stomach. The doorknob is chrome. Awful pain. Getting worse. Three tall candles all quenched and the wax going yellow. A nearly dead plant, off-white, like bits of torn skin. Awful pain. Wires in her, prongs. Zigzag, zigzagging. Pain going from the front to the back and around again. A hoop of steel, like a hoop on a cask. Tearing. She is stuck to the chair. What is happening. She does not know. Should she call them. What is happening. The chair cover is starting to be damp, slowly at first, like the tide swerving slowly up onto dry biscuity sand.

It's ... It's ... It's coming out. Pouring out. The leather of the chair all ooze now and sticky like warm puree. She is holding the chair next to her. What to do. What to do. Should she shout out. She rips the tablecloth off to stuff it around her. Her insides are mad now. Askew. It's coming down along the legs of the chair. Wet and clots. Both. Trying to call them but unable. Trying to get up. Unable. The chair up with her, a trio, the chair and her and it. Trying. So small a creature able to wreak such pain. There is a nest of brass buttons, brass beading along the side of the chair next to her and she puts her fingers to them, for something to touch, to implore of. The tablecloth is soaking, a flag after battle, bloodied through and through. The pain is wild, there is vengeance in it. It is going now, going out of her, departing, a nebula out into nowhere.

The key is being turned and they are coming in. They won't take this. They won't have this.

They're in.

JUDGEMENT

'What has she done ... What have you done?' Roisin asks.
'She's taken something, Roisin,' one of them says.
'What have you taken?' and without waiting for an answer they turn her pockets inside out, delve into her handbag, pitching things out, her comb, chewing-gum paper, her rosary beads.

'Tell us what you have taken,' Roisin says, and with a cold undeviating conviction says that it must be stopped, it must be counteracted at once.

'She's miscarried,' a voice says in a whisper and others stand in the doorway, staring as if at some tournament.

'May you rot in hell ... You have murdered it ... You wanted that baby dead ... You willed it ... You'll pay for it every day of your life ... Women crying out for babies ... They'll curse you and God will curse you,' Roisin says, standing over her, livid now, deprived of her victory, shrieking, nothing else mattering, nothing of why lives have to be so hard, some harder than others, or if the love of God is greater or lesser for those who suffer more, those whom he causes to suffer more, or if sometimes he shows a mercy.

'It is God's will ... It must be,' Mrs B says, crossing to hold her. In the doorway the girl with the club foot has her mouth wide open, longing for a peal of laughter which she has to suppress. No one has told Mary what the court has decided, no one has thought to. Mrs B is holding her, telling her not to be afraid, saying the same words again and again, 'You won't die ... You're not going to die,' and two women carrying sheets and towels pile them around the leg of the chair and the sodden carpet.

'We better pray ... That's all we can do now,' the nun says.

'Kneel,' Roisin says.

'I can't,' Mary says.

'Kneel down and confess before God that you did this.'

'She can't get up ... In God's name will one of you call an ambulance,' Mrs B says, because she sees the look in the eyes, the look she does not like, and in concert with their prayers she holds her, the small frame – askew – whispering in her ear – 'You're not going to die ... You're not ... Going ... To die.'

LOVE IS TEASING

It has begun to snow but inside all is a cave of colour. Golds. Silvers. Platinums. Thu-thump. Thu-thump. Thu-thump. Sweeter pulses within it. The press and sway of bodies all around. Love. The cosmos. Galaxy love.

Mona is on the stage preparing to sing, the foil at the back moving and trembling in silver gusts, a diadem for her, swirling, stroking her lamé haunches, sucking for an instant on the little locket which hangs from her neck, then the arm with the braided bracelets being raised to signal that she will commence.

Mary sits at a centre table, people milling and moiling, men stooping to get the wink, the love wink. Nowhere the face that she is searching for. The face she does not yet know. But would know the moment it materialised. And will know. She closes her eyes for an instant, thinking how it might be, how unimaginably beautiful it might be, that there would be a someone to whom she could tell it all, all of it, down to the last shred, but that there would be no need to tell it because it would be already known and that would be love, that is what love is, such as those milling people were dreaming of and drinking themselves insensible to gnaw at, such as her own mother and her own father had dreamed of in the long ago, such as all people dream and go on dreaming in the cold crucible of time.

'Care to come out, ducky, for a few minutes.' A drunk man with chapped hands stands above her.

'No I wouldn't.'

'Suit yourself,' he says, umbraged, badgering a young woman going by, tumblers brimming, brass gold, slopping them as she rebuffs him.

As the lights change so does Mona. She is a mermaid, necklaced in seaweed, one bare shoulder the melting fawn of fudge, the out-stretched arms weaving, willing them to her. A milkmaid calling home her kine at dusk, a woman pleading with her betrothed then all of a sudden taunting them with being so laggard with the words.

> 'She's sun and rain
> She's fire and ice
> A little crazy but it's nice
> And when she gets mad you'd best leave her alone
> 'Cos she rages just like a river.
> Then she'll beg you to forgive her.
> She's every woman.'

The crowds are already cheering, the rapt faces of the men near the stage groping to get to her body, a pelt of lamé, magenta, the gleam of fish scale, licking wet, from the river and the single trigger words – New York, LA, Christmas Nights, Temptation.

Her hair is a halo, for falling gleams of sequiny dust, moon-dust, star-dust; the disc jockey fencing with the men, upbraiding the cheeky bucks, and all the while Mona cool and bewitching in sil-houette. When she has finished the disc jockey kisses her, hands her an envelope, and flushed, lightly gliding, she makes her way back to their table, opening the envelope en route, gives yell because she has won money and not a gift token, then turning to a sleepy-looking young man in a vest she asks him to be an angel and get two nice girls two large vodkas and white lemonade.

'You were great,' Mary says.

'You'll be great,' Mona says.

'I won't be up there.'

'Do you want to bet.'

'OK. OK. Ladies and Jamesons,' the disc jockey says, donning a red fez, to wild applause. 'OK. OK. The only way to get a prize is to participate ... Strut your stuff like Mona Lisa did ... Tommy McHale, can you come up here like a good man ... OK. OK. I hear you Mrs Dubrinksi. Tommy, is it a coincidence or are sick jokes in ... You what ... You want to win a mobile phone and you want to tell a joke ... You've just won a weekend for two in Benidorm ... What more do you want ... What ... A woman ... The place is full of women ... Colleens ... Take your pick ... But don't take Mrs Dubrinski ... She's booked ... Isn't that so, Esmeralda ... Oh, Tommy, not the sick joke you told last Christmas ... That's a terrible joke altogether that one about the guy who keeps dipping his chips in a leper's sores ... Excuse me, Tommy, you're out of order ... There's a nice man down there with a good, clean joke ... By the name of Eamonn ... Come on, Eamonn ... Come on up ...'

The crowd boo and hiss as soon as Eamonn begins because it is a joke they already know.

'Don't mind them, Eamonn, press on.'

'There were two men in a doctor's waiting room and one says to the other, I've got a green ring on my dick and the other says, I've got a red ring on my dick and the guy with the red dick is called in first. Drop your pants, the doctor says. Has a look. Big smile. Go off and enjoy yourself. Second man goes in. Same procedure. Drop your pants. Jesus Christ. Major surgery. Second man goes down to the seafront to throw himself in, meets first man who is having a stroll, says, I don't understand it ... You're told to enjoy yourself and I'm down for major surgery. Ah, says your man, there's an awful big difference between lipstick and gonorrhoea.'

As they ridicule him and throw bits of bread and sausage, the disc jockey tells them what hard men they are, hard men and no mistake, and calls out to Mrs Dubrinski to come to his aid, which of course she does – 'You want me to tell you a joke ... You'd like to hear something about the old sod ... Well, I'll tell you about Farmer Joe ... Poor Farmer Joe down the country having to wring turkeys' necks for our Christmas dinners. Gobble. Gobble. Gobble. Having to get the wee blood up to the top of the neck so we don't spoil our palates ... Oh dear oh dear ... How we do pamper ourselves and what nicer song to go with that turkey than the one I learned sitting on your knee, Esmeralda – 'Without you I've got no place ... I'll be lonely this Christmas without you, lonely and cold ... Without you to hold.' – Now that's a fitting song ... Would draw a tear from a stone ... What did I just hear ... D'you know what a man has come and whispered in my ear ... Shocking, shocking altogether ... That every time you have a wank you take a year off your life ... Saving your presence, Mrs Dubrinski, I might have to go and have a shower ... I can ... You what ... Marvellous ... for me alone ... A wee eggnog ... Oh, the night is young yet ... We'll smooch anon ... We'll mosey on down to Lily's in the lane ... Now you strenuous woman what are you taking your boots off for ... Saving your presence, Ladies and Gentlemen, Mrs Dubrinski is a card ... A top o' table at Lily's ... The toast of the crowd ... The famous men with their Kathleens at home a'bed, their curlers in ... Proper place for a wife ... Oh, the famous men and I will not name names were ready to drink straight from Mrs Dubrinski's slippers ... Oh, you're cross with me ... You didn't want me to say that ... I beg your parsnips ... I'll tell you what, we'll have a nice song and who will it be ... Who will be the little linnet ...' and scanning the tables he goes naw-naw, thinks maybe that woman in the polka dot dress except that she has a bad cold, leaps around the stage, inviting greenhorns, covers his eyes with his hands, levels a finger down into the crowd, then opens his eyes and shouts 'Mona's friend.'

'I can't sing,' Mary says.

'Can't is won't,' he shouts back.

'I've never sung before.'

'Ah, sure the worse you are, the more fun it is,' he says and laughs and the crowd laughs with him. Walking towards the stage a hand and then another reach out to give her courage.

Across the land the snow is falling, the silver-thorn flakes meshing and settling into thick, mesmerising piles, sheeting the country roads, looping the winter hedges to a white and cladded stillness, and down at home their house is empty, the vacant rooms waiting for life to come back into them, for windows to be lit up again and the sloshing crowd waiting too, the way she is waiting for the face to materialise, the face that she will sing the words to, sing regardless, a paean of expectancy into the gaudy void.

'Are you ready?' the disc jockey asks and gives a little tweak to it, pitying the scalding red of her earlobe.

'I'm ready,' she says.

Her voice was low and tremulous at first, then it rose and caught, it soared and dipped and soared, a great crimson quiver of sound going up, up to the skies and they were silent then, plunged into a sudden and melting silence because what they were hearing was in answer to their own souls' innermost cries.

Fallbrook Hosp.

760-728-1191   Calif.

Annaliese

Marg. Burnham
Avis Beardsley
L. Grant
T. Waldier
R. Black
R. Merkle
R. Arnott
Bev Eveleth
J. Cole
K. Bowen
Phil Brooks
H. Kupiec
Liz Wooten
J. Agathos
Deb Ouellette
Joan Paradis
Y. Cantara

S. Krahn
L. Thurlow
M. Turcotte